Dear Reader,

Christmas is our favorite season, and in our household we extend it all the way through Epiphany, culminating with a party and family game night at our church. Despite the hustle of travel and shopping and decorating and parties, Christmas is a time of reflection about the year coming to an end. The beautiful lights and decorations remind us of the simple joys in life, that we can overcome hardships and be open to new experiences. And in the midst of a dark, cold winter, we find warmth in company and companionship.

So it was a delight to work on this book about a Christmas discovery and to discover more about Anne, who has had her hardships to overcome, and who has the strength to find joy in the nooks and crannies of her new life in Blue Hill and share that joy with her family, friends, and neighbors.

Good tidings,
Jolyn and William Sharp
writing as Emily Thomas

Secrets of the Blue Hill Library

Nowhere to Be Found
Shadows of the Past
Unlocking the Truth
Theft and Thanksgiving

The Christmas Key

Secrets of the
BLUE HILL LIBRARY

EMILY THOMAS

Guideposts

New York

Cover and interior design by Müllerhaus
Cover illustration by Rob Fiore, represented by Artworks Illustration
Typeset by Aptara, Inc.

Printed and bound in the United States of America
10 9 8 7 6 5 4 3 2 1

Chapter One

"Come on, Mommy!" Liddie Gibson wormed her way through the post-service coffee hour crowd to grasp her mother's hand. "They're going to open the Advent cabinet!"

"The Advent *cabinet?*" asked Anne with a laugh, as she allowed herself to be dragged off. The parishioners around her smiled indulgently. Besides, they were all drifting in the same direction Liddie was tugging her mother.

Anne's son, Ben, appeared at her side. At nine, Ben was four years older than his sister and was often a solemn child, but Anne could tell he was excited as much as she was, truth be told. Though she still had trouble envisioning what they meant by an Advent cabinet, many of the parishioners had assured her that the church's special Advent ritual was one of the highlights of the holiday season. And now she would finally have the chance to see what they were talking about. A crowd was gathering at the far end of the community room, and Anne could see that Reverend Tom was already there, standing next to what Anne guessed must be the Advent cabinet.

When Anne got closer, it became apparent that the people of Blue Hill Community Church had been quite literal when they named it. It was an Advent calendar built in the form of a cabinet. It stood about five feet high, although most of that was in its legs.

The case atop those legs was perhaps two feet tall and three feet across. There were four rows of six drawers each for a total of twenty-four. To her librarian's eye, it looked like an old-style card catalog cabinet.

Except, she realized, those weren't drawers. They appeared to be little doors, each hinged to swing out and each with a small keyhole and a key in its lock. Anne wondered what was behind those doors. Some sort of cubbyhole? She noticed that, despite the cabinet's height, the piece had little depth—perhaps only eight inches or so. The wood was painted in festive red-and-green colors with pictures of Christmas-related scenes on each of the small doors.

"Friends." Reverend Tom's resonant voice carried through the room, quieting the coffee-hour chatter. "Once again the Advent season is upon us, and as part of our celebration in this joyful time of the year, we enjoy our church's unique tradition of the Advent cabinet!" With a flourish of his hand, he indicated the odd card catalog.

"Now, today is only December second," he continued with a twinkle in his eye, "so we have only two doors to open. But next Sunday, we will have a full week's worth. Shall we begin?" He stepped up to the cabinet, solemnly turned the key in the first door, and opened it. Anne could see that there was something inside the small space, but she couldn't make out what it was.

Reverend Tom removed it and held it up for all to see. "A Matchbox car," he announced. "Who has put it here and what is its message for us?"

"I did," said Helen Smith, on the far side of the crowd from Anne. "I put it there." Helen was the president of the church's board, and she stepped forward now. "It's to represent all the people who will be traveling during the holidays and to remind us to pray for their safety." Many heads nodded, and Anne recalled that Helen herself had a large and far-flung family who would be among those travelers.

Reverend Tom delivered a brief, impromptu message that began with the traveling wise men of the Christmas story and ended with the joys of seeing family and friends during the holidays. After a pause to draw out the suspense, he turned back to the cabinet and unlocked the second door, this time removing an origami swan. A collective *ooh* rang out from the kids, and Liddie stood on tiptoes to get a better view.

"Who takes credit for this treasure?" Reverend Tom held the tiny paper swan up in the palm of his hand so everyone was afforded a view. "It's lovely," he prompted when no explanation was forthcoming. "It's made with great care..."

After another pause, there came a small cough from somewhere behind Reverend Tom, and a shy teenager who seemed to be trying to hide behind unkempt bangs and her father's oversized sweater crept diffidently to Reverend Tom's side.

"I don't know...," she started, her cheeks crimson, but Reverend Tom put a hand on her shoulder and she seemed to draw strength from that. "I thought perhaps the swan would remind us of the Ugly Duckling and that sometimes a great thing starts out small."

"Excellent, Carrie," Reverend Tom's voice boomed, and he repeated what she had said for the benefit of the whole group standing around. "The promise contained in even the humblest situations—such as a babe born in a manger. Clever. Insightful. And perfect for the lessons of this season. Did you make the swan yourself?"

Carrie McAllister nodded, and, noticing all eyes turned to her, she instinctively shrunk back. Reverend Tom let her go and invited the group to join him in singing "Away in a Manger."

Next to the Advent cabinet was an open crate filled with toys and winter clothing and school supplies for needy families—another church tradition. As she sang with the others, Anne read the hand-lettered sign that explained the needs of the anonymous families who would receive the gifts, and she made a mental note to pick up a few of the items listed when she was out shopping for Ben and Liddie.

Following the carol, the crowd was ready to disperse, but Reverend Tom held up his hand. "One more bit of business, friends, please," he announced, adding with a twinkle, "It's a busy time of year, you know. Helen?"

Briskly, Helen Smith stepped forward once again. "Many of you have already heard, but when we went to take out the Christmas decorations this year, well, we had a bit of a surprise." There was general laughter at this. Helen went on to explain that a family of mice had nested in one of the boxes and reduced the contents to a glittery mess. "Specifically," Helen continued, "this was the box of ornaments for our tree in the sanctuary."

This news seemed to sober the crowd. "We'd like to ask your help in rectifying the situation." Helen paused and scanned the crowd. "If each member or family could contribute one ornament by next Sunday, we'll be back in business." Helen's gaze stopped on Anne briefly before she glanced away. "We're hoping that rather than buying something new, you will consider donating something from your own collection. This would personalize the tree in a way that I think would be very appropriate to the season." This suggestion was met by approving murmurs, and the crowd soon returned to its coffee-hour conversations.

While Helen was speaking, Anne had been casting an occasional glance at the Advent cabinet. The thing was fascinating and she wanted to get a better look at it. As the social hour resumed, she stepped up to examine it.

It wasn't exactly fine cabinetry — no fancy inlays or anything like that. But it was a solid piece of construction and seemed to have been built with care. Each of the twenty-four small doors featured a seasonal image that appeared to have been cut from a magazine and applied with shellac. She examined scenes of ice-skating parties, Christmas tree harvesting, and holiday feasting, among others. But it was the tiny locks and keys in each door that particularly fascinated her, and she leaned forward to peer more closely.

"It was built about a dozen years ago by a man named Anderson," said Reverend Tom, appearing suddenly beside her. "He donated it to the church, and we've been making good use of it ever since." He smiled and patted the cabinet fondly as he spoke, and for Anne the name stirred a vague childhood memory of a Mr. Anderson from church, a quiet and gentle man who even then seemed elderly. Noticing her interest in the keys,

Reverend Tom added, "Go ahead and look at one," and then he pulled one from a lock and handed it to her.

The key was delicate—long, thin, and wiry. It seemed to Anne to be Victorian in style. It flared out at one end for the metal to wrap around a white enamel disk on which a number was painted. Seeing her take note of this, Reverend Tom said, "Each one is unique. The keys are not interchangeable. Remarkable, aren't they? I speculate sometimes that they are what gave Mr. Anderson the idea. He had this set of little locks and keys lying around, and the Advent cabinet kind of grew from there."

"They're exquisite," Anne said, shaking her head. She reached to return the key to its cubby and then hesitated. There now seemed to be two locks without keys. One key she held in her hand, but where was the other? She checked the number on the key she held, and then looked questioningly at Reverend Tom as she restored it to its lock.

"Ah, yes, well. Things do go missing over time," he said with a smile. "It's the way of the world, I'm afraid. Somehow it went missing last year. Number seven must now remain the locked cubby."

Anne, who hated to see a set of books lacking a volume, frowned in concern. "Wouldn't it be possible to have a replacement made?" she asked.

Tom waved his hand in a dismissive gesture. "Where can you look to find someone who would do work like this nowadays?" He turned slightly as if to step away.

"Surely we could at least get the cubby open?" Anne said. "Call a locksmith? Or a cabinetmaker? If we could remove the lock, wouldn't it possible to make a new key to fit it?"

Reverend Tom paused and blinked slowly at Anne, frowning slightly. "Sometimes we just have to work with what we have," he said somewhat distractedly, and then his genial smile returned as he looked past her shoulder and said, "Ah, Helen. Here's Anne. I think you wanted to talk with her?"

Anne turned to find Helen Smith smiling at her. "I did, Anne, if you don't mind?" Reverend Tom was already stepping away as Anne smiled acquiescence. Helen drew her to the edge of the room. "I had two things to speak with you about, actually. You heard about our little...misadventure with the mice."

Anne nodded, though it had been more a statement than a question.

"Well, I wanted to ask...that is, I was particularly hoping that you would be willing to donate some ornament of Edie's for the church tree. This is our first Christmas without her, of course, and she was such a beloved figure in the church. I just thought it would be especially appropriate if we could have something on the tree in memory of her. Would you...," she faltered, "would you be willing?"

"Of course," Anne said quickly, touched yet again by the affection and respect that the community retained for her late great-aunt. Then, since Helen seemed self-conscious about making such a request, Anne added, "Would you like to come by the library to help pick out something appropriate? I was planning to bring the boxes out of storage tomorrow."

"Oh well, I wouldn't want to intrude," Helen said, but Anne could see that she was pleased by the idea so she pressed the invitation until Helen said, "Thank you, dear, I would love to."

After a moment, Anne asked, "And what was the second thing?"

"Oh yes," Helen said, more businesslike now. "The second thing is the Nativity play. It's an annual tradition—for the children, you know. It's cosponsored by the children's program and the church board. We were hoping that Ben and Liddie would participate. Most of the children do."

"That sounds wonderful!" Anne exclaimed. She looked around for her offspring, but they had drifted back over to the refreshment table.

Anne had been giving a lot of thought to how her family could build new holiday traditions in their new home, and the Nativity play sounded like an excellent outlet for her kids' excess energy and excitement in this season. "They've never participated in one before, though," she added.

"Not to worry, dear." Helen patted her arm and began to lead her across the room. "Suzanne has done them many times, and with many children." Suzanne Brady was the children's program director, and Helen was now leading Anne in Suzanne's direction.

As they approached, Anne saw that Suzanne was deep in conversation with Brad Trowbridge, a seminary student who was currently doing an internship with Blue Hill Community Church. He was a tall, stocky lad with wavy brown hair and dimples when he smiled, which he seldom did, and he spoke with a very slight stutter. Though many in the church considered him earnest and well-meaning, Anne knew that some people found Brad a bit too distant and intellectual in his approach to the ministry. Then again, she reflected, given the congregation's deep love for Reverend Tom, in their eyes even a paragon would come up short by comparison. Anne suspected, though, that the young seminarian was scared to death and that eventually he would come to have the same facility with a congregation that Reverend Tom had with Blue Hill Community Church.

"Anne says yes," Helen announced gaily as Suzanne approached.

Suzanne shifted her attention away from Brad to Helen and Anne. She looked pleased and relieved. "Yes *and* yes?" she inquired, cryptically.

"Well, only one yes, so far," Helen replied. She turned back to Anne. "I'm afraid the Nativity play is a two-part request..." When Anne raised her eyebrows, Helen continued, "We're also in need of a few adult volunteers to help supervise during rehearsals."

Anne hesitated, foreseeing a significant time commitment, but she remembered her own participation in church and school events. She had always grown nervous when she got near a stage, even in rehearsals, but when her parents were involved it had a calming effect on her. She would make time.

"You see," Suzanne added, "we have an extra-large children's Sunday school department right now. The McAllisters will be formally joining the church in January, and we'd like to have their three older children participate in the Nativity play as well."

Anne nodded. The McAllister family was already quite established at the library. Jason and his father shared an enthusiasm for spy novels and had requested various classic, if now obscure, authors from the interlibrary loan. And their daughter Carrie had formed a rapport with Sherri Deveraeux, one of the library's growing number of volunteers, over their shared love of poetry.

Suzanne tipped her head toward Brad Trowbridge and continued, "And with the participation of the older kids who can handle speaking into the microphones, Brad has incorporated more speaking parts and extra elements into the play."

"We'll be bringing forward more of the historical context this year," Brad explained, tucking his chin as he lectured. "The hardship of Mary and Joseph as they traveled to Bethlehem to participate in the census, their daily life in an occupied country..." Behind Brad, Suzanne rolled her eyes and glanced away. "The kids and the audience will empathize with Mary and Joseph, and the miracle of the birth of the Savior will be that much more intense."

"So, you see?" Helen said, "we'll need extra help with the play this year." She gave Anne a meaningful look, and Anne realized what was behind Helen's request. Brad was young, and Helen was afraid that pushback from Suzanne or the other parents when the play wasn't done "the way we've always done it" would dampen his enthusiasm for the ministry. "In fact," continued Helen, "we're in need of more volunteers yet, so if you think of anyone you think would be suitable...?"

Anne nodded. "I'll keep an eye out." But inwardly, the new task of recruiting more volunteers became yet another item on a very long to-do list.

Anne didn't think her sigh was audible when Helen and Suzanne turned away, but a calm voice behind her said, "It just *seems* overwhelming. By the end of the season you'll be surprised at all you've accomplished." Anne turned to find Mildred Farley, Aunt Edie's dear friend for many years, standing next to her. The older woman was elegantly attired today in a lavender sweater set and pearls.

Anne smiled wanly. "I know. It's just that Christmas was always so hectic in New York, and I thought in a small town things would be different. And now there's this play. And I just agreed Friday to have the Dickens Night celebration finish up at the library..."

Mildred nodded. "Yes, I heard. Which is why I'd like to offer to bake cookies for it."

Anne shook her head. "I couldn't ask you to do that!"

"It's no trouble," Mildred insisted. "I've already started my Christmas baking and have three different kinds of cookie dough in the freezer. You just tell me how many you need." She cocked an eyebrow at Anne.

"Er, maybe eight dozen?" Anne guessed hesitantly.

"Better have twice that." Mildred gave her a knowing look.

"Mildred, I don't know how to thank you." Anne could hear the tinge of relief in her voice.

Mildred patted her on the arm. "You know I love a challenge. And I know Edie would be pleased as punch to see the library take off the way it has."

* * *

The Blue Hill Library was a new and growing endeavor. Upon her passing, Edie Summers had left Anne and the people of Blue Hill, Pennsylvania, her rambling Victorian home, along with a sufficiently large endowment to transform it into a thriving library. To Anne's delight, her great-aunt had also stipulated that Anne herself take the position of librarian. For Anne, it was perfect. As the mother of two who had been widowed just a few years before, and more importantly, as a librarian who had just been laid off in one of the world's most expensive cities, Anne was thankful to return to her hometown and take on the intriguing task of turning her beloved aunt's familiar home into something altogether different.

It had been quite a journey. The building required extensive renovation, of course, to make it suitable for its new role. And she'd had to build all the book collections from scratch, a daunting but infinitely satisfying task. But now the work was done and the library was open to the public, and she was constantly challenged to find ways to firmly embed this new institution in the life of the community.

And then, of course, there were other challenges. As a college-bound young woman, Anne had left Blue Hill for more urban environments, and there were times she still missed her vibrant Brooklyn neighborhood and the energy and endless variety of New York. But even more, she worried about her children's adjustment to this new life, since they had never known anything but New York.

Both Ben and Liddie were proving themselves to be resilient, however, and Anne was proud of the way they had adapted.

Still, she couldn't help but think that the first Christmas in a new place might be particularly difficult, and so she was determined to create an experience for them that would combine familiar elements of their old life with new traditions.

So, when they arrived in Blue Hill, Anne carefully stored in the attic the Christmas decorations they had used in Brooklyn. This morning, she brought these out, along with boxes of decorations her aunt Edie had accumulated in her travels over the years, and hauled them to the elevator on the third floor and transported them to their private living room at the back of the second floor. Once Anne had arranged the boxes so that she could access their contents, they took up half the living room. Fortunately, before she could begin to feel overwhelmed, Helen Smith arrived.

Soon Anne was kneeling on the floor with her arms up to her elbows inside a large box, while Helen sat in a nearby chair and sipped tea, looking on. "I think these must be the tree ornaments," Anne said, adding a grateful *finally* in her mind. They had already looked into several boxes that held Edie's decorations for the rest of the house, but so far, nothing for the tree. But now, at last… "Here we go." Anne pulled out a smaller box, stuffed with individually wrapped ornaments, clearly intended for the tree.

They were a mix of store-bought and handcrafted ornaments. There were delicate glass birds, some finely crocheted snowflakes, shiny red-and-silver candy canes, and a collection of musical instruments tied with gold ribbons.

Anne laughed when she came to a crude papier-mâché Santa, and she held it up for Helen to see. "I think I was six when I made this one. It was my gift to Aunt Edie that year."

Another box held four mismatched, handblown glass balls.

"How about this one?" Anne said, holding up one hand-blown orb. It was a heavy, clear bulb with blue-and-white swirls encircling it like clouds over the earth, and a closer look revealed small flecks of red, gold, and green in the clear glass.

Anne registered a fraction-of-a-second delay before Helen said, "Oh no, Anne, that's much too nice. You should keep that one for your own tree." But Anne could tell from the gleam in Helen's eyes that she had already picked just the place for the ornament on the church's tree.

"Nonsense," Anne said, rolling back onto her haunches. "The church tree ornaments can't just be a bunch of cast-offs. Besides, you said you wanted something in memory of Aunt Edie. I happen to know that she had this one for many years, because it's one I remember from my childhood. In fact, if I remember correctly, there was a set of these, but this one" — she leaned over the box of ornaments and peered in — "appears to be the last of its kind. So there you are," she smiled triumphantly at Helen, "I think this would make a fine tribute to Aunt Edie."

"Well, all right, Anne," Helen replied with no great reluctance, "if you're sure." She took the ornament and held it up to admire it.

Meanwhile, Anne dived back into the box. "We seem to have hit a trove of particularly fragile items," she observed. "Everything is so carefully wrapped." She continued to rummage through wads of tissue paper, until she noticed a piece of slender wire. "*Hmm*, well, except this."

But when she grasped the thin piece of metal and drew it out, it proved to be not wire, but a long, thin, wiry key that flared out at one end to encircle a small white porcelain disk, on which was painted the number seven.

She held it up, incredulous, to show Helen, who exclaimed, "It's the missing Advent key!"

CHAPTER TWO

Helen stared at the tiny, ornate key. "But how can that be?"

Anne was too dumbfounded to reply. She continued to twist the key about, looking at it from various angles, as if some different view would suddenly explain its presence. Finally, she said, "Do you think this really is it?"

After her initial surprise, Helen was regaining her customary no-nonsense practicality. "It certainly looks like it, though we'd need to take it to the church and test it. If it opens door seven, then it's the right key. Though really," she added, eyeing it narrowly, "I don't see how it could be anything but."

She glanced at her watch. "Now, I would love to go with you to check out your find, but I'm afraid I don't have time this morning."

Anne looked at her own watch. "Oh my goodness!" she exclaimed, "I've got to open the library!" She clambered to her feet, then added, "But I'd be glad to have you with me to check out the key. Would you be free to meet at the church this afternoon?"

Helen agreed and thanked Anne again for the ornament and the tea on her way out.

Anne rushed downstairs and had no sooner unlocked the library doors than Sherri Deveraeux, one of her newer volunteers, arrived to staff the desk. Sherri had recently recovered from a long illness that had caused her to miss much of her senior year of high school. Though still recovering her strength, she was determined to get back on track, studying for her GED and simultaneously preparing to apply to college. She had also wanted to find a job, but her parents didn't think she was ready, so she had begun volunteering at the library. Sherri was drawn to Anne because she yearned to visit New York City and hoped to go to school there. She loved to quiz Anne about life in the Big Apple.

Sherri's presence gave Anne time to haul more boxes from the attic in order to set up her holiday book displays. For the Fiction Room, this was merely a matter of some classics like Charles Dickens's *A Christmas Carol* or an illustrated edition of the O. Henry story *The Gift of the Magi*, as well as DVDs of favorite holiday films like *It's a Wonderful Life* and *Miracle on 34th Street*.

But of course things were different in the Children's Room. Here, she still had a couple of unopened boxes of books that she had ordered when she was initially building her collection but which she had stored away until now.

During her years as a librarian in New York, Anne had developed a standard Christmas display that she called "Season's Readings," and though she tinkered with it and updated it every year, most of the books it featured were now old friends. It was both comforting and energizing to create a version of her traditional display here in this new context.

Three different illustrated versions of Clement Clarke Moore's *The Night Before Christmas* made up the core of the display. Around these, she arranged a wide variety of favorites. Some of these were seasonal offerings featuring beloved characters, such as *Madeline's Christmas*. Some were fantasy adventure stories, such as *The Polar Express* or *An Adventure in Latkaland*. Some were just heartwarming, like *Li'l Rabbit's Kwanzaa* or *Favor Johnson*. Her favorites featured lots of humor, like *How the Grinch Stole Christmas* or *The Best Christmas Pageant Ever*.

When she had finished the display, she stood back to admire her work. Fortunately, Monday mornings at the library tended to be quiet, so she had been able to devote her full attention to unpacking boxes and arranging displays. And she had also spent more time than she should have flipping through old favorites to remind herself of their stories. Before she knew it, it was eleven o'clock, and she heard a familiar woman's voice calling from downstairs. "Anne?"

She went to the top of the stairs and shouted down, "Up here, Grace." Soon, she could see a large, colorful box bobbing on the lower landing, but then the box turned slightly and Grace Hawkins smiled out from behind it. From the way she carried it, the box was clearly empty, albeit awkward.

Grace called out, "Merry Christmas, Anne!" and gamely continued up the stairs.

Anne backed out of the way and stood by her display of children's books. "Can I help you with that?" she asked, though it was clear there was little she could do.

"No, no," said Grace laughing. "It's not heavy." She carried the box to the display table and set it down on the floor. "Whew! I can't thank you enough for doing this, Anne."

The box was wrapped in red-and-green paper with repeated images of Santa, elves, snowmen, and other figures. There was a slot cut in the top and a sign affixed to the front with the words Letters to Santa on it.

Grace was the editor of the *Blue Hill Gazette*, the town's weekly newspaper, and each year, the paper invited children to submit their letters to Santa, which were then published in a special section. Parents loved to see their children's names in the paper. But while in the past they had collected such letters through the mail, Grace had always wished she could have some heavily trafficked drop-off point as well. Post office regulations had not allowed her to set up a box there, and few people had proven willing to make a special trip to the newspaper's office. Now that there was a library in town, it was the perfect spot.

"Very nice," said Anne, studying the colorful box. "Did you make it?"

Grace laughed again. "Yes. Fortunately, it doesn't need to pass a very close inspection. As long as it keeps the letters in one place, it's doing its job. Oh, and look at this!" She admired Anne's display, commenting on books that had been her own favorites in childhood. Picking up *Favor Johnson*, she said, "I don't think I know this one," and began to leaf through it. "Oh, there's a dog," she said, quickly closing the book again. "It's going to make me cry, isn't it?" She spoke as if it were a foregone conclusion.

"Probably," Anne said, smiling. "Coffee?" She motioned toward the stairs and they headed down.

When their coffee had finished brewing, Anne and Grace took their mugs to the circulation desk so Anne could relieve

Sherri, who went to shelve some returns before leaving for the day. "So, how many letters do you expect, anyway?" Anne asked as she lifted her mug to her lips.

Grace shrugged. "Hard to say. We usually get about a hundred, and they're already starting to arrive through the mail. I don't know if having the box will increase the numbers or if it just means we'll get the same amount through a different route. I figure many people will still mail them, since that's what they're used to."

"It's just...that's a pretty big box."

Grace laughed. "Yes, well, that's more about visibility than capacity. I wanted something nice and visible for the photo op when Santa comes to collect them." Suddenly concerned, she added, "Is it too big? Will it be in your way?"

"No, no," Anne assured her, "it will be fine." She waved to Marian and Douglas Pauthen, two regular patrons who had just come through the door. They returned the greeting but, seeing that Anne was busy, didn't stop to chat. Turning back to Grace, Anne said, "I have that list I promised you." She pulled a piece of paper from a drawer.

"Oh, good, thank you," said Grace, and she scanned the sheet. She was writing a feature story on holiday books and Anne had promised to provide recommendations.

"Basically, it's just the list of books I have on display upstairs," Anne said.

Still reading, Grace said, "Is the one about the dog...? Oh yes, I see it." Looking up, she said, "Thank you so much, Anne, this is a big help. And you've annotated it! You've practically written the article for me."

"Recommending books is my business," Anne said with a wink, though in truth, she was a little thrilled to think that her recommendations would appear in the newspaper. And it would be good publicity for the library.

Grace set down her empty mug, folded the sheet of paper, and put it in her bag. "Well," she announced, "I'd better go and see what mischief the good people of Blue Hill are getting into." But when Anne returned from taking the coffee mugs to the kitchen, she found that Grace had slipped upstairs and brought down the copy of *Favor Johnson* she'd been looking at. "I'll just check this one out," she said, almost sheepishly, "for the article, you know."

Grace left, and Anne began decorating the circulation desk with a small tree and some green garlands.

"It's beginning to look a lot like Christmas," Douglas Pauthen said with a smile.

Anne looked up from her work and smiled. "Are you looking for something for the holidays?" she asked, though she knew what he actually wanted.

He laughed. "No, no. My reading interests are not especially seasonal. But I was wondering if the next volume of the Johnson biography was in yet?" But even as he said it, Anne was pulling the book from the Holds shelf. Douglas had been awaiting the arrival of this book for a couple of weeks, and he beamed with pleasure when he saw it.

His wife joined him as he flipped the book open to its table of contents. "Good morning, Anne," she said, setting down three mystery novels. Not only were the Pauthens regular patrons of the library, they were also fellow members of Blue Hill Community Church.

"So, are you folks ready for Christmas?" Anne asked as she checked their books out.

"For us, that's mostly just a matter of buying enough eggnog," said Douglas with a smile.

His wife said, "There's a bit more to it than that, Douglas." She turned back to Anne. "We have fifteen nieces and nephews, and we send them each a little something. But we've got those presents all bought and they'll be shipped this week." She turned back to her husband, "Won't they, dear?"

"Yes, yes," he responded, with a wink at Anne. "Though we'd be spending a lot less in shipping if you'd gone with my idea." It was his turn to address Anne. "All any of these young people want is gift cards anyway."

"Will you be seeing any of them for Christmas?" Anne asked.

"Goodness, no," said Douglas, aghast. "That's why we buy them the presents, so we won't have to host them." He had retrieved Marian's coat from the rack and was now holding it up for her.

"He says that," Marian slipped her arms into the coat sleeves, "but you should see him when we all get together in the summer."

"Annual family picnic," Douglas put in. "Get 'em all at once and get it over with."

"He has all fifteen lined up, organized, and off on adventures. They all think the world of him and will do whatever he says. It amazes their parents."

"They just need to take a firmer hand with 'em," Douglas said with another wink.

But Anne was suddenly reminded of a promise she'd made. "You know," she said, "I told Suzanne Brady I'd help with the Nativity play this year, but I know that they are in desperate need of additional adult volunteers. Do you think you two would be interested?"

Douglas gave Marian a speculative look, and Anne realized that whatever gruff front the retired Army captain might put up, the decision would actually be hers. "Suzanne does quite a job with those kids...," she said tentatively.

"I gather that this year there's a larger group than usual," Anne continued. "My Ben and Liddie will be participating, and there are some other new families as well."

"Sounds like they could use some help, Mare," Douglas said quietly.

Marian's face brightened with decision. "Well, perhaps we will then. I'll just give Suzanne a call to get a better sense of the time commitment, but yes, perhaps you'll see us there as well." She collected her three mysteries from the desk. "But I'll warn you, it may cut into my reading time."

The Pauthens left, and Anne felt relieved and thankful to have found more volunteers for the Nativity play so quickly. She was also thankful that Bella Miller was coming in to cover the afternoon shift. Bella and her twin sister Remi were Anne's two paid employees, and it was Bella's turn to take Monday. With Bella on hand, Anne calculated that there would be enough time before the kids got home from school to run up to the church. She had planned to use the time to continue decorating the library and her residence, but she decided those could wait. She was intensely curious to see whether this key was what it appeared to be.

* * *

Anne pulled into the parking lot just as Helen Smith emerged from her own car. "That was good timing," Helen greeted her as Anne jumped from her car and pulled her coat more closely around her. From the look on Helen's face, Anne thought that she must be as curious about the key as well.

The church offices were behind the main building with the entrance just off the parking lot. They entered to find Sophie Wise sitting behind a desk, a bank of filing cabinets behind her and a work table off to one side.

Helen hesitated when she saw her and said, "Sophie," a note of uncertainty creeping into her voice. Anne didn't know Sophie well, but she had noticed that most members of the church treated her with a degree of wariness that Anne didn't understand.

Sophie had only recently begun to act as the church secretary/receptionist, though Anne understood that she had been a member for some years. The church had never had a receptionist before, and there was some mystery about this appointment that Anne had yet to fathom. She wasn't sure, for instance, whether it was a paid or volunteer position. But at the moment, the new receptionist appeared flustered by the arrival of visitors.

Recovering her composure, Helen said, "Good afternoon, Sophie. Is Reverend Tom in?"

"No. No, I'm afraid he's not," said Sophie, sounding as if she'd been caught at something. "He's out visiting parishioners all afternoon. Monday is his day for that."

"*Hmm*," said Helen frowning, "I suppose it doesn't matter. We're just going down to the Community Room."

Though this seemed perfectly innocuous to Anne, Sophie opened and then closed her mouth, as if she wanted to object. Helen had already turned away, so in an effort to make some further explanation, Anne added, "We may have found the missing key to the Advent cabinet." She had already drawn the key from her jacket pocket and she held it up to illustrate her claim.

Helen gave a slight frown, but Sophie's eyes widened. "Really?" She was almost childlike in her amazement.

With a slight sigh, Helen said, "Would you like to come with us to try it out?"

Sophie all but scuttled out from behind her desk. "Perhaps we'll find some sort of treasure in there," she said as she followed along.

"Most likely we'll just find a few dust bunnies. Not my idea of a treasure," Helen said, adding, "Though, having a complete set of keys again will be a treasure."

They arrived at the cabinet, and Anne paused a moment to exchange a glance with Helen. Then she carefully fit the key into the lock on door number seven. It turned smoothly, and the door swung open.

Helen uttered a soft, "Huh."

There *was* something inside.

CHAPTER THREE

Anne retrieved a small box, perhaps two inches square, out of the cubbyhole and found that it was covered with some sort of fabric with a very fine nap. The box opened clamshell fashion, so she rocked the top back on its hinge. Nestled inside was a gorgeous ring with a gleaming blue stone.

"It looks like a sapphire," Helen whispered after they had all stood a moment in shocked silence.

"A real one?" asked Sophie, but Helen could only shrug her shoulders.

"But how did it get in here?" Anne asked Helen. "Does it belong to the church?"

Helen shook her head. "I would say it must have been Edie's."

"Edie's?" exclaimed Sophie, and Helen explained how Anne had found the key. "Oh well, then," she said, satisfied, "it must have been Edie's. She put it there."

"But why?" Anne asked, not at all convinced. Neither of the other women could offer an explanation.

"Did she put anything else in there?" Sophie asked, but they could see at a glance that the shallow cubbyhole was otherwise empty.

Anne's brain shifted out of stunned puzzlement and into gear. "Okay," she said slowly, "if not *why*, then *how*?" She looked up at the other two women. "If Aunt Edie did lock this ring into the Advent cabinet, how could she have done so? She could only do it sometime around the holidays, right? When it's out here?"

"Oh no," Helen shook her head decisively. "The storeroom where the cabinet is kept is not locked. Anyone in the church could get at it any time they wanted. In fact, we make a point of keeping the space around the cabinet fairly clear, since it has to be hauled out every year. We try not to let it get buried under things."

"Okay, so the ring must have been locked in the cabinet sometime last year before Christmas, because the key was gone by then. Or actually, before December if that's when the key was found to be missing. Right? Was the key already missing when the cabinet was brought out from storage for the season last year?"

Helen frowned. "I'm not really sure when we noticed it." She shook her head. "At some point, somebody realized the key was missing, but I couldn't say who, or when. Reverend Tom said he would look around for it, but he never found it."

"Well," said Anne, pointing to the cubby's position in the cabinet. "Was the key there on the seventh of last year?"

"Ah," said Helen, catching the significance. "No, the key was definitely gone by the day that we wanted to open the cubby."

"Which would have been the following Sunday? Whatever that date was?"

Helen nodded.

"Okay," said Anne, "so that's…a little inconclusive, but it's something. But I'm assuming that the key was *not* missing the year before?" Both Helen and Sophie shook their heads. "So, sometime between January and approximately December seventh of last year, somebody put this ring into the cabinet and took the key away. And apparently anyone in the church could have done so."

Helen nodded, but Sophie insisted, "Edie put it there."

Anne frowned. "I just can't...," she began, then said, "Perhaps I should leave this for Reverend Tom."

But Sophie immediately shook her head. "But he's not here," she said, in a slightly urgent tone.

Confused, Anne began, "But I could just—"

Sophie shook her head. "I don't want to take responsibility for it. Besides, it's Edie's ring." She sounded convinced of this, even if Anne was not.

Helen supported Sophie. "I think you'd better take it, Anne. Edie had the key, so she must have been the one who locked the ring in the cabinet. I can't imagine why, but Edie generally had good reasons for whatever she did." After a pause, she added, "Perhaps she left a note. There was a lot of paper in that box, and a note might have become separated from the key."

This was a reasonable suggestion, though somehow Anne couldn't believe that the ring belonged to Edie. Anne herself had never seen it before, and it just didn't seem to be her aunt's style. But she had to admit that Edie was the most likely person to have locked it in the cabinet since the key had been found among her things. Perhaps the ring came to Edie from someone else? In that case, she had a responsibility to try to find its owner.

Anne closed and locked the cubby door, leaving the newly found key in place. She closed the ring box and slipped it into her pocket. "Well, then," she declared, "if the missing Christmas key has turned up a mysterious ring, I'll just have to see what I can learn about it."

* * *

Anne returned to the library just in time to welcome Ben and Liddie home from school. After a quick check-in with Bella to make sure all was well, Anne asked the kids to get ready to take Hershey for a walk, their regular after-school chore. As usual, the dog, still something of an overgrown puppy, was excited to have the kids home again.

They slowly made their way down Bluebell Lane, their breaths materializing as little clouds of vapor as they walked. If it weren't for the absence of a horse-drawn sleigh in the scene, Anne could almost believe that she and her children had been transported into a hand-tinted Currier and Ives lithograph. Anne cherished moments like these with her children, and, bundled up against the crisp, cold air as they were, this moment felt especially cozy and comfortable as they talked. Ben kept a tight leash on the dog, and Anne kept a watchful eye on the proceedings while she talked over the day with her children. As usual, their stories about school were excited and energetic but at times slightly confusing so that Anne had to go back and establish some key piece of information they'd forgotten to mention. But as they burbled on, Anne reflected with relief that, after the first few months, they seemed to have settled well into Blue Hill Elementary.

When they'd first enrolled, most of Ben's comments about the school had focused on the ways in which it was different from his neighborhood school back in Park Slope. And though as a kindergartener, Liddie had no former school to compare hers to, she had often imitated her brother by focusing on differences between their new lives and the lives they had known in Brooklyn.

Now, however, their talk was all about Miss Reed, Liddie's kindergarten teacher, Mr. Layton, Ben's fourth grade teacher, and their new friends and activities at Blue Hill Elementary.

After they had each reviewed their school day, Anne asked, "So what do you think about the Nativity play?"

She had broached the possibility of Ben and Liddie participating in the play when they got home from church the day before, but she didn't want them to feel it was something they were being forced into. So at the time, she had merely asked them to think about whether they would like to participate.

This turned out to have been a wise decision, because Ben immediately said, "Ryan's going to be in it." The involvement of Ben's friend was a much stronger inducement than any Anne could have offered. And if Ben was in, then his sister would be too.

She decided to treat the matter as settled. "That's great," she said. "He's been in it before, hasn't he?"

Ben nodded and said, "Uh-huh," but if Ryan had shared any insights about the experience, Ben wasn't passing them on.

"And I bet some of Wendy's kids will be in it too," Anne added. Of the new friends that Anne had made since returning to Blue Hill, Wendy was perhaps her closest. A voracious reader and tireless volunteer, she was a strong supporter of the library. And with seven kids, Wendy's brood could practically do the Nativity play by themselves. Anne chuckled to herself over that thought, then continued to her children, "So don't forget, the first rehearsal is Wednesday after school. You'll need to come straight home and get Hershey walked so that we can get down there."

At the sound of his name, the dog raised his head and wagged his tail hopefully. Ben gave him one of the treats he carried in his pocket. "We will, Mom," he promised.

* * *

Helen's theory about a note that went with the key was reasonable, but it turned out to be sadly unfounded.

On Tuesday, after covering the morning shift in the library, Anne indulged her curiosity in the afternoon and spent some time trying to find some information about the mysterious ring.

First, she sifted through every last decoration and minute scrap of paper in the box that had held the ornaments, but neither a note nor any other clue about the key or the ring revealed itself. As she packed it all away again, she thought about what other lines of inquiry she could pursue.

Once she'd cleaned up her mess, she went to her desk and took out the file of documents related to Edie's estate. Her aunt's executor had been extremely thorough, something for which she was grateful, and the estate inventory was sufficiently detailed that it listed the more valuable pieces of jewelry separately. Anne did not consider herself much of a judge of jewelry, but it appeared to her that the mystery ring must be worth enough to have made this list. Reading through the inventory, however, she found no mention of a ring that sounded even remotely like this one.

Besides, as she knew perfectly well, she had already checked the list against the contents of the jewelry case she'd inherited, and there had been nothing missing. But her intrinsic thoroughness had her double-checking the list nonetheless.

Once Anne had completed her review, she felt vindicated in her sense that the ring had not belonged to her aunt at all. But then she recalled her own line of reasoning as to the timing. Clearly, the ring had been hidden in the cabinet at least some months before her aunt died, so it wouldn't have been among her possessions at the time the inventory was made. Realistically, she shouldn't expect to find it on the list. The executor might very well not have known of its existence.

So the fact that the ring did not appear on the estate inventory did not settle the question of whether the ring had belonged to her aunt, though Anne clung to her unfounded conviction that it had not.

She sat and pondered for a few minutes and then rose and went to her closet, where she removed a black velour blouse from its hanger. She laid this on the top of her desk and set the ring on it. The black material made an excellent backdrop against which to display the ring. She used her cell phone camera to take several pictures, showing the ring both by itself and in its box.

She fired up the phone's e-mail application and sent the pictures to both her parents with the message, *Call me*.

Soon, Anne's mother was on the line. "Anne," said Charlene Summers in a quizzical tone, "did you buy a new ring? I mean, it's very nice, but it must have been expensive."

Anne laughed and reassured her mother. She explained the whole story of the Advent cabinet, the missing key, its unexpected discovery among Edie's things, and the surprising contents of the locked cubbyhole. Then she asked her mother to take a good look at the ring.

"I don't know, dear" said Charlene after a few moments. "I'll ask your father—Edie was his aunt, after all—but I have to say that I never saw Edie with a ring like that." Anne waited while her mother paused thoughtfully. "Edie had a few nice pieces of jewelry, but I never would have described her as someone especially interested in such things. For the most part, her nicer pieces were family heirlooms, and I think she showed me most of them at one time or another. This just isn't something I recognize."

"Somehow it didn't seem like her style to me, either," Anne said.

"No, I think you're right," her mother said slowly. "At least, this isn't something I would have picked out thinking she would like it. But I'm sorry, dear, I can't say for sure." She paused, then changed the subject. "So," she asked eagerly, "how are the kids?"

Anne relaxed and tried to dismiss the ring from her mind. "They're starting to get excited about the holidays. Now that it's finally December, it feels like we're actually getting toward

Christmas." She paused and added, "Oh, and they're going to participate in the Nativity play at church."

"Oh, how nice," Charlene exclaimed. "What will they be playing?"

"I don't know yet. The organizing session is tomorrow after school. I've promised to help supervise."

"I wish your father and I could be there for the performance," she said wistfully. "You don't suppose you could make a video, do you?"

"I don't know, Mom," Anne said, wincing. She felt that parents who were always filming their children made spectacles of themselves. "I'd feel a little…self-conscious." And besides, Anne didn't really need another task to worry about. But she also knew that her parents would be disappointed to miss it, and she sighed. "We'll see."

"Thank you, dear. Now, your father isn't here right now. He's out on the golf course." Anne smiled. Her father had become an avid golfer since his retirement a few years before.

"Okay, Mom. But you'll ask Dad to have a look at that ring when he gets back, won't you?"

After hanging up, Anne glanced at the clock. The kids would be home from school soon. The ring and the box were still before her on the desk, nestled in the fabric she'd laid out. She picked up the ring and brought it close to her eyes. The blue stone flashed as it caught the light. Could it really be a sapphire? Anne was no judge of gems, but it was certainly pretty.

And the ring itself was lovely, delicately shaped. On impulse, she peered at the inside of the band. It appeared that there were some markings there. With one hand, she groped around inside her desk for a magnifying glass, and finding it, raised it to her eye to look again at the underside of the ring. Yes, there were some letters etched there. After much squinting, she made them out as the letters *JH* and *DC* and some numbers.

She studied them until her eyes began to water, then she set down the ring and the magnifier and closed her eyes to rest them. What could the letters and numbers mean? Might the numbers be a date? If so, it would be a date early in the previous year. And the letters, initials? But without more information, more context, how could she determine their significance?

The afternoon was wearing on. She took the ring and settled it back into its box and closed the lid. Then she sat there for a bit, turning the box around in her hand. Finally, after she had turned it over two or three times, she realized that there was something printed on the bottom. It appeared to be some sort of symbol, two interlaced, script Ds, beginning the words "Diamond District."

Anne sat back. That must be the name of the store where the ring was bought. Or at least the name of *a* store where the box originally came from. But she'd never heard of it. The only jewelry store she knew in Blue Hill was Kepple's. Come to think of it, Kepple's was the only jewelry store that she'd ever known Aunt Edie to patronize. Another indication that this ring had not belonged to her great-aunt.

But what about this Diamond District?

Anne did a quick search on the Internet and found that there was a store by that name in Blue Hill. It appeared to be out on the west side of town. Anne pictured the neighborhood for the address given, but it was a part of town that had changed and grown a lot since her day, and she didn't know it well. Studying the store's Web site, Anne realized that the Diamond District was actually a chain of jewelry stores, apparently family-owned, with stores spread across Pennsylvania, although most of them were located farther to the east.

Well, Anne reasoned, if the ring was sold by this store, and especially if they had also done the engraving, which suddenly seemed a much more valuable clue, then perhaps they would have a record of who bought it and when. And that might help her get it back in the hands of its rightful owner, whoever that might be.

But her reflections on the ring and the store were interrupted when Hershey, who had been sleeping quietly, abruptly awoke and raised his head and thumped his tail. She knew that in a moment, she would hear the sound of Ben and Liddie rushing up the stairs.

CHAPTER FOUR

O n Wednesday, the sound of rushing feet reverberated in the front hall of the library.

"Benjamin Eric Gibson!" Anne's voice was not loud, but it was laced with authority. Ben and his friend Ryan Slater stopped in their tracks. "Try that again." She didn't object to the boys using the library entrance, but she drew the line at them disrupting library patrons.

The boys, who had just come bursting through the library's front door and racing down the hall, looked at each other for a moment, then retreated more sedately toward the vestibule to shed their coats. But Anne was sure that she heard some giggling as they went.

"I'm so sorry," she said to the woman who was checking out a recent novel.

The woman gave her a sympathetic smile. "It's the time of year," she said. "They can't help getting a little excited." As the woman left, Anne wondered whether the phrase "a little excited" really extended to "running pell-mell into the library."

The boys returned, smiling, their faces still pink with the cold.

"Where's your sister?" Anne asked Ben.

"She already went upstairs."

"Right. Are you two ready?" They both nodded. "Did you take Hershey out?" They nodded again. "Go upstairs and tell Liddie it's time to go." This precipitated a barely controlled dash for the stairs.

Anne turned to the volunteer helping her at the desk. "You'll be okay closing up, Sherri?" And when the young woman assured her she would be, she said, "Thanks so much for doing this. With rehearsals twice a week, I can see that this play is really going to put a crimp in my schedule." Fortunately, she thought, the Sunday rehearsals wouldn't conflict with the library's schedule.

But this was Wednesday, the afternoon of the organizing session, and Anne had to fulfill her promise to help supervise. Since she had to take Ben and Liddie down anyway, she had also agreed to take Ryan, the nephew of her old friend Alex Ochs.

Actually, Alex was something more than an old friend. He and Anne had been a couple in high school. When Anne returned to Blue Hill to convert her aunt's home into the library, Alex was the contractor who had done the work, and Anne had been grateful for his familiar face and the chance to renew their friendship. She was also happy that Ben and Ryan had hit it off, since Alex was raising his late sister's son.

All three children were excited on the drive down to Blue Hill Community Church, and when they entered the sanctuary, they found that a fair number of people were assembled. As soon as they walked in, Anne was unsurprised and pleased to see her friend Wendy Pyle, who indeed was there with five of her seven children. A five-foot-one, raven-haired bundle of energy, Wendy made a beeline for Anne as soon as she saw her. She greeted Ben, Liddie, and Ryan as they moved past her to join the gathering children, then without preamble, greeted Anne with, "Do you have your shopping done yet?"

Anne blinked, then laughed. "No, I'm afraid I haven't even started!" Wendy had lately been asking Anne this question every time they met. What she really meant was, "You'd better get busy on it." Looking around, Anne spotted Suzanne Brady already herding the kids together while Helen watched and Brad conferred with the older kids. Anne saw shy Carrie listening intensely while simultaneously pulling up the cowl of her sweater as if it were a mask. She also saw that the Pauthens were there, and she gave them a wave before turning back to Wendy. "I haven't even done my cards yet," she admitted.

"Well, don't let the time slip away from you," Wendy warned her. "Been there, done that, and it's not pretty." She moved into one of the pews and sat down, patting the cushion for Anne to sit beside her. "I'm glad you're helping out with the play this year," she said as Anne did so. "I know it helps keep the kids focused to have some adults around, but there's not really that much for us to do. It will be nice to have someone to talk to." She eyed the milling group at the front of the sanctuary. "They've got a big group this year, don't they? One year, my kids made up half the cast."

Meanwhile, Helen and Brad had been conferring while Suzanne finished rounding up the kids. Anne watched as they separated and Brad took a seat in the front row of pews. Helen made her way down the aisle to Anne and Wendy and they slid over in the pew to make room for her. Helen smiled a greeting but didn't speak because Suzanne was just beginning to address the assembled students. "The wise men are the best parts," Wendy whispered to Anne. "They get to carry gifts, so they have something to do with their hands, and they only have to learn a couple of lines each."

Once Suzanne had the kids settled, she welcomed everyone and thanked them for participating. "Some of you have done this before, and some of you are here for the first time," she said. "This year we have the luxury of working with a larger group than usual, and we'll be making some changes to take advantage of our greater numbers."

Suzanne turned and motioned to Brad. "Also, you all know Mr. Trowbridge," Brad stood and gave a quick nod at Suzanne's mention of his name, but she continued on without further fanfare. "Brad is spending some time with our church while he prepares for the ministry. He also has some ideas for this year's performance." Suzanne nodded toward the other adults. "And we're very lucky to have the assistance of some other members of the church as well," she added, acknowledging Helen, Wendy, Anne, and the Pauthens.

Suzanne relaxed as her focus returned to the children. "I'm so glad you've all agreed to participate," she said. "We're going to have a good time. There are a lot of jobs that need doing. Some of them are on stage and some of them are backstage, but they are all crucial to the success of the production. Okay?" She looked around at the nodding children with a smile of genuine pleasure on her face. Then, seeming to remember something, she added, "Um, Mr. Trowbridge? Did you have anything to share with the children?"

Brad slowly unfolded himself from the pew and made his way to Suzanne's side. "Hello, ladies and gentlemen," he said in a friendly if somewhat formal manner. The smaller children giggled at being addressed as grown-ups, and Anne saw him take the opportunity to peek at an index card he held in his hand. "You know, the Christmas season is a time of great celebration," he began, and for some minutes he droned on about the long history of plays and performances as important aspects of public celebrations and festivals. It was not uninteresting, Anne thought, but it was perhaps a bit much for the fidgety children.

Finally, he concluded with an assurance to the teens and the children that their participation in the Nativity play would be a contribution to the community celebration of the joyous season. There was a palpable relaxation of tension as Suzanne once again stepped forward.

She was carrying a large stack of papers, which she handed to one of the teens with a murmured instruction. Turning to the group, she said, "We're going to assign the roles now, and I've asked Simon to hand out the scripts. But I want to emphasize one thing—whatever role you're assigned, it's vital that you read and understand the entire script. Don't just go through and look only at your own part or your own job in isolation." She paused and gazed around to emphasize her point. "It's important that everyone understands how the whole show is supposed to go. That's how we all work together. Any questions?

"All right, then. I'm going to give you all your assignments, and then we'll spend the rest of the rehearsal unpacking the props and scenery and getting everything set up. I expect that by our next rehearsal, you will all have studied your parts and will be ready to begin work on the performance."

Suzanne pulled out another sheet of paper and began reading the assignments, which she had apparently determined ahead of time. She read the backstage jobs first and then the onstage roles. Two of Wendy's children were cast as wise men, and Anne saw her friend nod in satisfaction. Liddie's face lit up as she learned she was cast as one of the angels. Ryan Slater was cast as a shepherd, and Ben was cast as one of the sheep. The one surprise, really, was that shy Carrie McAllister had been cast as the narrator.

Suzanne allowed them to chatter among themselves for a few moments, comparing jobs, and then she started organizing them to bring out and unpack the scenery and props that they used every year. Anne didn't notice exactly when he stepped in, but suddenly Douglas Pauthen was among the children, directing them with a quiet but authoritative word here or a gesture there.

Wendy sat back with a sigh. "Well, that's done," she said. "Justin may not be too pleased, but he'll have to wait his turn." Her six-year-old son had also been cast as a sheep. Turning to Anne, she added, "Liddie will make a beautiful angel."

Anne was about to reply when she heard a noise behind them, and they turned in the pew to find Reverend Tom approaching. The door behind him into the vestibule was just closing, and Anne thought she had caught the briefest glimpse of a person who was leaving. Oddly, she had the impression that it had been Alex Ochs, but of course, she knew that Alex had another commitment elsewhere — that's why she'd been the one to bring Ryan to the rehearsal. So if it was him, what was he doing at the church?

As Reverend Tom neared, he gave them his usual benevolent smile. "Good afternoon, ladies. How goes the rehearsal?" He sat down in the pew in front of them and turned to face them. All three women leaned forward slightly so that they could converse without disrupting the proceedings.

"They're off to a good start," Helen said and Wendy nodded agreement. Since Anne had never been through this experience, she didn't feel qualified to comment.

"And how is our young intern doing?" Reverend Tom asked.

There was a moment of strained hesitation before all three women offered a weak "Fine" at almost the same moment. Reverend Tom gave a small nod but refrained from further comment.

In the silence that followed, Anne was aware of the sound of Suzanne's voice as she directed the young people in setting up the scenery. Suddenly, Helen threw out a new gambit. "So you must have heard about Anne's amazing discovery?"

The smile left Reverend Tom's face and he sat very still for a moment before shifting his gaze to Anne. "Ah, yes, Sophie told me," he said. "The ring."

Seeming disconcerted, Helen filled the silence. "Well, yes, the ring and also the key! Imagine finding the lost key that way. And yes, finding the ring was certainly odd as well, but isn't it so nice to have all the keys again? I could hardly believe it when it actually worked."

"Ring?" asked Wendy. "Key? What are you all talking about?"

Anne filled her in about finding the key in Edie's things and then the discovery of the ring locked in the cabinet. As she spoke, Anne watched Reverend Tom's face. She sensed that something about this incident troubled him, and she feared he was upset that she had taken the ring away with her. After all, it was found on church property.

When Wendy had finished exclaiming over the story, Anne said to Reverend Tom, "I tried to leave the ring with Sophie, you know, but she wouldn't let me. She was convinced it must have belonged to Aunt Edie, although I haven't been able to confirm that."

"Well, of course it must have," said Helen. "If Edie had the key, then she must have been the one to put the ring in the cabinet."

"But maybe the ring belongs to the church," said Anne, still watching Reverend Tom. He seemed lost in thought.

The pastor shook his head distractedly. "No, no. It doesn't belong to the church."

Anne looked at him even more curiously. "You sound very sure," she said. "Does that mean that it *does* belong to Aunt Edie?"

Slowly, Reverend Tom refocused on Anne and then smiled. "Oh, I don't know that," he replied with a chuckle. "I just know that the church doesn't own any jewelry."

Before Anne could say anything further, they were interrupted by a voice from the front of the sanctuary. "Helen?" Suzanne was calling, "Reverend Tom?"

They all looked in her direction. As the Pauthens and the kids organized scenery and props, Suzanne stood in the midst of the bustle with her hands on her hips, looking about her with a puzzled expression.

"What's wrong, Suzanne?" Helen asked as she and Reverend Tom both rose and started toward her. After a moment, Anne and Wendy followed out of curiosity.

"Where on earth...?" Suzanne was muttering. Then she said to a few children who were standing by her, "You keep looking, okay? A large cardboard box." To the approaching adults she said, "What did we do with the costumes last year?"

Immediately, they all began to look about the floor as well, Anne included, even though she had no idea what she was looking for. As the Pauthens and more of the children came over to join the search, Suzanne said, "They were in a big box"—she indicated its dimensions with her hands—"and it was clearly marked Costumes on all sides."

Reverend Tom frowned. "I seem to recall that box was getting pretty ratty last year, Suzanne. Is there any chance that we got a new one?"

Suzanne shrugged, still looking around. "It's possible," she conceded, "but I don't remember doing so." She sighed. "Each year seems to bleed into the others," she muttered. "I can't...Who was Joseph last year? That's the only way I can tell one year from the next."

But before anyone could supply the name of last year's Joseph, Helen gave a small, "Uh-oh." They all looked in her direction. "I remember what we did with the costumes last year," she said.

And then, as if Helen had somehow telepathically communicated the information to her, Suzanne's face fell, and she said, "Oh."

For the benefit of the others, Helen explained, "Eleanor Jameson took them all away to be cleaned."

This didn't sound like such a terrible fate to Anne, but judging from the crestfallen expressions now shared by Wendy, Reverend Tom, and the Pauthens, she decided there was still something here she didn't understand.

"And she never...?" Reverend Tom asked.

Helen shrugged, and Suzanne added, "Apparently not."

Sensing Anne's confusion, Wendy quietly filled her in. "Eleanor had a stroke. She's eighty...eighty-six, I think, and she has never fully recovered. She's been in a rehab facility ever since."

"Well," said Helen, after a moment, "no need to despair just yet. I can ask her daughter Emily about them."

Suzanne took a deep breath and nodded, but the rehearsal ended on a somewhat somber note, with Suzanne looking troubled.

Out of the corner of her eye, Anne saw Douglas turn to his wife and raise an eyebrow, but she merely tipped her head to one side and neither spoke.

* * *

On the drive home, Liddie talked excitedly of her role as an angel. "I'm going to get to wear wings, right?" she asked.

"I don't know," Anne replied, laughing. "Probably. You'll have to ask Mrs. Brady that."

"Usually the angels do wear wings," offered Ryan.

"Wings!" cried Liddie, clapping her hands together. "I'm gonna have wings and a halo!"

"I don't think they do halos," Ryan said uncertainly, but nothing dampened Liddie's enthusiasm.

Anne glanced with concern at Ben, who had so far been silent. "How 'bout you, Ben? Are you looking forward to the play?"

Ben said nothing for a moment, and then, "*Baaaah.*"

Anne laughed. "Well, I guess I'll take that for a yes."

"He's just mad because he has to be a stupid old sheep," said Liddie with satisfaction.

"Honey? You don't mind being a sheep, do you?"

Ben made no reply.

"It's still an important part," Anne tried. "If there were no sheep then there'd be no shepherds."

Ben remained silent.

"Someone's got to be the sheep," she added, "and you'll be on stage almost the whole time."

When Ben still didn't respond, Anne decided that she had better let him work out his disappointment, if that's what it was, on his own.

But Ryan, apparently also discontented, spoke up to say, "At least you've got a line. A shepherd does even less than the sheep!"

"*Baaaah*," said Ben.

CHAPTER FIVE

Anne had intended to work on her Christmas cards on Thursday because she had one of the Miller twins available to cover the library during the day. The conversation at the rehearsal, however, had rekindled her curiosity about the ring's ownership, a question she had allowed to drift to the back of her mind after her failure to find an explanation among Edie's papers. She now made up her mind to visit the Diamond District to see what she could learn.

She had learned from Wendy that the jewelry store was part of a development on the west side of town that had gone up not long before the last recession. The intent had been to create a small, upscale shopping plaza that would attract boutique tenants from Blue Hill and surrounding towns. Despite lots of tasteful landscaping and cozy retail spaces, however, the development had struggled to retain high-end tenants, especially when the economy went sour, and it now hosted a more eclectic mix of shops and offices, which struggled to compete with Blue Hill's thriving downtown.

At least there was plenty of parking, Anne thought, as she pulled into the lot.

The Diamond District had been one of the first stores to commit to the development and enjoyed a prime location, but when Anne entered the store, it appeared to be deserted. She gazed about at a vast array of gleaming display cases, many arranged in small groups with a central square in which a clerk could stand. The December light filtered weakly through slightly tinted windows and was supplemented by dim fixtures. A sleek, black lacquer cabinet and shiny mirrored panels on the walls made the light cast a cold, almost institutional ambience to the jewelry store. Anne didn't see another soul until a figure rose slowly from behind a counter at the back of the store. "Good morning." he said without warmth.

Anne returned the greeting and made her way past the glass-topped cases toward the back. The man was middle-aged and tall but stooped, and he had a haggard, defeated air. He eyed her as she made her way to the back, and though he continued to stand, he gave the impression that he'd much rather sit. As she approached, Anne gave him a smile that was not returned, and when she finally stood before him, she said, "I wonder if you can help me?" She found herself unsure how to continue.

He looked at her expectantly.

Finally, she tried, "Are you...the owner?"

"I'm the manager," he replied. He had a harsh, croaking voice. "Henderson Brockhurst."

Anne nodded. "The thing is, you see, I've...found a ring. I think it may have been lost and I'm hoping to return it to its..." For some reason, she hesitated over the word *rightful.* "...former owner."

The man spread his hands in a "How does this concern me?" gesture.

Anne pulled the ring box from her pocket and turned it over. "You see, it looks like the ring may have been purchased here. Or at one of your other stores? I thought you might have a record of it." Brockhurst made no move. His unresponsiveness was getting under Anne's skin. "Do you do engraving? Because the ring has some, and I thought that's something you might have a record of as well." Finally, she forced herself to stop talking.

After a moment, the man sat back down at the desk and motioned for Anne to take a seat, but she declined. She felt as though she needed to stay on her feet in case she needed to run.

After another moment, Brockhurst held out his hand. "May I see it?"

Anne handed over the box and he placed it rather precisely in front of him. Then he drew over a large magnifier on a flexible arm. The lens was set in a round frame that had a light built into it. He switched on the light and peered through the device to open the box. For a large man, he handled the box with a delicate touch.

As soon as he opened the box, Brockhurst gave a faint grunt—of surprise, Anne thought—but he quickly recovered himself, drew out the ring, and set the box to one side. He examined the ring minutely and for a long time, paying particular attention to the engraving on the inside of the band. As he continued to turn the ring over and over, however, Anne began to get the sense that his attention had wandered off, that he was simply turning the ring about while he considered some other matter.

Abruptly, he ceased turning it. "This is a very fine ring," he said, reaching for the box and carefully tucking it back inside. "Unfortunately, I'm sorry to tell you that this is a ring that was stolen from this very store last year." Without warning, he slid open a drawer in the table at which he sat, set the box inside, and slid it closed again. "We're very happy to have it back."

Anne stood in stunned silence for a moment, consternation and indignation rendering her mute. "Excuse me," she said at last in a rising intonation, "but what are you doing with that?"

At last Brockhurst looked up at her, a dark scowl on his face. "As I say, madam, we are very grateful for the return of our stolen property." His face assumed a knowing look. "We are prepared to...drop the matter here. Not pursue it any further." He clicked off the light on his magnifier.

"Not pursue..." Anne was rendered almost inarticulate by his insinuation. "Mr. Brockhurst, if you are implying that *I* had something to do with the theft of your ring, I can assure you that is certainly *not* the case. So you need make me no promises of 'dropping the matter here.' Just the opposite, in fact. If this ring is stolen property, then it should be with the police, to be used as evidence in your case."

Brockhurst seemed taken aback by her vehemence. "Well," he mumbled, looking away again, "the suspect has not yet been...apprehended."

"All the more reason why they should have it, then," Anne quickly retorted. "It's evidence in an ongoing investigation. You give that ring back to me right now, and I will take it down there myself, so that I can also tell them how it came into my possession."

Once again, Brockhurst adopted a stern expression. "I will take the ring to the police myself, madam, when I have the opportunity to do so. As for your story..." But he stopped abruptly when he saw Anne draw her phone from her purse.

"No time like the present," Anne said. "I'm calling the police right now and asking them to come down while I'm still here. We can tell them the story together." As Anne had regained her self-control, she had become increasingly suspicious of Brockhurst's behavior. Pulling out her phone had been intended as much to see how he would react to an actual intent to call the police. But she'd now made up her mind not to leave the store while the ring was still in that drawer, and bringing in the police would ensure that.

She hesitated over the keypad. She didn't know the number of the police department, and somehow this situation didn't seem to her to rise to the level of an "emergency." After a moment, she made up her mind and pressed the nine key. But in her moment of hesitation, Brockhurst had pulled open the drawer, and he now removed the ring box and placed it on her side of the desk before she had a chance to dial the one.

"Fine, then," Brockhurst said. "*You* take it to the police. But I warn you," he blustered as well as he could under the circumstances, "I'll be checking with them to make sure you do."

* * *

"So you think, what, that he was trying to steal the ring from you?" Officer Michael Banks looked up from his notebook to gaze at Anne with concern.

"Wouldn't you?" she asked.

Anne had been so shaken by her encounter with Henderson Brockhurst that she had indeed gone straight from the Diamond District to the police station. There, she had been lucky enough to find Michael Banks, a good friend from her high school years with whom she had reconnected since returning to Blue Hill. Shakily, she had spilled out her story, and he had taken her to a conference room and settled her down with some tea in a Styrofoam cup.

After leaving her for a few minutes, he had returned with a file folder but had set that to one side on the conference table. He was now leading her more slowly and calmly through her story. But his question brought Anne up short. She had certainly found Brockhurst's behavior suspicious and upsetting, but what, in fact, did she suspect him of? He'd returned the ring, and he had not tried to stop her when she snatched it up and all but ran out the door. She hadn't liked or trusted the man from the moment she'd set eyes on him, but that didn't constitute a crime.

When Michael didn't respond to her question, she added, "Well, what do you think?"

Michael pursed his lips and pulled over the file folder he'd brought in. "The thing is, Anne," he said as he opened the file and gazed at the top sheet, "he really did report a ring stolen from his store. Almost" — his eyes searched the page — "eighteen months ago."

"This ring?" Anne asked, surprised.

Michael didn't answer immediately, but he drew over the ring box, which was sitting open on the table, and flipped a couple of pages in the file. He studied one page, occasionally flicking his eyes to the ring. After a moment, he shrugged and said, "It fits the description."

He continued reading in the file, and Anne began to feel intensely curious about what he had found there. Focusing on the file helped to take her mind off the incident in the jewelry shop, and she sipped her tea more calmly.

Leafing through the pages, Michael said without looking up, "Does the name *Courtney* mean anything to you?"

"As a first name or a last name?"

He looked up at that. "Last," he said.

But Anne shook her head. "No. Who is it?"

Michael returned his gaze to the file. "Possible suspect, apparently," he replied and turned another sheet. "*Hmm.* Cleared by Philly PD," he muttered, but he flipped the page impatiently over and back again. "You'd think they could provide a bit more detail," he muttered under his breath and continued reading his way through the file.

But there was little more in the folder, and after a moment, he closed it again and gazed at it thoughtfully. For a second, he looked to Anne just like the teenager she had known long ago, puzzling over some math problem in his homework.

"So how do you explain his behavior this morning?" she finally asked.

He gave a slight shake of his head, as if to clear it. "People respond to stress—to the unexpected, let's say—in funny ways." He paused a moment before continuing. "Let's take him at face value for a moment. He's had a ring stolen, more than a year ago. We believe this because he filed a police report at the time. And then one day a strange woman comes into his store with the very same ring, asking him if he can tell her anything about it."

"Okay," Anne said, "so he freaks out and his first thought is to get his ring back, so he tries to simply hang onto it. But I won't play along with that and he realizes his position is untenable. But why not let me call the police to come down?"

"Well, for one thing, because he's got your ring in his drawer, which might not look good when the police arrive. But also..." His voice trailed off.

"Spill it, Banks," Anne said in a poor attempt to imitate a television police interrogator.

Her attempted humor sailed past Michael, who was scratching his chin and gazing thoughtfully out the window behind her. At last he said, "There's also the insurance. Presumably he filed a claim on this ring months ago and has already received payment. And now, all this time later, the item suddenly resurfaces. So you see"—he shifted his gaze back to Anne and shrugged—"it might be one complication too many. So he lets you walk out with it. If you go to the police, as you say you're going to do, well, fine, he'll file whatever additional paperwork he needs to and he'll have his ring back. And if you don't, if you simply disappear again with the ring, well, that might just save him some hassle and nobody would be the wiser. So he decides to sit back and let things take their course."

"And now I've gone with option A," said Anne.

Michael nodded and pulled the ring to him for a closer look. "Now I'll be the one paying him a visit, and we'll see how he reacts." He pulled the ring from the box and held it up to gaze at it. "I'll have to hang onto this, you know."

Anne nodded, then said, "So it's valuable?"

Michael didn't respond but continued to study the ring.

"You know what I'd like to do," she continued after a moment. "I'd like to have Hank Kepple look at it and tell me what he thinks."

Slowly, Michael straightened and looked at her. "That," he said, "is a very good idea."

CHAPTER SIX

Anne had to plead with Michael Banks to let her go with him when he had Hank Kepple examine the ring. Finally, he said, "I tell you what: I'm due for my lunch break. We'll make an unofficial visit. If it proves worthwhile, I'll go back and make an official one." And so together, they strolled out of the station and made their way to Kepple's Jewelry Store and the only other person in town capable of giving them some expert guidance on the ring.

They walked in to find both Hank and his wife, Heidi, in the store, and since Hank, Anne, and Michael had all gone to school together, they exchanged some warm greetings. Hank led them to the back of the store, leaving his wife to tend to customers. Unlike the cool, minimalist decor of the Diamond District, Kepple's was warm and inviting. The cases were well lit and the glass tops and sidings recently cleaned. Anne glanced sideways at a display of wedding rings as she and Michael followed Hank through the store. The soft wood paneling and the wheat-colored carpet muffled the sound of their footsteps and voices. Anne imagined it allowed couples a little privacy as they selected what might be the most expensive item of jewelry they would ever buy.

Hank motioned for Anne and Michael to sit on two cushioned stools stationed in front of a glass-topped counter. "So, what can I help you with today?"

"We're just some old friends popping in for a visit," Michael said, then added, "but, as long as we *are* here, I'd appreciate your opinion on something, Hank."

Hank shrugged. "Sure." Michael pulled a plastic evidence bag from his pocket, extracted the ring box, and handed it over. Hank furrowed his brow at the sight of the bag but took the box without comment. He turned it over to reveal the Diamond District logo on the bottom. "Are you sure I'm the one you want to talk to?"

"I've already—" Anne began, but Michael cut her off with a gesture.

"If you could just have a look at what's in there," he said.

Hank nodded and pulled the ring from the box. After looking at it a moment, he moved to a desk and drew over a lighted magnifier much like the one Brockhurst had used. He examined the ring carefully for some time, taking note, Anne saw, of the engraving. Then he finally switched off the light and pushed the magnifier away.

"It's a nice ring," he said with a shrug. "The mount is very well made. The stone is gorgeous. It almost looks real. I'd say this ring is worth a few hundred dollars."

He studied Michael as he said this, and the police officer quickly asked, "Hundreds? Not thousands?"

"Oh no," said Hank. "The ring would have to have a real sapphire to be worth that kind of money."

Michael frowned, and Anne said, "Brockhurst reported it stolen as a real sapphire, didn't he?" Michael flashed her a reproachful look and Hank gave a little cough and discreetly turned his head away. "Sorry," said Anne, abashed.

Michael sighed and said to Hank, "Would he do that, in your opinion?"

"Henderson? Deliberately file a false claim?" Hank hesitated and shrugged. "What can I say? I don't know the man that well. Plus, he's a competitor, so anything negative I might say would have to be viewed in that context." He spread his hands. "Between you and me, personally, I wouldn't put it past him. I don't really care for the man, I guess in part precisely *because* I wouldn't put something like that past him."

Anne could see Hank struggling to be fair and honest. At last, he added, "I'll tell you one thing, though: He ought to know the value of his own ring."

Michael nodded and stared down at the floor as he thought. Anne and Hank gazed at one another for a few moments, until finally Hank asked, "So what's your interest in this, Anne?"

Anne glanced at Michael, who nodded, so she told him the story of finding the Advent key and then the ring and of her visit to the Diamond District that morning.

Hank let out a low whistle. "So Edie had some hot property and hid it in the church, huh? That's bold." He grinned. "Do you think she was a fence?"

Anne smiled, but Michael made an impatient gesture. "The question is, how did she come to have it?"

Hank picked up the ring and began to examine it again. "So this is the ring that was stolen?"

"That's what Brockhurst claims."

"Sounds like your department," said Hank.

"If it was shoplifted," Michael said, "it probably would have been sold along quickly so that the thief could convert it into cash. You might normally expect them to take it out of the area to try and avoid detection, though jewelry is awfully hard to trace. After a couple of transactions, it could easily have ended up with someone who didn't even know it was stolen."

"So Aunt Edie could have had it innocently," Anne said, sounding defensive to her own ears.

"But you don't think it was hers?" Hank asked, and Anne shook her head. "Well, I can tell you there are lots of ways jewelry goes missing without being stolen. A lot of women take their rings off to wash their hands or help with the dishes after a dinner party, and it gets left by someone's sink. I sell a lot of replacement rings after such incidents."

"So you're saying it could have come to Aunt Edie by accident," Anne mused, "after she had hosted a luncheon or something. But then"—she picked up the box—"it wasn't just the ring. It was inside the box. You might slip off a ring and accidentally leave it beside someone's sink, but putting a ring back inside its box, that's something you do at home. And nobody lived in Aunt Edie's home except her. And none of that explains why she would have hidden it in the Advent cabinet."

"Well," said Hank thoughtfully, still turning the ring about in his fingers. Then he shrugged and carefully placed the ring back in its box. He started to slide the ring box toward Anne and Michael but pulled it back abruptly and examined the bottom of the case more closely.

Finally, he rested the box back on the glass. "I don't know if this is a helpful clue or not," he said, "but the Diamond District redesigned their logo about a year ago. It wasn't a drastic change in look, but they started using a more modern font. They went for a more Art Deco look rather than the curly type font you see here."

Anne and Michael both considered the information but could draw no conclusions from it.

Michael picked up the box and put it back into the evidence bag. "One thing is clear: I need to have a talk with Henderson Brockhurst. Hank, thanks very much for your help."

* * *

By the time Anne got home, it was time to meet the kids and get their supper prepared. Thursday was the library's night to stay open late, and Anne's volunteers were leaving for the day, so she had to cover that shift herself. As she often did, she took Ben and Liddie down to the library's first floor with her, and since it was a quiet evening, she was able to help them with their homework until it was time to close up.

But the result was that on Friday, when she had no volunteers, she found herself at the circulation desk, not doing library work but facing her stack of still-unwritten Christmas cards. She enjoyed writing cards, but it was a long task and promised to be longer than usual this year, since she had to convey so much news about her relocation to Blue Hill. Though she welcomed photocopied holiday letters from others, she had an aversion to producing one herself. It had been a prejudice she'd shared with her aunt Edie, in fact. But that meant that almost every card would require a fair amount of writing. She knew her pleasure in the task would be offset by tedium, as well as thoughts about the mysterious ring, and she found herself looking for excuses to delay.

One excellent excuse was the beckoning latest edition of the *Blue Hill Gazette*, and she eagerly turned to the feature on gift books that she had supplied information about to Grace Hawkins. Every suggestion she had made was included and her descriptions had mostly been reproduced verbatim. Grace had been both gracious and effusive in acknowledging Anne's contributions and in promoting the library. Anne was thrilled.

It occurred to her to check and see if the article appeared in the online version of the newspaper. To Anne's delight, she discovered it did. After she e-mailed the link to her parents, she decided that she ought to post the link on the library's Facebook page as well. At last, she felt ready to start in on her cards.

Just as she was about to start, however, the library's front door opened and Wendy sang out, "*Woo-hoo!* The Blue Hill Library zooms into the digital age."

"So it came through okay?"

Wendy slapped a stack of extra copies of the *Gazette* down on the desk before shucking off her coat. "Yes, it did," she said, "and you already have several 'likes.' But what you need to do," she continued, "is get more followers for your page, so that when you post a link like that, people will know about it."

"Followers?" Anne blinked. "I'm not sure I like the sound of that. What am I, the Pied Piper or something?" But in response to her friend's look of exasperation, she continued, "Okay, seriously, how do I go about getting followers?"

"There are any number of things you can do," Wendy said, sitting down. "For one thing, you could just put up a sign here on the desk that says, 'Follow Us on Facebook.'"

Anne had to admit that that sounded both easy and sensible.

"You could also add it to your e-mail signature," Wendy continued. "Put it on bookmarks. All kinds of things."

"Okay, you're right," Anne admitted, "I should do more. But I'm telling you one thing right now," she adopted a mock stern tone, "I am *not* tweeting."

Wendy gave a dismissive wave of her hand. "Tweeting is for the birds." They both had a good laugh.

"But, Anne, listen," Wendy continued after a moment, "there's something else I want to talk with you about." She looked around to make sure there were no patrons around so they could talk in peace for a moment. Anne waited, but Wendy seemed uncharacteristically puzzled about how to begin. "I don't know what your custom was with your friends in New York," she finally began, "whether you exchanged Christmas gifts or not. And I don't want to sound presumptuous or anything, but in case you were thinking of getting anything for me? Well, I'd rather you didn't."

"I see," Anne said. She had indeed entertained the idea that she'd pick up a little something for her friend.

"Now, it's just, well, I say this to everyone. You know with *seven* kids," she said, emphasizing the number, "I've already got quite a few presents to buy, and it just makes my life so much simpler if I don't have to worry about exchanging gifts with my adult friends." She looked at Anne anxiously, then added, "I hope you don't mind?"

Anne laughed. "No, of course not. I'm afraid that I hadn't really thought of it that way myself, and perhaps I would have if I were more considerate, but it makes perfect sense. We don't have to give each other gifts if you don't want to."

Wendy laughed with relief. "Well, thank you," she said. "I always worry that I sound ungrateful or presumptuous or something when I say that, but it really is a big help." She was already standing and putting her coat back on. "I have to be off again," she said. "The first week of December is almost gone, and I still have so much to do. I'll see you on Sunday, if not before."

"Thanks for the newspapers," Anne called after her.

But Wendy's talk of gifts had spawned another thought in Anne's mind. Wendy helped out quite a bit with the library, but she was not the only volunteer. In fact, Anne relied heavily on Library Guild volunteers, including Mildred, Betty Bultman, and Sherri, not to mention her two employees, the Miller twins, to keep the library running smoothly. And for the holiday season, she had pleaded with them for as many hours as they could spare.

As a friend, Wendy was a special case, but for the others, Anne realized that she ought to acknowledge their assistance and dedication with some small gift—not enough to embarrass them but enough to express appreciation.

She sighed inwardly. Something else to add to her list.

CHAPTER SEVEN

A nne was in the kitchen with a casserole heating in the oven and water about to boil for tea when the phone rang. When she answered it, she wasn't surprised to hear her mother's lilting voice. She cradled the phone between her ear and her shoulder as she grabbed a mug and tea bag.

"How are you holding up, dear?" her mother asked. "I know the holiday season can be stressful, and as a librarian you are probably doing double duty by making sure that the library is a festive place."

"It's not just the library, Mom. It's also the play and the Dickens of a Christmas, and I've been trying for two days to get my cards written, and I have no shopping done," Anne said. She realized that she had somehow left off the one item that was starting to consume the lion's share of her mental energy. She wondered why that would be.

"Are Liddie and Ben okay?"

"They're fine, really. It's just..."

"Why don't you start from the beginning, dear, and tell me everything."

Anne asked her mother to hold for a second while she grabbed the kettle off the stove before it started to whistle and poured the hot water into her mug.

"Well, you know the mysterious ring in the pictures I sent?" she asked.

"Oh yes. Your father says he doesn't recognize it, by the way. And he agrees with you that it doesn't look like Edie's style. In any event, he's pretty sure it's not a family heirloom."

"Yes, he sent me an e-mail."

"Have you been able to find out anything more about it?"

"Not exactly." Anne sighed and did as her mother suggested and told her about visiting the Diamond District and Mr. Brockhurst's claim that the ring was one that had been stolen from his shop, then about her visit with Michael Banks and their trip to have Hank Kepple evaluate the ring.

"But the oddest thing, Mom—" She paused to sip her tea and to peek around the corner at Ben and Liddie. The kids were lying on their stomachs on the floor in the living room. Liddie was watching cartoons on television, and Ben was studiously writing something on a pad of yellow legal paper. She turned back and settled down at the kitchen table. "When Hank looked at the ring he pointed out two things: The setting is very high quality, but the stone is fake."

"Oh, that's not so odd," Charlene interjected.

"It's not?" Anne settled down at the kitchen table to hear her mother's explanation.

"I'd say it was a starter ring. Real stones are expensive, but you can start with a really nice setting and plan to add the diamond or—sapphire, wasn't it? You start with a good foundation and build from there."

"Huh. Well, that's something to think about. Though, why would Aunt Edie have a starter ring?" Anne continued. "And there's another thing—there are some initials inside, and a date, though the engraving is hard to make out."

"*Hmm.* Hold on, dear. Here's your father coming in. Let me get him to pick up the other extension. Dale—"

Anne could hear a muffled conversation as her mother quickly filled her father in.

"Hello, Anne! How's my favorite daughter? No luck with that ring?"

Anne smiled. Sometimes it seemed that the farther away her parents lived, the younger she was in her father's eyes. "Not yet, Dad."

"Well, why worry about it, then? I told you I don't think it was Edie's."

"I know, Dad, but if the ring wasn't hers, then it must have belonged to someone else. And that someone else might very much like to have it back. I feel like I need to find the real owner."

"Well, the most obvious thing to me," Anne's mother interjected, "is that Edie meant for the ring to be one of the Advent treasures. Why else would it be in the cabinet? And in that case, there may not be a 'rightful owner.' Perhaps you're overthinking this, dear."

"I suppose that's possible," Anne said slowly.

"Of course it is," her father agreed. "Your aunt probably picked up the ring at a thrift store to put it in the cabinet. It's not unheard of, for people to find fine items among costume jewelry."

Anne brushed a wayward strand of hair from her face as she considered this. "But how could I confirm something like that?" she asked plaintively. "It's not likely there'd be a receipt around for something like that."

"Well, dear," her mother replied in a patient tone, "why don't you ask Mildred? If Edie had bought such a thing for that purpose, Mildred would likely have been with her."

Of course. Why hadn't Anne thought of that already?

Anne called Mildred immediately after her conversation with her parents, but the older woman didn't answer. Anne hung up when the call switched to voice mail. She didn't want to leave a recorded message, so she planned to call again after she'd put the kids to bed. However, once she'd cleaned up the kitchen after supper and supervised Ben's and Liddie's bedtime routine, she feared it was too late to call Mildred. The call would need to wait till morning. Instead, Anne scoured her great-aunt's papers and records of charitable contributions for a receipt of some sort from the local Goodwill or consignment store, but she found nothing.

The next morning, Saturday, she awoke with the intention of calling Mildred as soon as she found a few moments in the day, but her intent turned out to be moot, as the woman herself showed up at the library in the middle of the morning to check out a book. Her arrival was doubly welcome because Anne had been about to make another stab at her Christmas cards. She happily set those aside, however, when her aunt's longtime friend entered.

The library was unusually quiet. Anne supposed that this was because families were out shopping or skiing. She was glad to have a moment with Mildred, who was always easy to talk to.

Anne got her settled into a chair with some tea, but before she could begin to question her about the cabinet and to explain about finding the ring, the front door clattered open and two boisterous boys rushed through and skidded to a stop in the foyer. They peered up at the bookcases and around corners with suspicious looks.

When the older of the two spotted Anne, he shouted, "Hey, where's Santa's mailbox? We got letters for Santa!"

Anne resisted the urge to bring her finger to her mouth to signal for him to lower his voice. Just then the boys' mother stepped inside and joined them.

"Tommy! Inside voice, inside voice," she remonstrated. She ducked her head a little when she saw Anne, as if in apology for her boys' behavior.

Anne and Mildred couldn't help but chuckle. Anne sent the boys upstairs to the Children's Room, and they raced each other there. Anne noticed the shy woman was shivering a bit, so she invited her to have a cup of tea also. The woman explained then that the boys hadn't seen a library outside of school. "We aren't readers, you see," she explained and asked if it was still okay if they dropped their letters in Santa's mailbox anyway.

"Of course. The library is here for the whole community," Anne said immediately, "And it's free to get a library card, you know. I'll just have you fill out a form—"

"Oh, uh..." The woman shrugged again. "I don't have my glasses with me." She bit her lip in indecision. "But I can tell you all the information if you wanna write it down for me."

Anne nodded. In New York, she'd assisted countless patrons who'd "left their glasses at home." Anne made a mental note to look into a literacy program for the library once the hustle and bustle of the holidays had gone by.

Just then, what sounded like boxes being thrown down the stairs interrupted her thoughts, and the boys suddenly appeared at the corner of the desk, each with a book from her Christmas display. Anne filled out a membership form for each of the boys and reminded them of the due date, and they ran out as noisily as they ran in, but this time they were excited about having a book to read and a library card. The woman gave Anne a grateful smile as she followed the boys out.

Anne turned back to Mildred, who had finished her tea and was fishing about in her handbag. She paused and cocked an eye at Anne. "Do you know her?"

Anne gestured at the registration form on the desk. "She said her name was Dolly James, but that's all I know."

The old woman nodded and settled back, whatever she'd wanted in her purse apparently forgotten. "Her mother used to clean some of the houses around here. Her father died in a mining accident, and the mother took the kids out of school after that. Dolly's mother had always been…fragile, mentally, and the accident, well, it was too much.

"At some point the state stepped in and broke up the family, put the kids in separate foster homes. So Dolly grew up and got married and had those two boys. And then her husband died. Cancer. Thankfully, Dolly didn't fall to pieces the way her poor mother did. The boys seem to be doing okay, though I don't know how they get by." Mildred sighed. "She's had a hard life."

Thinking back to New York again, Anne said, "I think it's especially hard to be poor and have a family at Christmastime. What if the boys don't receive what they asked Santa for?"

Mildred gave her a sympathetic smile. "I wouldn't worry about that too much, Anne. Someone at church has taken Dolly James and Tommy and Jayden under his or her wing." She shook her head at Anne's questioning look. "Someone anonymous. But this person buys their heating oil in the winter and, let's say, points Santa in the direction of their house."

Relieved, Anne sat back down behind her desk, while Mildred stood and stepped over to browse the New Arrivals shelf and select her reading for the week. As she returned to check out, Anne asked if she could stay a minute more.

"What's on your mind, dear?" Mildred asked, resuming her seat.

Anne told Mildred the story of the missing Advent key and the surprising find in the locked cubby.

"So the key was with Edie's Christmas decorations?" she asked with satisfaction. "Well, who would have thought it? I'd heard that you found the key, but there seems to be several different stories going around. That Edie!" she said, shaking her head and smiling fondly. "Even now she's full of surprises."

"Do you know why she had the key?" Anne asked. "Or anything about this ring?" She took out her phone and pulled up the pictures she had sent to her parents. Mildred took the device and studied the pictures carefully, with Anne reaching over to swipe from one image to the next.

After a while, Mildred handed the phone back and shook her head. "I'm afraid not, dear. She never said anything about the key, even when it was found to be missing last Christmas and everyone was talking about it."

As to the ring, Mildred had no memory of Edie buying it or saying that she intended to donate such a thing as one of the Advent cabinet treasures. "I suppose it's possible," she added, "that Edie just never happened to mention it. The cabinet treasures are meant to be fun, not something that she would brood over." She thought for a few moments. "On the other hand, I do recall her telling me all about some of the other treasures she put in over the years."

A question suddenly occurred to Anne. "What becomes of the treasures, anyway? After Christmas?"

"Generally, Reverend Tom gives them back to whoever put them in the cabinet to begin with. Sometimes, if he sees a particular use for something, he'll ask if it can be donated to the church, but I don't think that happens very often. Sometimes people save them and put them back in the cabinet for another year. There are two or three that are favorites with the children, so they have to come back every year."

"But what about something valuable, like the ring? Would Reverend Tom ask to have that as a donation?"

Mildred looked at her uncertainly. "I don't think it's ever come up. Reverend Tom always insists that people choose objects with — what does he say? — 'symbolic not intrinsic' value."

"So if Aunt Edie had bought it in a thrift store with the Advent cabinet in mind..."

"She would have assumed that it was not very valuable," confirmed Mildred. "And all this talk reminds me, I signed up to supply a treasure for one of the days next week. I don't have a clue what I'm going to get." She cocked an eyebrow at Anne. "Suggestions welcome," she said. "Edie and I used to swap ideas every year."

But Anne was still preoccupied with the ring. "Which makes me think," she said, "that if Aunt Edie *had* bought this ring for the Advent cabinet, you'd have known about it—probably would have been with her when she did it."

Mildred shrugged. "But what other explanation would there be?"

"There are two questions," Anne said. "The first is, who put the ring in the cabinet? The most obvious answer is Aunt Edie, because I found the key with her things. But we don't know that for sure. Somebody else could have put it there and asked her to hold onto the key for safekeeping.

"But if we assume that she *is* the one, then the second question is, how did Aunt Edie come to have the ring? My parents don't recognize it, you don't recognize it, I don't recognize it. And we all seem to agree that it's not really her style, anyway." Mildred added her agreement with a nod. "It wasn't lost or forgotten because it wasn't just lying around loose. It was in its box. Or in *a* box, at least.

"But I can't imagine why someone would give such a ring to Aunt Edie or ask her to hold it, especially if they may have thought it was valuable. And it's not like there were any other women living in her house." Anne stopped, chewing her lower lip as she tried to think the situation through logically.

"Well," said Mildred thoughtfully, "except for Julie, of course."

Chapter Eight

All other thoughts vanished from Anne's mind as she gaped at the older woman. "Who on earth is Julie?" she demanded.

"She was Edie's lodger," Mildred explained.

"Aunt Edie had a lodger?"

Mildred seemed taken aback by Anne's surprise and dismay. "Well, perhaps that's not quite the right word, but my dear, surely you knew Julie, didn't you?" She was leaning back away from Anne and twisting her hands together in her lap. "Or knew of her, I mean. Edie must have said..."

"Never," said Anne. "Not a word." Her thoughts flailed about as she tried to absorb this piece of information. Finally, she spluttered, "How — how long did she live here?"

Mildred appeared to recover more quickly than Anne. "Well, yes, let me think. It was only for a few months. Early last year." She looked at Anne with concern. "Are you all right, dear? I didn't mean to give you a turn." She reached out and patted Anne on the hand.

Anne sat without responding, coming to terms with the news. At Mildred's touch, she drew her attention back to the older woman. "You know, it's funny. I always used to tell her that she should take in a lodger. She had this big old house, after all. It would have brought in a little income, not that she needed it, but also, you know, company. And somebody right there in case...anything happened."

Anne laughed. "She told me that I fretted too much. And that she liked her privacy. She said if anything happened, you'd know." She smiled at Mildred. But as she continued to think, her smile changed to a frown. "But you know, I've been through her papers, and I don't recall seeing anything about this. Like a lease or a rental agreement." She looked up with a puzzled expression. "What can you tell me about this woman, Mildred?"

"Oh well, you must understand, dear, that I actually only met her once or twice, and Edie didn't talk about her all that much. Indeed, I think Edie didn't see her all that often. She spent almost all her time down at the university. She was a very smart girl." Mildred leaned forward conspiratorially. "She had a doctor's degree."

The state university was about half an hour down the interstate from Blue Hill and, in recent years especially, the town had benefitted from this relative proximity as more and more young professors and staff people had chosen to settle there, where houses were cheaper and life was quieter. Some in Blue Hill worried that the town was becoming little better than a bedroom community, but the university employees brought some stability to the town's economy.

"So she was a professor?" pursued Anne. "You say she had a doctorate? What was her field—her area of study?"

"Something to do with art, I think," Mildred replied, thinking back. "But no, she wasn't a professor. I remember, because that was my first thought too. She explained it all to me the first time

I met her. There was some term for what she was doing." Mildred thought some more but couldn't seem to come up with it. "Post...something," she finally said.

"Postdoctoral fellowship?"

The older woman's face lit up. "Yes, that was it! What is that, dear? I'm sure Julie explained, but I don't think I quite followed it."

"It's a temporary position that academics sometimes take between getting their doctorate and getting their first job as a professor. But the point of a postdoc," she continued thoughtfully, "is that it runs for a set time period, usually a year or two I think, and then it's done."

"That's right," Mildred said, her memory jogged. "That was the case with Julie. She only had a few months left on hers. But she'd been renting a room with a family closer to campus, and something happened that they couldn't put her up any longer, so she came to stay with Edie for the last few months."

"Do you remember what happened?"

Mildred grew circumspect. "Well, I believe they had a daughter and it suddenly became necessary for the daughter to move back home with her parents. I don't know the details," she added, appearing uneasy, "but Julie had been staying in the daughter's room, you see, so she needed to find a new place to live."

"But if she'd been living closer to campus, why did she come to Blue Hill?"

"She already had some connection to town," Mildred said, appearing to search her memory again, "or perhaps it was her young man who did. Anyway, even though she didn't have much free time, she was already spending some of it up here. She'd come to our church a few times and had gotten to know Reverend Tom, as I recall. He was the one who connected her with Edie."

"So Edie rented a room to her?" Anne asked. "I'll have to look through her papers again, but as I think about it, I'm pretty sure she didn't claim any rental income on her taxes last year."

"I don't think it was anything as formal as that," Mildred said, shaking her head. "Julie only needed a place for a few months. I think they worked out an arrangement where Julie bought the groceries and, I don't know, paid the electricity bill or something. Edie said she still felt guilty because Julie was forever buying all this food and then was hardly ever around to eat it."

It felt odd to think of someone else living in the house with her aunt Edie, even if only for a few months. Anne thought back to the conversations they'd had on the subject. "You're just rattling around by yourself inside that enormous house," she would say to her great-aunt.

But Edie would only laugh at the suggestion. "I'm much too old and set in my ways to try to accommodate myself now to a bunch of strangers, even if they are paying rent," she'd say. And at some point, Anne had stopped making the suggestion.

But now it appeared that Edie, in a way, had acted upon it after all, near the end of her life. As was typical with Aunt Edie, however, it appeared the arrangement had come about to meet Julie's needs, rather than her great-aunt's.

Anne sighed. "Is there anything else you can remember about her? Her field was art, you say? Do you mean art history?"

Mildred said she thought that Julie's degree might have been in art history, but she wasn't sure. And no, she couldn't really remember anything else about Julie, though she would keep trying. But, Mildred was quick to point out once again that she had only met the young woman a couple of times, and even Edie hadn't seen that much of her.

"So what was Julie's last name?" Anne tried.

After a moment, Mildred again shook her head. "I'm sorry, dear, I can't seem to recall that either. It was an odd name. I think it had a z in it." Her voice trailed off a bit, but then she shook her head again.

"It started with Z?" Anne asked.

Mildred hesitated just a moment. "No, I don't think that's right. It just has a z in it." She heaved a slight sigh.

Anne suddenly recalled how they had gotten onto this topic to begin with. In her surprise at the news of the unknown lodger, she had forgotten about the ring. She reached for her phone and brought up the pictures once again. "Well, so maybe this belonged to her then?"

Mildred pursed her lips. "Well, of course I can't really say. But I have my doubts."

Anne's optimism deflated a bit. "Why do you say that?"

"Well, it's a nice ring, even if it's not a real stone. Julie was the sort of girl who, if she were to splurge on something, would buy a pair of comfortable shoes."

"I see." Anne sat for a moment, thinking. Then she asked, "Didn't you say Reverend Tom introduced Aunt Edie to Julie?"

Mildred nodded. "That's right, dear. That's what Edie told me. Perhaps he can tell you more about Julie."

* * *

Before asking Reverend Tom about Julie, Anne had determined to see what her own parents might be able to tell her. "How come you didn't tell me about Aunt Edie's lodger?" she asked into the phone.

The silence on the other end was finally broken with her mother's response. "What are you talking about, dear?"

Anne realized that she was still a little upset by this latest revelation and she tried to calm herself. "Apparently Aunt Edie took in this young woman last year as a lodger. She never said anything to me about it. What was going on?"

"I don't... Are you sure, Anne? I don't recall anything like that."

"Mildred just told me about it," Anne said. "She was surprised that I didn't know."

"Hold on, dear. Let me get your father to pick up." But when Anne put the question to her father, she got the same result.

"What was this woman's name?" asked her father.

"Julie."

"Julie what?"

"Mildred couldn't remember," Anne admitted.

"Well, I don't remember Edie saying anything about renting out rooms. Why would she do that? She certainly didn't need to."

"Dale," said her mother, "there was that young woman at the university. Wasn't her name Julie?"

"Oh. Well that was just some girl who stayed with your aunt for a short time. While she finished some program or something at the university. When was that, Charlene? Last year? The year before? But she wasn't a *lodger*, as you call her."

"Well, what was she then?" Anne asked, feeling a little exasperated.

"Just someone who stayed with your aunt for a little while."

* * *

Later that afternoon at the library, Anne was still mulling over the unexpected news about Edie's houseguest when she was surprised to see Michael Banks appear, in uniform and apparently on duty. He didn't bother to take off his coat but walked straight to the desk and gave her a somewhat formal "Good afternoon, Anne." To her astonishment, he pulled out the ring box and set it before her on the desk.

She gave him a questioning look and then—she couldn't help herself—quickly opened the box to peek inside and see if the ring itself was there. It was. She looked at Michael again and after a moment said, "Don't you need this?"

A look of vexation crossed the police officer's face. "Mr. Brockhurst," he said, "is now telling us this is not the stolen ring after all." Anne glanced around, but none of the library's current visitors were nearby. Michael's face relaxed a bit, and he shook his head ruefully. "I went to talk with him yesterday and told him that you had turned in the ring. I reviewed the original police report with him, and when I confronted him with the fact that the gem was not a real sapphire, as he claimed, he asked to see the ring again. Then he said he'd made a mistake and this wasn't the stolen ring after all." Michael shrugged. "He was very apologetic."

"That's convenient," Anne observed.

"Perhaps. But for the moment, there's not much else I can do about it."

"What if this *is* the ring?"

"Then there's a good chance that Brockhurst is guilty of filing a false police report as well as insurance fraud. But he swears that this is not the ring, and for all I know, he's telling the truth. I can't prove otherwise, at any rate." He sighed and shook his head. "Anne, listen to me carefully," he looked at her intently. "There is no evidence that Brockhurst has committed any crime. Got it?" She nodded. He gestured toward the ring. "And if this is no longer evidence in an investigation, I have no justification for holding onto it, so I'm returning it to you."

Anne looked at it pensively. She hadn't liked Brockhurst, but she chided herself that personal feelings were not evidence either. "As far as that goes," she said somewhat reluctantly, "I remember he reacted to the ring almost as soon as he opened the box. I noticed it at the time. Maybe he jumped to a conclusion and then had trouble letting go of it." She looked back up at Michael. "Not that I want to make excuses for him."

"It's a fair point," he responded with a shrug. "Anyway, I hope you'll keep this safe. And if you learn anything more about it, or if you ever decide to get rid of it or give it to someone or do something with it, I hope you'll let me know."

"Of course," Anne said quickly, and her gaze returned to the ring box. Then, with determination, she added, "But I am going to keep trying to find the ring's owner and how it came to Aunt Edie." She found herself grinning as she thought of an appropriate book reference. "You can just call me Frodo."

Michael gaped at her for a moment and then laughed. "You mean from *Lord of the Rings*?"

"Sure," said Anne. "Someone else with a ring and a mission."

Chapter Nine

After the church service the next day, Anne, Ben, and Liddie were all eager to see what would be revealed in the Advent cabinet cubbies. Now that they had reached the second Sunday of December, there was a whole week's worth of doors to open, and each small treasure drew some fun association to Christmas.

Reverend Tom, however, only selected one item for a short homily—a toy telephone. A young man hefting a child on his hip, standing next to his wife, explained he had placed it in the cabinet because it made him think of God speaking to Joseph and Mary, preparing them for the birth of Jesus.

"A 'calling.' Excellent," Reverend Tom said, holding the small phone above his head so everyone could see it. "God called on Joseph and Mary to raise his Son, to accept this herculean task of being a parent. They could hardly understand what was happening in the moment, and yet they heard the call and answered it. This week, let's each be aware of God calling us—in a loud strong voice, or in a still, small one. Let's listen to each other, and to God."

There was a moment of quiet after this, as if everyone, even the children, were listening for the still, small voice. Then Reverend Tom turned to Brad and invited him to say a prayer.

Brad was obviously prepared for this. Still, Anne sensed his nervousness. He cleared his throat and began with a poetic and carefully thought-out invocation. He thanked God for the insight of Reverend Tom and for the support of the congregation of Blue Hill Community Church, naming each of the board members as he did so. Then he thanked God for the children. Next, he made a plea for the health of the congregation — and as if on cue, two or three people sneezed — and success for the church's missions, including the Christmas play...It was a rather long prayer, as if Brad was afraid to leave anything out. But the congregation was patient and prayed along with him, with a hearty "Amen!" resounding at the end.

Shouting over the shuffling of feet as congregants prepared to leave, Helen asked, "Will someone take these last pieces of pound cake home with them?" Soon the community room was filled with the noise of chairs being put away and dishes being washed and children dodging and chasing one another around and among the chattering adults.

* * *

"Well, I don't trust this Henderson Brockhurst one bit," said Wendy decisively. At that afternoon's rehearsal for the Nativity play, Anne updated Wendy, Helen, and Reverend Tom on her efforts to identify the owner of the ring. Though they sat in the back of the sanctuary, they kept their voices low. Anne and Reverend Tom sat in a forward pew and both were turned to look back at Wendy and Helen, who sat behind.

"Judge not...," murmured Reverend Tom vaguely.

"You know him?" Anne asked Wendy, puzzled.

"No, but just the way you describe him...," Wendy responded, unabashed. "Clearly he tried to take advantage of this theft to claim a much more expensive ring was stolen. And now that the ring itself has turned up, he's in trouble."

Anne, who until this moment had strongly agreed with this assessment, paradoxically found herself wavering when she heard it articulated by someone else. She recalled her own comment to Michael Banks about the possibility that Brockhurst had jumped to a mistaken conclusion.

As if reading Anne's thoughts, Reverend Tom interjected, "Now Wendy, there's no evidence to support that charge. That's why the police had to return the ring to Anne."

Wendy looked ready to argue but then sighed. "Still...," she muttered, discontent tinting her words.

"And besides," said Anne, "none of that sheds light on how Aunt Edie came to have the ring." A further thought struck her. "As far as that goes," she continued, "the fact that she had the ring makes it less likely that this is the ring that was stolen."

Reverend Tom nodded. "Edie was not in the habit of harboring stolen goods."

"No," agreed Wendy, but she added, "not if she knew it was stolen."

Anne looked at Reverend Tom. "And what can you tell me about this Julie, anyway? Mildred says you were the one who introduced her to Edie."

Reverend Tom's gaze flicked away for an instant, then returned. "Oh...well...," he said, "Mildred had the basic facts correct. Julie had a fellowship down at the university and she suddenly found herself in need of a place to live for the last few months. She didn't want to sign a year's lease on an apartment because she expected to be moving back to Philadelphia before then. I mentioned her predicament to Edie and the two of them came to an arrangement." He shrugged.

"But do you think this ring could have been hers?" Anne pressed. When Reverend Tom didn't respond immediately, she continued, "Because the more I think about it, the less likely it seems. If she was doing a postdoc, that means she'd just gotten her PhD not long before. That is, she was only a year or so away from having been a poor graduate student. Mildred made the same objection, and I know that when I was in graduate school, I certainly didn't own anything as nice as this ring, even if it's not a real sapphire. It just doesn't say 'recent grad student' to me." After a pause, she added, "Unless she came from a wealthy family?"

Tom hesitated a moment and then said, "No. No, I don't think her family is wealthy."

Anne nodded as if her suspicions had been confirmed and looked to Wendy and Helen. "What do either of you remember about her?"

"I remember her coming to church a few times," Helen said, "but I'm afraid I only spoke to her on one or two occasions and even then we said nothing substantive. She struck me as very studious, maybe even a little absentminded. I knew she'd stayed with Edie for a while and that Edie seemed to like her, but that's all I ever heard."

"Yes, I also heard Edie say how much she enjoyed her company. She seemed to be surprised at that," added Wendy, "and she talked about how little she saw her. She joked that they spent more time together at church then they did at home." She thought for a moment and then shrugged. "But that's it."

Anne opened her mouth to ask another question, but she became aware of Reverend Tom stirring slightly beside her. His attention seemed fixed on the back of the church. She looked in that direction and saw Alex Ochs slipping silently through the doors into the sanctuary. But she was surprised to see that he was carrying his toolbox, which he carefully and quietly stowed behind the rearmost pews.

Looking up, Alex found all four of them staring at him. A grin spread across his face, and he strolled down the aisle rubbing his hands together. He seemed to have already removed his coat and gloves. "Well," he said in a stage whisper when he was close enough, "how goes the rehearsal?"

"Everyone is working hard," Reverend Tom praised.

The rehearsal, which had been going forward all during their conversation, had started out very well indeed. Suzanne and Brad had begun by gathering all the kids in a circle for a read-through. "See how much you can do from memory," Suzanne encouraged them, though they all held tightly to their scripts.

Still, it soon became clear that they had made good progress learning their own lines, even if most had ignored Suzanne's plea to familiarize themselves with the entire play.

"It happens every year," she said to Anne's group when she wandered back during a break after the read-through. Helen and Reverend Tom nodded sagely. "They want to get away with the bare minimum. But I try it every year, and usually there's a few who will make the extra effort."

They all congratulated her on the read-through, which seemed to them to have gone very smoothly. "Could you tell which parts were added by Brad?" she asked with concern in her voice. "He's really expanded some of the material."

Wendy, Helen, and Reverend Tom all shook their heads. "I've seen this play I don't know how many times," said Wendy, "But I didn't notice anything unusual. It all seemed to flow together to me. Apparently he writes quite well."

"There's going to be more music this year too," Suzanne continued fretfully.

"It will help us take advantage of our unusually large cast this year," Helen reassured her. "It's a blessing that we have so many people who want to participate. I think it will be lovely."

"But what about the length?" asked Suzanne. "The congregation may start to get restless."

Tom gave her a benevolent smile. "It will have to be a long production indeed for parents to get tired of seeing their children perform."

Even Suzanne smiled at that. "They're good kids," she said, giving in, and then suddenly she gave a violent sneeze.

"Uh-oh," said Wendy laughing. "Don't tell me you've come down with something right before the performance!"

Suzanne shot her a dark look. "Don't even joke," she warned, followed by another explosive sneeze. She sighed deeply and pulled out a tissue.

When she put it away again, she gave them a wan smile with watery eyes and then grasped the back of the pew ahead of her. "The show must go on." She pulled herself up out of the pew and then turned back to them. "Helen, perhaps I'll take you up on your offer? Not right this minute, but in a little while."

Helen nodded. "Of course." She had arrived at rehearsal with good news from Eleanor Jameson's daughter Emily. Apparently the costumes had been cleaned last year as promised, and returned to the church. But Emily's husband had put them down in the basement, not knowing where the other Nativity play supplies were kept. Looking enormously relieved, Suzanne had decreed that the costumes would be handed out at the end of this rehearsal. Though she had at first declined Helen's offer to go down and fetch them, it appeared she was now ready to accept the assistance.

Suzanne, who had been standing in a slightly stooped posture, straightened her spine and made her way back down to the front of the church.

Tom watched her with some concern, but before he could do anything, Alex tapped him on the arm and the two of them excused themselves to step out into the foyer.

"What are they up to?" Anne asked suspiciously, but Helen and Wendy shook their heads absentmindedly, their attention focused on the rehearsal.

At the front of the sanctuary, Suzanne and Brad began working with the kids to block out the movement and the flow of the play's action. Initially, Suzanne set them all briskly in their places and moved them about so smoothly that Anne felt this must be the familiar, traditional presentation. But gradually, Brad spoke up more and more frequently, suggesting additions and variations which the kids would try and which everyone would then need to discuss.

Meanwhile, it started to become clear that Suzanne's energy was flagging. Noticing this, Brad cut himself off in the middle of describing a new idea that he'd had and suggested that it might be a good time to work on a little of the music. For just a moment, Suzanne's back stiffened, but then she agreed. As she made her way to one of the front pews and settled down, Brad got his guitar out of its case, tuned it, and began warming up the singers.

Helen slipped out of her pew, apparently preparing to head down to the basement. Anne and Wendy both looked at her inquiringly, but she waved them down to keep their seats. "I'll come back if I need help," she whispered, "or we'll get some of them to do it." She gestured with her head toward the front of the church.

Though several children had solos, Brad announced that they would focus on the carols that everyone would sing. Despite the familiarity of the carols, at least to the adults, it quickly became clear that the children were not nearly as prepared with the music as they'd been with their lines. And the less familiar carols were practically incoherent. It took them a long time to struggle through the entire set even once, and when they were done, Brad gave the distinct impression of trying to put a brave face on things.

Still he congratulated the kids and praised their hard work, promising that they would spend more time on the music before the performance. He seemed at a bit of a loss as to what to do next, when Helen came rushing into the sanctuary, her face contorted with disgust.

"Ugh," she said. "I've got to go wash my hands."

Everyone was quiet while they awaited her return. "This can't be good," Wendy whispered to Anne, and they stood up to move to the front of the church. Alex and Reverend Tom appeared, seemingly from nowhere, but they asked no questions and apparently already understood that something was wrong. When Helen returned, she looked at the group with dismay.

"Well," she said slowly, "you remember the problems we had with the Christmas decorations? I'm afraid this is even worse."

* * *

"I don't remember mice being one of the plagues," Wendy whispered to Anne, but she didn't dare share her comment with the others, since the loss of the costumes had created quite a bit of consternation.

Alex had taken a strong light down to inspect the damage and had returned with a grim report indeed. "It's not just the damage to the clothes and the nests they've built," he said, "there's a lot of other, uh, stuff that you don't normally want in your clothing."

"Well, they can be washed," Wendy said, and she was immediately confronted by the horror-stricken faces of the kids who would be wearing these costumes. "Mom!" said her son Justin reproachfully.

Reverend Tom, repressing a smile, said, "So do you think the old costumes are damaged beyond repair, Alex?" He gave a little nod as he said it.

"Yes," Alex said, "yes, I do."

But Suzanne, still seated in her pew, groaned at this news. "How are we possibly going to replace all the costumes at once?" she asked.

They all looked at one another. "I could send a mass e-mail to the parents," Wendy suggested. "Perhaps if each child's parents took responsibility for their child's costume?"

"Can we really put such an unexpected burden on them at this time of year?" asked Helen.

Everyone stood for a bit, trying to think up options. Then Marian Pauthen spoke up. "I'll do it."

They looked at her incredulously. "All of them?" said Helen.

"Mare used to do the costumes for a little regional theater group we belonged to down South when I was stationed there," her husband said, pride evident in his voice. "She can run you up some costumes, no problem."

"But with what material?" Anne asked. "Do we need to reach out to the parents and ask for donations?"

Marian shrugged. "I'll be happy to take what I can get, but finding extra material isn't that difficult."

They all looked at her in silence for a bit, and then Suzanne said, "Tha— Than—," and broke into a prolonged sneezing fit. Finally, she managed to wheeze out a "thank you" that sounded no less heartfelt for being stuffed up.

CHAPTER TEN

M onday morning, Anne once again opened the library by herself. She was in a good mood because she had finished decorating the library and thought that it had turned out very nicely, if she did say so herself. She had splurged on an evergreen garland to drape over the entrance to the History Room, and the aroma was soothing and pleasant. Marian Pauthen and Mildred had gathered a group of kids last week to help make a colorful paper-chain garland, which brightened the Children's Room.

Her good humor was only slightly dampened by the nagging internal voice that reminded her of her still unwritten cards and not-yet-started Christmas shopping. But she did, after all, still have two weeks. She was also getting much more anxious about the Dickens of a Christmas event, which was coming up on Thursday.

But lifting her spirits above all her concerns was the fact that Ben and Liddie were excited and happy about the holidays. Her worries about their first Christmas in a new place were, so far, unfounded, and they seemed to be really enjoying the new experience of the Nativity play in particular. As long as the kids had a good holiday, any number of other challenges could be dealt with.

Monday was always a big day for deliveries, and Anne was in the middle of rearranging the New Arrivals shelf when she heard the door open, quickly followed by Reverend Tom's booming, "Good morning, Anne!"

She slipped behind the circulation desk and smiled in greeting. "Good morning, Reverend. Finished the Supreme Court book?"

"I have," the pastor said, handing the book to her, "and it was very good. But I thought I'd look next for something a bit lighter for the holiday season. I may have to wait until the new year to dive back into the more serious stuff again."

Anne smiled but did not reply. Reverend Tom read a lot of history, politics, and current events, and she doubted his ability to stay away from these topics, even if it was a busy time of year. She decided to wait and see what he actually brought to the desk.

Fifteen minutes later he wandered back from New Arrivals, flipping through a book about conditions in the slums of India. "I've heard about this," he murmured as he turned the pages. "It won an award, didn't it?"

"That's right," Anne replied brightly, "the Light Holiday Reading Award."

After a beat, the pastor looked up with a confused expression. Anne kept her own face perfectly straight, but Reverend Tom's brow quickly lifted and he laughed. "Yes, well," he said, "the best-laid plans and all that." He put the book down on the desk. "I've heard too much about it not to have a look."

Anne smiled and checked the book out for him, noting his silence while she did so. Normally, he kept up his friendly banter during this process, but when she looked up to hand the book back to him, his posture seemed to have stiffened and he gave a strange impression of being ill at ease.

He'd been holding his coat over his arm and now, setting the book back down, he made something of a show of getting it on. In the midst of this, with an air of studied casualness, he said, "I thought the rehearsal went well yesterday."

She gave him a quizzical look, as if to say, Were you at the same rehearsal I was?

"I mean," he fumbled, "it's still early. These things have a way of pulling together. I'm sure it will be fine. But, what I meant to say was that I've been thinking about our talk yesterday. About your latest, um, interest." He shot her a quick glance. "The ring."

Puzzled, Anne merely smiled and said, "Yes?"

"Have you given any thought to the possibility that it might belong to the Andersons. You know, the family of the man that built the Advent cabinet?"

Anne sat back in her chair, her mind racing to try to grasp the various angles of this possibility. "No, none at all," she said. "It never even occurred to me." She paused and thought a bit more. "And offhand, I guess I don't see why it might have, why they would have any connection to it." Her eyes refocused and she glanced at him sharply. "Do you have an explanation as to why they would?"

"Well," Reverend Tom said slowly, his gaze fixed on the far wall behind Anne as he thought, "I was just remembering how Elizabeth Anderson—she was Patrick's daughter-in-law—how she and her kids stayed so involved in the tradition of stocking the cabinet with the treasures. Because of the family connection, you know.

"These days, of course, the whole congregation really gets into it, but I gather there was a time when, like a lot of traditions, it was in danger of dying out. When I arrived in Blue Hill, Elizabeth and her kids were still carrying most of the burden of finding the treasures and putting them in the cubbies. I remember how committed to it they were, though never in a pushy or demanding way." As he reminisced, Reverend Tom's face relaxed. "But they were determined to keep it up in memory of the old man. I wish I'd had a chance to meet him. I gather he was quite a character." Reverend Tom shook his head sadly. "He died shortly before I arrived."

The pastor's voice trailed off a bit in memory, and after waiting for him to continue, Anne finally said, "Is the family still in the area?"

Startled, Reverend Tom replied, "No, no. I'm afraid they are not. They moved away last year, you see. Young Patrick, Elizabeth's youngest son — they call him Pat — was off in college, and she decided it was finally time to move someplace warmer, as she'd always meant to do. So no, I'm afraid they're all gone now."

"But they left last year," Anne said thoughtfully. "So you're suggesting that Elizabeth might have put the ring into the Advent cabinet before she left?" She looked at Reverend Tom, but his face bore a carefully neutral expression. "So that, what, the congregation would find it come Christmas?" She was beginning to find a narrative in the idea that appealed to her. "Sort of a last farewell to the church and the cabinet?"

Her lips pursed, and she gazed down at the desk before her as she tried to work out the possibilities. "But then, why didn't it work? Why wasn't the ring discovered at Christmas? And how did Aunt Edie come to have the key?" Another thought occurred to her. "And besides, that ring is an awfully expensive thing to place in the Advent cabinet." She looked back up at Reverend Tom. "I thought the whole idea was that the items should be symbolical, not valuable."

"Well, yes, that's true," Reverend Tom agreed but said no more.

"Even though the stone's not real, that's still a nice ring," Anne mused, "and not exactly cheap. Was she wealthy?"

"No," Reverend Tom replied, "I wouldn't have said so."

"But I suppose even still, if it was some sort of parting gift to the church, she might have thought something special was called for. And she might have wanted to set up a little surprise for the congregation. But then, why didn't she say something when the ring wasn't found? She must have heard whether or not her surprise worked. Surely she would have checked with someone. Does she still have family in the area? She must still have friends and acquaintances around. Do you have an address for her?"

Tom shook his head. "There's no family left around here. That was another reason why she wanted to move, to be closer to her sister. And no, I'm afraid I have no current address for her."

"Do you know where she moved to?"

Tom hesitated. "Somewhere out West," he said at last. She continued to look at him expectantly until he finally added, "Perhaps near Arizona?"

"But you think she might have been the one to leave the ring in the Advent cabinet?" Anne persisted.

"I didn't say that," Reverend Tom replied, "I...merely suggest an alternative possibility for you to consider. Since you appear to be so interested in this. But as I say," he hurried on, "the people involved have moved away. It might just not be possible to learn how the ring came to be in the cabinet. It may need to remain a mystery." He gave her a sympathetic look.

"Oh, now, Reverend," Anne replied thoughtfully, "there's no need to be defeatist." She smiled at him. "After all, I'm a trained librarian with Internet access. I can find quite a bit of information when I need to."

When Reverend Tom left, Anne was, at long last, ready to start writing her Christmas cards. She had unpacked the deliveries, gone through the mail, and posted to Facebook about the Dickens of a Christmas event.

Carefully, she arranged her supplies before her on the desk—boxes of cards, pens, stamps, her address book, and her phone, because some addresses she didn't have in the book but only in the phone's address book function. She needed to get those sorted, she told herself sternly.

She reached for a card and a pen.

"Excuse me." She looked up to see a man in a business suit. "Do you have the latest John Grisham books?" She directed the man to the mystery section.

She turned to her address book and copied an address on the first envelope.

"Sorry, where's the box?" A frazzled looking woman was clutching some envelopes in her hand. "For the letters to Santa? I promised my kids..." She waved the envelopes vaguely and Anne directed her up the stairs.

She opened a card and wrote the date in the upper right corner. "Dear—" The phone rang. It was the school librarian wondering if Anne had a copy of a book that was already checked out from the school's collection. She did, and she promised to hold it for the student who would be by to pick it up after school.

When she returned the handset to its cradle, she sat still and looked about for a moment. Was her fourth attempt the charm? She reached again for her pen, picked it up, and began to write.

CHAPTER ELEVEN

Despite her boasts to Reverend Tom, sadly neither Anne's training nor her Internet skills proved as effective as she'd hoped when she sat down the next day to apply them. Anderson, after all, was simply too common a name, even when she could couple it with specific first names. The family's prior connection to Blue Hill proved of little help, and Anne simply had too little information about their current whereabouts. She wished she had thought to ask Reverend Tom where young Patrick had gone to school—anyone with a university connection was a cinch to find. But her attempts to get the pastor on the phone were unsuccessful, and an e-mail to him asking the question went unanswered.

It turned out that there were a lot of current and recent college students out there named Patrick Anderson, with no way to determine which was the one she wanted.

Too bad it wasn't as simple as typing "Who put the ring inside the Advent cabinet?" into the Internet search engine.

She was staring at the computer screen when Alex Ochs walked into the library. "So," he said in what was becoming the ritualized greeting of the season, "got your shopping done yet?"

She shot him a look through narrowed eyes. "No," she said. "I just barely got my cards done yesterday."

He set a bag down on the desk and removed his gloves and then his coat. "Well that's progress then. I can't wait for mine." Then he studied her for a long moment. "What's wrong?" he asked, concern creeping into his voice.

Anne scowled and shook her head to clear it. "Just not finding what I'm looking for." She raised her head and looked first at Alex and then at the bag. "What's that?"

"Costumes," he announced, smiling broadly.

"Costumes?" she exclaimed, incredulously.

"Well, potential costumes, anyway," he said. She pulled the bag closer and peered inside. "In fact," he admitted, "sheets."

"Sheets," she confirmed. "White sheets. Umm, more or less."

"Yes, you know, white like angel robes. White like sheep." She arched an eyebrow at him and he shrugged. "I'm donating them to the cause. If Marian can do anything with them, she's welcome to the lot."

"And you've brought them to the library because...?"

"Ah, well, I can't make it to the rehearsal tomorrow. Do you think you could take them with you? And perhaps that nephew of mine as well?"

Anne smiled and put the bag away under her desk. "Of course."

He grinned. "Thanks. So what's up with this?" He gestured with his chin toward her computer. "The Internet not cooperating?"

Anne sighed. "Oh, it's this business with the ring," she said.

"The one from the Advent cabinet? Still no clues as to the owner?"

"Reverend Tom came by yesterday with a good suggestion, but somehow I just haven't been able to make it work."

"What was his suggestion?"

"That the ring might have something to do with the Anderson family. You know, the family of the man who built the cabinet. But I can't seem to find any information about them. Anderson is such a common name, you see. Apparently they have no family or friends left in Blue Hill, nobody who might have an address or a phone number, and now they're lost in the midst of the country's great host of people named Anderson." She gestured toward her computer.

"Reverend Tom told you that?"

At his tone of voice, Anne looked up sharply. "Elizabeth Anderson, the daughter-in-law, moved away last year," she said, "and there's at least one son, Patrick, who is apparently a college student someplace, though I can't tell where." She scrutinized his face. "Why do you look like that? Do I have that wrong? Or was it not their family that built the Advent cabinet? Another Patrick Anderson? Older?"

"Oh yes, he built it. But Reverend Tom told you they had no friends left in Blue Hill." It was a question couched as a statement.

Anne thought. What exactly had Reverend Tom said? Slowly, she replied, "He said there were no family members left in the area. And that he didn't have a forwarding address for Elizabeth."

"Ah, well," said Alex, his face clearing, "that's true enough, I suppose. There are no members of the family left around here. But there are certainly people they were friendly with, some of whom I would think would have their new address."

"Like who?" Anne asked eagerly.

"Well, for starters," Alex said thoughtfully, "you might try the Corrigan girl, Jenny. She used to date young Patrick. In fact, I was under the impression they were still a couple even when he went off to college."

"Jenny Corrigan," Anne said, making a note on the back of an envelope on the desk. "Do you know where Patrick went to school?"

But Alex only shrugged. "Someplace in Boston, but I don't remember which one. And his mother moved...out west someplace. Maybe New Mexico? I don't really remember." Anne made some additional notes, her discouragement dispelled. "Anne." Alex looked at her curiously. "Why are you so worked up about this, anyway?" Alex finally asked.

"The ring belongs to somebody," Anne said. "I'd like to get it returned to its owner. If Aunt Edie is the one who put it in the cabinet, the rightful owner may not even know where it is. I just, you know, want to make sure that it's all right. And I can't help it. I'm curious why Edie had that key and what her connection was to the ring." She hesitated, then added, "Besides, isn't this the season when we should be particularly willing to do things for other people?"

"I see," said Alex, with a smile, "you want your own little personal Christmas miracle."

She gave him a frown, but something else she'd been wondering about came into her head. She glanced down again at her desk and tried to adopt a casual tone. "Anyway, shouldn't you be down at the church?"

But her attempt to surprise him into an explanation of why he was carting his tools around in the church fared no better than her search for the missing Andersons.

"Down at the church?" he replied in a tone of exaggerated innocence. "Why would I need to be down there?"

He began donning his coat and she was about to press him before he could make his escape, when she caught sight of Douglas and Marian Pauthen entering the library. Alex turned and followed Anne's gaze. "Well," he exclaimed, "look who's here."

The Pauthens approached the circulation desk and greeted both Anne and Alex cordially. "Perfect timing, I'd say," Alex interjected, "I've just been asking Anne to take something to you tomorrow. I can't make the rehearsal."

Anne hauled the bag back out from under her desk so that Alex could present it. "In case you can use them for the costumes," he explained.

"Angels and sheep," Anne added with a smile.

Marian turned a gracious smile on him. "Why thank you, Alex. That's very thoughtful of you."

"As a matter of fact," said Douglas, "we're going shopping for fabric this afternoon."

"Shopping?" asked Anne and Alex together. Alex, now more serious, continued, "I'm sure Reverend Tom wouldn't want you to be going to a lot of expense over this. It's already generous just to make the costumes. I'm sure there will be other donations of fabric, not just..." He finished by lamely gesturing toward the bag.

"Well, not shopping, exactly," Marian said.

"Not to worry," Douglas added with a wink. "We're going to an estate sale over in Deshler. You can get lots of old fabrics for almost nothing. Used and stained, nobody wants them. But they work great for costumes."

Anne and Alex exchanged an uneasy glance. "That sounds very clever," Anne said at last.

The Pauthens cheerfully excused themselves to browse for books to borrow. When they had moved off, Alex arched his eyebrows. "Maybe my old sheets aren't looking so bad after all," he said with a wink. "I gotta go," he said and picking up his gloves, he left with a little wave.

She watched him go with a smile. And then suddenly something he'd said came back to her. When she'd mentioned her Christmas cards, he'd said that he couldn't wait to receive his. And she had sent him a card, of course, but the remark collided in her mind with the conversation she'd had the week before with Wendy about exchanging gifts with friends.

Should she be thinking about buying a gift for Alex? Might he be thinking of buying one for her?

* * *

"Aw, Mom, carrot soup *again?*" Ben asked when he entered the kitchen and saw his mother standing over the stove. Anne's last batch had provided dinner for three days. Both Ben and Liddie had liked the soup very much the first two days, but even Anne herself was glad to see the last bowl of it.

"Don't be so hasty to make assumptions," she said, turning around to wink at him. Ben was settling in at the table beside Liddie and pulling his math book from his backpack to finish up his homework while waiting for supper. "This big pot," Anne explained, "is for another favorite—spaghetti."

"And meatballs," Liddie added.

In uncharacteristically quiet moods, the kids were content to focus on their homework while Anne cooked. She wondered how much their moods related to the shortening days as Christmas approached. Even Hershey was curled up quietly under the table.

The extent of Liddie's homework was only a fraction of Ben's, so when she finished, Anne suggested Liddie start her letter to Santa while Ben wrapped up his math problems. "Remember, Santa's coming to collect them the day after tomorrow."

Actually, Ben had appeared to be daydreaming more than multiplying and dividing, but the prospect of writing to Santa spurred him to finish quickly, and soon both children were absorbed in the task. Facing the stove, with her back to the kids, Anne nevertheless kept her ear cocked while the two of them quietly conferred over their wish lists. Liddie was deciding between asking Santa for a scooter or a new dress for Cleopatra, her beloved doll. Ben was pretty certain he wanted an iPad.

Oh, brother, Anne thought. *He's way too young for that.* Yet she knew teachers took computers to their classrooms more and more. Still, she would need to think about what would be just as exciting on Christmas morning.

"What do you want for Christmas, Mommy? Did you write your letter to Santa yet?" Liddie asked.

Anne turned and glanced down. Liddie had a list for Santa that filled an entire page, though when she looked, Anne saw that the handwriting was Ben's. She smiled at her son. "You've been helping your sister!" But he merely grumbled and redoubled his focus on his own list.

Anne returned her attention to Liddie. "Wow, sweetie. Isn't that a lot of things? Santa has many children to deliver to, you know."

"We know that," Ben explained. "We're working together so we can give Santa some choices." Anne glanced over his shoulder at his list, also very long. Ben covered his letter with his hand. "Mom! No peeking!" He giggled as Anne tousled his hair. "You didn't answer Liddie, Mom. What do *you* want?"

"Oh, I don't know..." Anne drifted back to the stove. "A giraffe might be fun. Or a camel, for getting around town."

"We can't have animals like that! We don't have a barn!" Liddie protested.

"Oh well, then. I'll have to ask Santa for a new barn."

"A giraffe would be cool, or a camel," said Ben wistfully. "Or another dog?"

"Ben, we've talked about this before. Now, if you two are done with your letters," Anne continued briskly, "I need you to clear the table for dinner, please. Put your homework in your backpacks now, so you won't forget to take it with you tomorrow."

Liddie scooted off her chair and started gathering all her papers at once, until Ben pointed out that she'd put her letter to Santa in her backpack along with her homework.

"Give it to me," Anne heard him say, as she was filling up their plates. And before she knew it, Ben had gathered both his and Liddie's letters and dashed through the door that led into the library to drop them in the letter box in the Children's Room.

Over dinner, she tried to engage the kids on the contents of their letters. Liddie was forthcoming. She preferred a scooter that had sparkly purple paint and streamers coming out of the handles. And for her doll, she wanted a sundress and straw hat—her old one had ripped when she was sliding down the stair railing.

"And why was she sliding down the stair railing, when it's forbidden?" Anne asked.

But Liddie had a ready answer. "Only actual children have been forbidden to slide down the banister. Not dolls."

"I see." Anne did admire her daughter's quick wit. She wondered if someday she'd be interested in a career as a lawyer. But, she reminded herself, that was down the road. She first had to worry about—in addition to everything else—how to sew a doll dress in the middle of the night once the children had fallen asleep.

"Come on, Liddie," Ben said. "You can help me with the play some more. May we be excused?"

Anne reminded them to take their plates to the sink, and when they'd finished the task, they raced from the room.

As she began to clean up, something came back to Anne from her earlier conversation with Ben. Her comment about being hasty to make assumptions had come off the top of her head, and yet, she realized, she herself had been quick to make assumptions at times. Anne thought about that in light of recent events. Was she making unwarranted assumptions about the ring? She would need to be on guard herself against such behavior.

But in the meantime, thanks to Alex's tip, she'd been able to get in touch with Jenny Corrigan and had an appointment to see her the next day.

Chapter Twelve

The next morning, Anne sat in a diner on the outskirts of Deshler, some twenty miles from Blue Hill and home to the regional hospital. As she sipped her coffee, she darted nervous glances through the plate glass window. The weak December sunlight was making slow headway against the night's frost, and the air outside looked cold and brittle. The warmth and bustle of the diner made a reassuring contrast with the chilly view outside the steamed window.

Anne turned the cup in circles on the table before her.

The bell over the door chimed with the entrance of another customer, and a young woman in hospital scrubs entered. Anne sat up straight and stretched her neck to catch the nurse's eye, and when she approached Anne's booth, asked, "Jenny? Jenny Corrigan?" When the woman smiled in acknowledgement, she continued, "I'm Anne. Thanks so much for agreeing to meet me."

As Jenny slid into the booth, a waitress appeared brandishing a menu. "Coffee, hon?"

Once she had her own steaming mug and Anne had a refill, Jenny gave Anne a tired, uncertain smile. "I'm still not really sure what this is about," she said. "Something about Pat?"

Anne realized the girl was younger than her blunt features and tousled hair had suggested. Probably not a nurse yet, she decided, but perhaps on her way to being one. Her ready smile suggested amiability and a willingness to help, but her distracted manner showed that she did not feel too personally invested in questions about the Andersons.

"Yes," Anne said. "I'm trying to contact him or someone in his family." But she could see that this bald statement merely kindled suspicion in the young woman's mind, and she tried to think of an approach that would sound more reassuring. "I'm a member of the Blue Hill Community Church," she said after a moment, and Jenny nodded in recognition of the name. "I'm told that Patrick and his family were also members, when they lived here?" Jenny nodded again, and Anne said, "In fact, it was Patrick's grandfather who built a... well, a special cabinet for the church."

Jenny began to relax once again, and leaning back in the booth, she gave a chuckle of fond indulgence as she said, "The Advent cabinet."

"That's right," Anne said quickly, wanting to build on this connection. "The thing is, you see, we've found something in the cabinet, and I'm trying to determine if it might belong to Patrick's family."

The suspicion was now gone from Jenny's eyes, replaced by a deep puzzlement. "What have you found?"

"Well," Anne said, "this." She drew the ring box from her pocket and placed it on the table. She had hoped to build up to this moment more gradually, but she didn't want to appear unnecessarily coy or withholding.

Jenny gave her a glance and then reached out to open the box, though leaving it where it was on the table. "Oh my," she said drawing her hands back. Almost immediately, she started to reach for it again but then paused and looked at Anne. "May I?"

Anne nodded, and Jenny tugged the ring from its box and held it closer to her eye. "It's gorgeous," she said after a moment.

"It's not a real sapphire," Anne said, almost apologetically.

"Still," murmured Jenny. She continued to turn it about and study it for a moment, but then she returned the ring to its box, shut the lid, and pushed it back a few inches across the table toward Anne. "I still don't understand," she said, looking again into Anne's face. "Pat's family moved away about a year and a half ago. The last time any of them were in Blue Hill was when Pat came to visit me last fall.... But you've just found this now? What makes you think it could be theirs?"

Anne described the locked cubbies, each with its own key, and how one key had been lost for a while, and the ring discovered when the missing key was unexpectedly found. Jenny nodded in understanding. Anne hesitated, then said, "I don't mean to pry, but are you a member of the church yourself?"

Jenny shook her head. "No. I used to go when I was seeing Pat, but I never joined."

"Do you perhaps remember my great-aunt, Edie Summers?"

Jenny frowned in thought. "Isn't she the woman who left her home to be a library?" And then, comprehension dawning, "Ah! You're the new librarian."

"That's right," said Anne, pleased, and she went on to describe how she had found the missing key among Edie's Christmas decorations.

"But if your great-aunt had the key," Jenny objected, "why do you think the ring might belong to Pat's family?"

"That's just the thing. I'm not sure," Anne admitted, "except that Aunt Edie was the kind of person whom people naturally trusted. But Reverend Tom—you must remember our pastor?" Jenny nodded. "He suggested the possibility of a connection with the Andersons, since they were so closely associated with the cabinet. And now I'm just trying to find a way to contact them, to check it out." She waited a moment, and then said, "What do you think? Could this ring have belonged to, say, Patrick's mother?"

Reluctantly, Jenny reached out and flipped open the top of the box, but she didn't extract the ring. Instead, she lifted the whole box and examined the ring again but then put it back down with a sigh and a shake of her head. "I don't know," she said. "I remember Mrs. Anderson had some nice pieces of jewelry that she'd bring out for special occasions. I remember her showing me one or two pieces one time and telling me they were things she had inherited from her own mother."

"Was this one of them?" Anne nodded toward the box.

"No, this definitely wasn't. But you might say they were... comparable to this ring. But as a rule, she didn't wear much jewelry and it wasn't something we talked about, except for that one time. So I really can't say one way or the other."

Anne nodded. "You said that Patrick came to Blue Hill last fall to visit you? And the rest of his family had moved away by then?"

"Yeah, Pat was the last to go off to school. Once Mrs. Anderson had the, you know, empty nest, she started talking about moving to be closer to her sister. And finally, she did."

Jenny hesitated and then continued. "Pat and I, well, we were together during most of his time in college, but of course we couldn't see much of each other. And really, we kind of drifted apart." She shifted uncomfortably. "Then last fall, just as he was going into his senior year, he came back to visit. I could tell he was starting to get serious, to think about what he was going to do after graduation and all that. He talked about coming back at the semester break and spending the holidays with me. And I just, well, I realized it was time to break it off, as much for his sake as for mine. But he didn't take it very well. And then he went back to Tufts."

Anne nodded and looked at the young woman more carefully as she listened. Jenny was direct and plainspoken. She would make a good nurse someday. "Do you know how to contact him now?" Anne asked.

Jenny, who had teared up somewhat at the recollection of the painful episode, blew her nose and shook her head. "He graduated in June. I sent him a card, but I didn't hear from him. He had talked about staying in Boston because of the job opportunities. He worked with computers. But I don't know if that's what he did."

Together they stared for a while at the ring, still sitting in its open box on the table. "So you think that...?" Jenny indicated the ring with her chin.

"I wonder," Anne said softly, "if maybe that was intended to be your engagement ring."

* * *

"So you think he just left it there?" Wendy sounded skeptical as Anne recounted the story that afternoon at the next rehearsal of the Nativity play.

"He was upset," said Helen, also listening with rapt attention. "His girlfriend had just broken up with him."

Reverend Tom, the fourth member of their group, said nothing.

"I'm sure he meant to come back and reclaim it," Anne said. "But he probably figured it was safe for the moment. It was locked in the Advent cabinet, and Aunt Edie had the key to the cubby. It wasn't like someone would just find it there. And it was his senior year of college. I imagine he had many other things on his mind, and he probably thought that there was no particular pressure to get back to Blue Hill and collect it."

"And then Edie died," said Wendy thoughtfully, "which he could have heard about somehow, and he doesn't know where she put the key or how to go about finding it. But why doesn't he contact you? Or Reverend Tom?"

Anne shrugged. "He may not know I inherited the house. Or he may be embarrassed. Or he may intend to yet, but just hasn't gotten around to it. I can think of a number of reasons."

"But to get the ring back?" Wendy asked. "Something could happen to it."

"Young people tend to think they have all the time in the world," observed Helen.

"What do you think?" Anne asked the pastor.

He shrugged. "To try to guess what is in young Patrick's mind is beyond me," he said, "but I can honestly say that you have managed to pursue this lead, Anne, much further than I would have thought possible." He paused for a moment, and then asked, "Having come so far, I wonder whether it's time to pause and see if Patrick makes the next move?"

But Anne shook her head. "The more time and effort I put into this, the more determined I am to get the ring back to its rightful owner and understand Aunt Edie's connection here. If Patrick hasn't come looking for it, well, then maybe I need to look for Patrick."

Reverend Tom looked puzzled. "But I thought you had already tried to locate Patrick and failed?"

"Ah, but I have some additional information now. I've already sent an e-mail to his old student address at Tufts. I don't know how long the university will let him keep it, since he graduated in June, but it hasn't bounced back. I'm hoping he has it set up to forward his mail automatically to whatever his new address is. And even if that doesn't work, I have a few other things I can try, based on the additional information I got from Jenny."

"I see," Reverend Tom said, looking more troubled than impressed.

Wendy laughed. "I think it's amazing, the amount of information you're able to find on the Web. When I try to search for something, I mostly end up with sites trying to sell me things."

"It's persistence, mostly," Anne said, "a willingness to sort through that commercial haystack to find the needle or two. Though I'll admit," she added with a slight smile, "that a well-crafted search query can do a lot to help."

"I'll almost be sorry when you do find the ring's owner," Helen said. "Hearing about the search has certainly helped these rehearsals fly by."

The rehearsal had once again begun with a quick read-through of the play. The cast members still kept their scripts in front of them, but Suzanne was urging them to keep their eyes raised from the pages and only check their lines when absolutely necessary. Anne noticed that Ben was merely holding his script and didn't open it once, though as he had pointed out several times, his only line wasn't even a real word. Still, she hoped the fact that he wasn't following along didn't mean he'd lost interest in the play. So far, he had seemed quite enthusiastic.

Marian, meanwhile, was pulling the kids out one by one so that she could take measurements. Unfortunately, she'd reported earlier to Anne, the estate sale had been a bust as far as fabrics were concerned.

"Not to worry, though," Douglas had added cheerfully. "We've got a line on another one on Saturday." He'd patted his wife's shoulder consolingly. Nevertheless, Marian had asked Suzanne to make a general announcement seeking donations of old fabrics.

Reverend Tom was just excusing himself when the cast took a break and Suzanne once again came down the aisle to chat with the group. He waited and watched her approach, but it was Helen who anxiously asked, "How are you feeling?"

"Yeah," said Wendy, "at the last rehearsal, I thought you were really coming down with something."

"I am...highly medicated," Suzanne announced, and as she approached, Anne could see that she was looking wan.

"Are you sure you should be doing this?" Reverend Tom asked with concern as he helped her to sit in a pew.

"I'm fine." Suzanne waved her hand dismissively. "Truly, it will be fine. It's just a cold, it's not this flu that's going around."

They looked at one another uneasily, but no one wanted to contradict Suzanne. Finally Wendy said, "Boy, they say it's a bad one this year."

Apparently, the bug was starting to work its way through the school, and Anne worried again about it getting into the library.

Reverend Tom took his leave and the flu outbreak served as conversation fodder until Suzanne stood. "Time for me to get back to work," she said.

The cast resumed its work on the blocking and movement, and Anne noticed that Brad was becoming more confident about making his suggestions. At first, they appeared to be relatively minor, and several unquestionably made the stage business more economical or effective. It seemed to Anne that Suzanne went out of her way to praise and embrace these new ideas.

But as time went on, Brad became more excited and his suggestions more elaborate. Some involved basic changes in the positions of scenery and props, and as his ideas became more complicated, it took longer to explain them to the kids in order to try them out. Brad began rushing about the stage area, demonstrating what he meant, playing several parts at once. The younger children giggled while the older ones looked skeptical or confused.

Several times, after a new idea had been given a trial run with much confusion and rushing about, Brad himself would reject it and announce a return to the way they'd been doing it before. When Suzanne proposed taking another break, Brad suggested that, while they did so, he focus more intensively with a few performers for whom he had more specific suggestions.

Soon, some three quarters of the cast was idle while Brad worked intensively in a corner with the narrator, the boy playing Herod, and a couple of other actors. Suzanne's face looked strained and tired, and since Brad was monopolizing some of the key cast members, there was little she could do with the rest. Her frustration was plain as she sat and rested once again in one of the front pews.

Eventually, Suzanne tried to regroup the kids who were not working directly with Brad, and she set them to rehearsing other scenes as best they could. She filled in for the cast members otherwise occupied and looked surprised and grateful when Ben stepped up on a couple of occasions to do the same.

But by now the rehearsal had been going on for a long time and the kids' energy was flagging. They began flubbing lines that they had delivered flawlessly earlier. Suzanne was increasingly impatient, but Brad seemed completely absorbed in his own little project. Just as Suzanne seemed on the point of losing her temper altogether, Anne saw Douglas appear from nowhere and speak softly into her ear. Suzanne gave him a grateful look and nodded.

Raising his voice to parade-ground levels, Douglas called the kids to attention and began organizing them into squads. Rather than continuing their work on the play, he put them through some physical exercises that both woke them up and settled their nerves. After a while, he called over to Brad and asked whether it wasn't time to stand at ease. Flashing an annoyed look, Brad responded testily that they were still working out a bit of business. Douglas stiffened but did not respond, and the kids all drew in their breath. Suddenly Reverend Tom, who Anne hadn't seen return to the sanctuary, spoke quietly into the silence.

"Brad," he said with just enough sharpness to get his attention. "I think we've accomplished enough for tonight." Reverend Tom discreetly tapped an imaginary wristwatch, and as he did so, the doors to the church cracked open and a few parents poked their heads in to see if it was safe to enter and collect their children. Addressing the group, Reverend Tom said, "Very good work, everyone. Thank you for the effort you're putting into this."

The younger children jumped up and ran hastily around the sanctuary collecting coats and mittens and boots, followed by the teens, who were in a more subdued mood as they slowly filtered out into the cold December evening. Anne walked quickly up the aisle to her own children and Ryan, but they seemed less distressed than some of the others.

But as they made their way out of the church, she saw Reverend Tom and Brad huddled in one corner. The pastor had a hand on the younger man's shoulder, but Brad was hanging his head and looked embarrassed. And she saw Suzanne, looking pale and frazzled, giving the two of them a wide berth.

CHAPTER THIRTEEN

The next day was the day of the Dickens of a Christmas event, and Anne awoke filled with excitement.

As Reverend Tom often pointed out, Christmas is the holiday when we celebrate the birth of the Savior, but the manner in which we celebrate owes a great deal to our Victorian forebears. And if there was ever a town made for Christmas, Blue Hill, with its wealth of charming, well-preserved Victorian architecture, was it.

The town had ingeniously capitalized on this potential with the Dickens of a Christmas event, an annual date on the community calendar when stores stayed open late to offer special sales and serve holiday refreshments. Some people even dressed in Dickensian costume. The downtown streets would be closed off to become pedestrian malls, and the crowds of shoppers would socialize and be entertained by strolling carolers. The climax of the evening was the arrival of Santa on the "Polar Express," a nod to the town's rich railroading history.

The downtown shops had all strung lights, though there was a slight division between a few who favored festive colored lights and those who chose the more austere but elegant strings of simple white. Virtually every window that faced the street had a white electric candle burning in it, and the town had hung great green wreaths from every lamppost. In addition, a large white star stretched over Main Street.

Over the years, as Anne had learned since her return to Blue Hill, Dickens of a Christmas had become a hugely popular event. It was a chance for folks to catch their breath in the midst of the holiday bustle, to light some lights against the darkness of the winter cold, to socialize with friends and neighbors, and yes, to do a little Christmas shopping. The event attracted families not just from Blue Hill but from throughout the region, and Anne was proud that the library would be playing an important role this year.

It was true that the opportunity had more or less fallen into her lap, but she was determined to take advantage of it. Fortunately for her, the library solved a problem that had long plagued the event's organizers: how to provide a fitting close to the evening. Once Santa arrived, he would wander through the town and in and out of various shops. But the problem had always been, where would he stop? Because to have any sort of concluding event at a particular store would be seen by other merchants as some sort of favoritism.

As a community enterprise without commercial encumbrances, the library provided a welcome neutral ground.

For Anne, the event offered a chance to build awareness of the library and extend its service mission. She expected to have many new people coming in today, and her challenge was to encourage at least some of them to return as regular patrons. To that end, she had created a drawing based on library card numbers in an effort to encourage new patrons to sign up for cards. The winner would receive a selection of holiday books that had been donated for that purpose.

Anne had already been seeing some results. For the past ten days, children and families had been visiting the library at an increasing rate in order to drop their letters to Santa into the box. It was true that many times they simply made a beeline for the box, deposited their letters, and left the library again, but many others lingered afterward, browsing the books on display. In fact, she had already signed up a fair number of new patrons during this time.

She began to mentally review her long checklist of things to do. *Thank goodness for Mildred,* she thought. Baking cookies had been one of the biggest and most time-consuming chores on that list, and Mildred had blessedly lifted that burden from her. But there were still plenty of other things to do. Once the kids were off to school and Hershey was walked, she was able to focus on her preparations.

When dinnertime rolled around, the library was ready. Evergreen garlands draped from the foyer and fairy lights lit up the checkout counter. One room of the library was done up in a Nutcracker theme, while another had Victorian accents, and the Children's Room had a winter sports theme with papier-mâché snowmen and ice-skates and ski poles that Ben and Liddie had helped her arrange. Anne herself was dressed in a red tartan wool skirt and a black turtleneck sweater that showed off her necklace of tiny glowing Christmas tree bulbs.

As it happened, the library usually stayed open later on Thursdays anyway, so Anne could tell that tonight's crowds and excitement were far beyond the usual. The town had closed off Main Street at five o'clock, and the restaurants were now crowded with residents getting a start on the evening. The library began to fill with people and Anne soon lost track of time.

Mildred, intermittently assisted by Ben and Liddie, had assumed responsibility for the refreshments, ladling out cups of hot chocolate and hot cider and keeping the cookie plates replenished. Fortunately, Sherri had volunteered to come in to staff the circulation desk, which left Anne free to move through the crowd, answering innumerable questions.

Many people, of course, were curious about the renovations that had been carried out to convert a home into a library, and several times Anne wished that Alex Ochs were on hand to answer some of the more technical inquiries. In fact, she'd rather expected that he would be there. She'd seen his nephew, Ryan, slipping through the crowd with Ben, and she was a little disappointed to find that Alex wasn't there as well. But she did her best, drawing on her memories of all that Alex had told her about the work, and people were understanding when she was unable to describe some of the more intricate construction details.

She knew that this was a social event and a holiday entertainment for the kids, but she was gratified by the number of people who were still actually browsing the books. She found herself spending a great deal of time making suggestions for good books to give as Christmas gifts, not only for children but for adults as well. Many people praised the feature Grace had run in the newspaper and were eager to discuss in more detail the suggestions that had appeared there. Indeed, the requests for gift recommendations came so frequently, and people seemed so appreciative of her suggestions, that Anne decided to create a small handout for next year's event. She could even build a display around it.

"Well, he likes history," one woman was saying, "especially about the Civil War."

"Has he read *Team of Rivals*?" Anne asked, when from the corner of her eye, she saw Ben standing off to the side.

He waited politely until she was finished, but she could tell he was alive with excitement. Still, he managed to keep his voice down when he said, "Santa's here. Well, he's down on Main Street, but he's come in on the train and he's on his way."

Anne smiled. "We'd better get ready to welcome him. Go tell your sister that he's on his way." Ben nodded and dashed off, but Anne knew that Santa had to visit many stores in the village before ending up at the library, so she suspected he would not arrive for a little while yet.

Sooner then she expected, however — though she thought it had probably felt an eternity to Ben and Liddie — a ripple of anticipation ran through the crowd, and eyes turned toward the library's entrance just as a reverberating "ho, ho, ho" sounded. As Santa stepped into the building, the crowd broke into spontaneous applause. "Santa is in the house!" he called, waving.

Standing by the circulation desk, Anne realized that she didn't know what, if anything, she was expected to do. Was she supposed to greet Santa? Welcome him to the library? She stood, hesitating, but the crowd parted before Santa as he made his way in, and spotting Anne, he made his way toward her.

"And there's the lovely librarian!" Santa boomed, "Merry Christmas!" Reaching into a sack, he pulled out a large candy cane and presented it to her with a flourish.

Anne gave a small curtsy as she accepted it and thanked the jolly man. There was the briefest flash of a wink before Santa turned and addressed the crowd, announcing that he was going to look around the library a little bit before he went upstairs and collected the letters that all the good little boys and girls had written to him. As he moved off into the crowd, it was all Anne could do to contain her laughter.

Underneath the beard and fat suit, she had recognized Alex Ochs.

* * *

The library was now very crowded since many additional people had arrived with Santa. It appeared that some families had met him at the train and had been more or less following him about town ever since. The excited buzz of conversation and laughter had risen a notch or two, and Anne cast an anxious glance in Mildred's direction to see how she was holding out, but all seemed calm at the refreshment table and Mildred seemed to be enjoying herself as much as anyone.

There was a light touch on her arm, and she turned to find a vibrant Grace Hawkins with a camera slung around her neck. "What a great turnout," Grace said into Anne's ear.

"Is it always like this?" Anne asked, flushed with excitement.

Grace shook her head. "Not this crowded. I think this must be the most successful year yet. Of course, we're lucky the weather has cooperated this year, but I think having it wind up here at the library has helped too."

Anne beamed. "I'm happy to hear it."

"Let's go upstairs," said Grace, "I've got to be ready for the photo op."

They found the crowds upstairs as thick as down, though perhaps with a higher percentage of children as they waited for Santa to come collect the letters they had written. Grace moved off to check out the best angles for her photographs, while Anne resumed answering questions about the library.

"This is marvelous," exclaimed Reverend Tom, suddenly appearing out of the crowd. "What a festive night." Anne was happy to see that the pastor was once again back to his usual good-natured self. It had seemed to her lately that he often acted oddly uncomfortable or constrained in her presence. Tonight, however, he beamed in good fellowship at all around him.

The two of them stepped to one side to observe the throng. "I must confess, I'm a little overwhelmed," Anne said. "So many people! Grace Hawkins said she thinks this may be the best turnout they've ever had."

Tom nodded. "It has certainly been going very well indeed. And I must say, I'm very glad we've been able to add this stop here at the library. I realize this event was created by the merchants in town, and I certainly don't begrudge them their holiday business, but still, it's nice to have the evening end up someplace where the emphasis is not on the commercial aspect of the season." He smiled at the crowd. "I hope you'll be willing to do this again next year?"

"Oh yes," Anne said enthusiastically. "I'll look forward to it."

Tom nodded and continued to gaze benevolently at the crowd. They could hear Santa making his way up the stairs through the throng. Now that they were past the excitement of Santa's arrival, however, it felt to Anne like things had leveled out a bit, and when Alex, as Santa, arrived on the second floor, he did not make a beeline for the letter box but continued to circulate among the crowd. His natural rapport with children made him a delightful Santa.

Soon, however, she heard Alex excusing himself, saying that Santa needed to have a word with their "charming librarian" about some good books for gifts, and he joined Anne and Reverend Tom in their corner. Anne's bright smile threatened to explode into laughter at any second. "Well," she finally managed, "I had no idea you were living this double life."

"Let's just say pressure was brought to bear," he said. To the extent that Santa can glare, he did so in the direction of Reverend Tom.

The pastor beamed at Santa, not at all contrite. "This will go a long way toward getting you off the naughty list, Alex," he replied with a chuckle.

Alex sighed and gave a shake of his head.

Anne, feeling a slight itch of sympathy, said, "So why are you...?" She gestured at his costume.

"The past ten years, Barney Stockbeam has played Santa," Alex said, "but this year, he's down with that flu that's going around. So..."

"I hear it's very contagious," Reverend Tom sympathized. "It's hit the congregation pretty hard."

But Anne was forming the words to tease Alex. "Well," she said after a moment, "you wear the weight well," and almost burst into a fit of laughter.

But Alex groaned. "I'm not going to need this pillow pretty soon," he said, slapping his padded midsection. "Pretty soon, it will all be me!"

"What do you mean?"

Alex glanced over his shoulder and leaned in. "It's the cookies," he confided. "Not to be ungrateful, but every single place Santa goes, he's gotta have a cookie! Or six," he added.

Tom clapped him on the shoulder consolingly. "That's true devotion to the part, my friend. Staying in character like that. Great roles require sacrifices."

Alex shook his head. "I don't want to see another cookie until next Christmas."

Anne was struggling between teasing and sympathizing when a voice behind Alex piped up. "Santa," said Liddie, holding up a plate, "would you like a cookie?"

Anne had to turn her head away to hide her laughter, but she was still impressed with how smoothly Alex responded, "Why thank you, little girl. Santa loves cookies!"

CHAPTER FOURTEEN

The Andersons seemed nice enough, but I didn't really know them," Wendy Pyle had said to Anne. "Essentially, you're e-mailing a total stranger. So how are you going to approach this? 'Hi there. I happened to find a valuable sapphire ring. Any chance it's yours?' What is he gonna say?"

Anne's long-shot message to Patrick Anderson's student e-mail address had yielded a response. And while perhaps not as cynical as her friend, Anne took the point, so she responded to Patrick with a message that made no reference to the ring, but rather spoke somewhat vaguely of the Advent cabinet his grandfather had built for the church. Anne asked if they might be able to speak on the phone.

It appeared from his reply that Patrick had not stayed in the Boston area after graduating but had in fact joined his mother in New Mexico. He made a point of mentioning the time-zone difference but also expressed his willingness to talk. He suggested some times for the next day, Saturday, and Anne took care to free up her schedule for the first of these.

She found Ben and Liddie busy with video games when she went to warn them that she would be on the phone for a while. Absorbed, they barely looked up in acknowledgment, though Hershey gazed at her from the floor and wagged his tail. *At least somebody's listening to me,* Anne thought, and retreated to her desk.

Apparently, her call caught Patrick Anderson at a distracted moment as well, even though he had suggested the time. He seemed to have no idea for a moment who she was or why she was calling. But she mentioned the church and the Advent cabinet, and after a moment, he responded, "Oh. Right."

Anne waited for something further, but when nothing was forthcoming, she tried, "Your grandfather was quite a craftsman. Was it a hobby for him or is that how he earned his living?"

"Uh, I think it was just a hobby."

Now that she had him on the phone, Anne was having trouble zeroing in on the topics she wished to address. "We'll be opening some more of the doors tomorrow," she tried. "You know, after service. That's a tradition that started while you still lived here, right? Did you enjoy the whole Advent thing? Choosing little treasures to go into the cabinet?"

She could almost hear the shrug down the phone line. "My mom was really into it. She did most of that."

Anne was absently sketching the face of the cabinet on a piece of scrap paper as she focused on the conversation. She began adding little pencil dots to each cubby door to represent the keyholes. "Patrick, did you know that one of the keys to one of the cubbies went missing last year?"

"Missing?" For the first time, he sounded interested. "Which one?"

"Number seven." She began to doodle a sketch of the spindly cubby keys. "Number seven went missing sometime last year."

After a beat, Patrick said, "Well, that's too bad. I remember my mom saying that the keys are all different so I guess that means you can't use one of the others?"

"The thing is…Patrick, do you remember Edie Summers? She was my great-aunt."

"Oh, sure, the ol…the lady who lives in the big house. She's your great-aunt? She's cool."

"She was my great-aunt. She died last year. She arranged to have that house turned into a library for the town, and I'm its librarian."

"Oh. I'm sorry," Patrick said, presumably in response to Edie's death and not the creation of the library.

"The funny thing is, I was going through all these Christmas decorations that Aunt Edie left behind, and in among them, I found that key."

"Key? To the Advent cabinet? The missing one?"

"Yes."

"Wow. Weird." Patrick seemed content to contemplate the weirdness of this without exhibiting any further curiosity— as to what might have been found in the cubby, for instance. Anne waited patiently, determined that he should make the next move. "Well," he said at last, "but that's good, right? To find something that was missing? But why'd she have it?"

"Well, Patrick, that's what I'm trying to figure out." Either Patrick was playing it very cool indeed, or, Anne began to suspect, he just didn't know anything. She decided to try the element of surprise. "How did Aunt Edie come to have that key? And what connection did she have to the ring?"

There was a moment of silence, and then Patrick said, "Ring?" in a tone that sounded genuinely bewildered.

"When we used the key to open door number seven, we found a ring inside there. I'm trying to figure out who it belongs to so I can return it. I...thought perhaps you might have put it there, or at least, might know something about it."

"Me?" Patrick's voice had the alarmed tone of someone who has been accused of something. "Why would you think I did? I don't even live in Blue Hill anymore."

Anne began marking her doodles with large Xs. "I had a talk with Jenny Corrigan the other day. She mentioned you'd been in town to visit her last fall. I thought...maybe you'd brought the ring with you then. To, you know, use it to propose. I'm sorry," she quickly added, "I know it's none of my business. As I say, I'm just trying to figure out who this ring belongs to."

When he still said nothing, she continued. "I thought you might have hidden it in the cabinet that your grandfather made, perhaps as a surprise. I thought maybe that was how you were going to, you know, pop the question."

There was a long silence on the other end of the line. "Huh," he said at last, "well, yeah." For a moment, Anne's heart quickened. Patrick gave a doleful sigh. "Yeah, I visited Jenny and I was thinking about proposing. Well, planning to. But I guess she suspected, because she broke up with me before I could do it. And yes, I had a ring with me. But I didn't leave it in Blue Hill. I couldn't. I had to take it back."

Anne thanked Patrick and ended the call. She looked up from the phone to find Ben and Liddie watching her intently.

They seemed troubled about something, but Anne couldn't make out what it was. There were none of the telltale signs that they'd been fighting and were now looking for her to adjudicate some conflict. "All done with the game?" she tried.

"Mom," Ben said, a note of distress in his voice, "when are we gonna get a Christmas tree?"

* * *

The Penn Pines Tree Farm, about twenty miles outside of Blue Hill, came highly recommended by both Wendy and Mildred. Such snow as they'd had this season had disappeared from town, but out here there was still a thin blanket on the ground, and it covered the unpaved parking lot of the tree farm. Anne crept slowly down the crowded lot, looking for a parking space. She eyed one family as they piled into their car and switched on her directional to claim their spot. "You see," she said to the kids, "we're not the last people on earth to get our tree after all."

When the kids had asked, she had felt stricken that she'd neglected their own Christmas and had done some quick calculating. Christmas was less than two weeks away, she realized, and tomorrow there was church and play rehearsal. School vacation hadn't started yet, and if she waited until next weekend, they'd have their tree only a couple of days before Christmas. She'd spent so much time putting up the decorations in the library, she'd not been thinking of their own tree. Well, it looked like today was the day. It was a good thing she had arranged for extra hours from her staff and volunteers for the holiday season.

The tree farm folks seemed very organized. There was a small corral of cut trees off to one side, but clearly, most of the families were there to cut their own. Tractors pulling wagons were running in circuits, taking families out to the plantations and bringing them triumphantly back with their trophies. Anne wondered what the average time spent making a selection was. She steeled herself to patience.

In a large shed off to one side, the tree farmers offered coffee, hot cider, and homemade donuts, but it appeared that most people were waiting until after they had found their tree before indulging in these treats. It sure made for a change from New York, where dealers would truck in trees from Maine and Canada and set up on street corners to sell them at exorbitant prices. Ben and Liddie looked around in fascination.

"Are we going to get to go on one of those?" Ben's eyes shone as he pointed to one of the tractor-drawn wagons.

"It looks that way," Anne replied, trying to remember if either of the children had ever seen a tractor in person before. She was struck again by how urban their young lives had been. Anne had chosen the city after growing up in a small town, but the city was all her own kids had ever known.

They joined a queue of families waiting to board the wagons. When their turn came, Ben bounded up, but Anne hesitated a moment, looking down at Liddie. The young farmer driving the tractor, however, had slipped down from his seat and suddenly appeared at her side, hoisting Liddie up and swinging her into the wagon. "There you go, little girl," he said with a smile.

"Thank you," Anne said and climbed up herself as the young man moved off to tend to other duties. There were plenty of single-parent families, she knew, but she had already noticed that almost every family at the tree farm seemed to have two adults. Moments like these could still revive her ache of loss, but she didn't have time to indulge it right now because she had to get the kids settled onto the benches.

"You have to sit down," she said to them in a low tone. "The wagon is going to lurch a lot as it goes along, and it won't be safe to stand up." Liddie hesitated. "Sit down!" Anne said again and got them settled on either side of her. Most of the other parents were engaged in similar conversations.

The wagon indeed gave a mighty lurch when it started and Ben, who'd looked skeptical, gave an impressed "Whoa!" and grabbed the wood-slatted side of the wagon. The tractor trundled and bumped along, but the kids, normally impatient with anything that moved slower than digital speed, were entranced. They stared about as the farmer drove them through a large stand of tiny trees still too young to harvest and finally into a large plot of trees that were clearly part of this year's crop.

They stopped in the middle, where a smaller group was waiting for the ride back. The farmer invited everyone to take a hacksaw from the collection in a box at the front of the wagon, but Anne restrained Ben's eagerly reaching arm and took a saw herself.

They climbed down and looked around. The other families began dispersing in different directions, some of the children already racing from one tree to the next. "Well," said Anne, smiling down at Ben and Liddie, "which way?"

Liddie seemed a bit overwhelmed, but Ben immediately pointed in a direction at an angle to the tractor's worn path, and they set off.

Making a selection turned out to be less fraught than Anne had feared. At first, in their excitement, the kids were ready to take almost every tree they saw, but Anne encouraged them to first come up with three finalists and then choose from among those. When they had finally made their selection, Anne hefted the saw and prepared to kneel down but then paused and looked thoughtfully at her son.

"Would you like to try it, Ben?" His eyes shone and he nodded eagerly as he reached for the saw. Anne instinctively pulled it back out of his reach, then checked herself. "This is very sharp," she warned, and then shifted the saw in her hand so that Ben could take it by the grip. He squatted down and was about to place it immediately under the tree's lowest branch when Anne stopped him.

"Remember, Ben, the tree is going to have to go into the stand." He looked up at her, uncertain. "Leave room to put it into the stand," Anne continued. "We're going to need a good six inches of plain trunk to go down into it"—she made a downward thrusting motion with her hand—"so that the tree will be stable when we set it up."

A look of comprehension spread over his face, and he moved the saw down the trunk to just above the ground. "Good," she said. "If there's too much trunk, we can always cut more off, but if there's too little, we'd have to trim off some of the lower branches. Go ahead."

Ben set the blade against the trunk and began to draw it back and forth, producing the irregular wobbling and skipping of an inexperienced sawyer. "You see? You need to keep an even pressure, enough to keep the blade steady against the wood and get the teeth to bite in."

Ben drew a breath, squared his shoulders, and started again.

"Good," Anne encouraged.

It took him a long while, as the blade hung up once or twice, and he ended up cutting it off at a rather steep angle, but Ben's face glowed with pride when the tree separated from the base and Anne lifted it into the air. He was so pleased he didn't even object to handing the saw back. They dragged the tree to the rendezvous and the farmer, a different one, passed it up to them into the wagon. Ben grinned for the entire return trip.

Back at the yard, the farmers trussed the tree up with nylon netting to make it easier to handle and held it aside for them while Anne took Ben and Liddie to enjoy cider and donuts. They sat at a wooden picnic table, listening to carols warbling through tinny loudspeakers scattered throughout the area.

Pausing in the middle of his donut, Ben looked up at Anne with a smile and asked, "Can we come here to get our tree again next year?"

CHAPTER FIFTEEN

"Well, you gotta feel bad for the kid," Wendy said. "He comes back to Blue Hill all worked up to propose and he gets his legs taken out from under him." She, Anne, and Helen occupied their spots in the pews as Sunday's rehearsal commenced for the Nativity play.

"Under the circumstances," Helen replied, "I think it was quite kind on Miss Corrigan's part. She knew she wasn't going to accept and she spared him the embarrassment of actually going through with the proposal."

"Oh, no doubt," Wendy agreed. "But it still must have been a disappointment." They sympathized silently with Patrick Anderson for a few moments. "And speaking of disappointment," Wendy continued, glancing at Anne, "this kind of puts you back at square one in identifying the owner of the ring, doesn't it?"

Anne gave a rueful smile. "Thanks for that concise assessment. Blunt but accurate."

Wendy patted her arm. "Anne, you know I still have faith in you. You'll find the owner yet."

Reverend Tom, sitting in the pew ahead of them, turned and gave a slight cough. "Not that I wish to speak against faith," he smiled, "but I'm concerned about the toll this is taking on you, Anne. I'm not sure that it's worth it."

Anne laughed. "Do I look that bad?"

"He's got a point, hon," said Wendy.

"You're the one who just said you had faith in me!"

"I do," said Wendy stoutly. "I'm sure you *could* find the owner. I'm just not sure that it's worth what it's putting you through."

"If I just had a clear lead," Anne muttered.

"You know," Reverend Tom said thoughtfully, "perhaps further effort on your part isn't even necessary. At this point, pretty much the entire congregation has heard about the ring." He looked at Wendy and Helen, who appeared unabashed. "Word has gotten around. Perhaps at this point, you ought to just wait and see if somebody comes forward to claim it?" He paused, and then continued, "You know, if the responsibility for the ring is weighing on you, I'd be willing to take it and hold it. While we wait to see if someone comes forward?"

Anne looked up and smiled. "Thank you, Reverend Tom. I appreciate your concern, I really do. But at this point, I've invested too much time and energy in this project to give up quite yet. I just feel like if I give my brain a chance to process things a bit more, I'll come up with a new angle." She shrugged. "I don't feel defeated yet. Down, but not out."

"I'm sorry to disagree with you, Reverend," Helen said, "but it seems to me that if it were just a matter of waiting for someone to come forward, well, then they would have done so by now. As you say, it's been a topic of general conversation for more than a week now. If the owner hasn't come forward at this point, it seems to me that there must be a reason."

"But I still think," said Wendy, "that there must be someone here in the church who knows *something* about the ring."

"That makes sense," Anne agreed. "After all, it was found here. Who but somebody associated with the church would think to hide it here? Or would know of the Advent cabinet as a hiding place?"

"Maybe somebody knows something but they don't realize they know it," suggested Wendy.

Anne frowned. "How would that work?"

"Well, suppose the person who put it there is no longer around. But there would still be people here who know of that person, and who might know something about them that would pertain to the ring, even if they haven't made the connection themselves."

Anne grimaced. "We can't read minds. Or interrogate the entire congregation. If there really is such a person, they either have to make that connection themselves or it will never be made."

"So you're back to waiting," Reverend Tom noted, looking at his watch and rising from his pew. "Just set it aside," he urged, "there are plenty of other things to worry about during the holidays. And that being the case, if you ladies will excuse me..." He strode up the aisle.

Anne did not comment on the pastor's remark but sat for a while in thought. Finally, she asked, "How do things come to be in the Advent cabinet, anyway? What's the process?" She was surprised to realize that this question had not occurred to her earlier.

"The board coordinates it," said Helen. "We have a list of people who have expressed interest in doing this. Each year, we do the initial asking, and once we have enough people, then Reverend Tom handles the details.

"It's mostly the same people year to year, though you may remember that we had an announcement a couple of months ago inviting people to participate."

Anne nodded. She did remember, though vaguely. It was the first time she had heard of the Advent cabinet. She hadn't paid a lot of attention, since there didn't seem to be any urgency to it and she hadn't understood the request. She remembered that she had meant to ask about it but never got around to doing so. "So there's a list?" she asked. "A schedule? Specifically, a way to find out who was supposed to cover December seventh last year?" And then something else occurred to Anne. "They're thanked in the bulletin, aren't they?"

* * *

At the front of the sanctuary, a process not unlike musical chairs seemed to be going on. By now, several children had fallen sick with the flu and had been forced to drop out of the play. Suzanne, who seemed increasingly unwell herself, was busy trying to fill the missing parts. Unfortunately, whenever she moved one child into a new role, it opened up another opening to be filled. At the moment, she stood studying the papers on a clipboard in apparent dismay while the cast and crew stood and gazed at her. Brad, apparently chastened by his misbehavior at the previous rehearsal, sat quietly to one side and stepped in only when Suzanne asked him to do something specific.

Eventually, it appeared that Suzanne had every hole filled. "All right," she said, her hoarse voice brittle with forced cheerfulness, "let's try it now."

The play lurched into life. The children who had just been assigned new roles naturally did not yet know them, so they carried scripts with them as they tried to learn their new marks. Several, forgetting themselves, continued to respond to the cues for their previous role before remembering themselves and stopping midline. This also frequently resulted in two people trying to talk at once. In addition, they had an unfortunate tendency to bump into one another as they moved about the stage area, trying to read their scripts as they walked.

After a single long, painful run-through of the play, Suzanne called a break. Brad, who had been completely silent throughout, got up and slipped out of the sanctuary.

As the children tried to learn their new lines, Anne watched as Suzanne slowly made her way down the aisle toward the rear of the sanctuary and sat next to the pastor, who had entered behind them unannounced. Keeping an eye on the cast, she spoke in a low voice. "I don't know, Reverend Tom. Maybe we should go back to the way we've done it in other years. It was a lot simpler for the kids."

"Now, Suzanne, the children have worked hard to learn this new version this year. To change it now would confuse them even more than what we've just done by putting them in new roles. And it might give them the impression that you don't have faith in them to pull this off."

Before Suzanne could reply to Reverend Tom, however, Douglas and Marian, who had been absent until now, entered the sanctuary carrying some boxes and bags. "Perhaps our friends the Pauthens will have some news to cheer us up," Reverend Tom remarked, a little louder.

And indeed, Douglas called out, "Success at last" as the two of them made their way toward Suzanne. "We finally found a couple of estate sales worthy of the name."

They set down their boxes and bags in the aisle, and Marian said, "There's more, of course. But I just wanted to show you a few of the things we've picked up." The ladies in the pews all rose to get a better look as Marian began to pull fabrics from the bag.

To Anne's eyes, Marian had assembled the rattiest collection of drapes, curtains, towels, and slipcovers imaginable. They were ragged around the edges, had gaping holes in their centers, and sported a variety of stains, smears, and cigarette burns. But Marian seemed oblivious to these flaws. One by one, she held them up with remarks such as, "Look at the richness of the color," or "What a sheen this has."

Anne cast questioning glances at her companions and was relieved to see the same doubt on the faces of Helen and Wendy as she felt. Even Reverend Tom seemed nonplussed, though she would not have wagered on him as a judge of cloth anyway.

Anne smiled to herself as a thought came into her head. *Just because he's a man of the cloth, that doesn't mean he knows cloth.* She felt sure Wendy would appreciate the humor.

Seeing the obvious dismay on her friend's faces, Anne quickly tried to restore the impassivity of her own, and she could see her companions struggling to do likewise. "Well," Helen said, as if trying to find a silver lining in the cloud, "that's quite a collection, all right."

"And we didn't have to pay much for it at all," Douglas said happily.

Helen pursed her lips and nodded in response, and Anne felt sure she was struggling not to say, "I should hope not."

But when Anne cast a glance at Suzanne, she became concerned. The director had already been looking unwell, but she now looked shocked on top of that. The woman finally managed to croak out, "Are you sure...you'll be able to get costumes from those?" Anne had seldom heard a voice that sounded so faint and hopeless.

But Marian, normally such an observant woman, didn't seem to notice. "Oh yes," she said serenely, "these will do very well indeed."

After a while, Suzanne said, "Well, we'd better get back to rehearsing," though it came out with remarkably little conviction. Douglas and Marian packed all their fabrics back up again while Suzanne rounded up the kids and began another read-through. Her listlessness seemed to be communicating itself to the children, however, and the reading went along even more poorly than the first read-through.

At one point, when it had more or less ground to a halt, Douglas spoke up and said, "I wonder if I might make a suggestion?" Reverend Tom looked at him with interest,

Suzanne with something between hope and desperation. "Since some of the troops need time to learn their new parts, perhaps for right now we should return to the music, the carols that everyone sings. You'll recall from the other day that we still need to work on that. Yet that's less dependent on who has what role."

Tom smiled, and Suzanne looked like the drowning woman who'd been thrown a life preserver. "Thank you, Mr. Pauthen," she exclaimed. But then she looked about and frowned in vexation. "Where has Mr. Trowbridge gone to? Has he still not returned? This is his area. I can't very well lead any singing with my voice the way it is."

Douglas volunteered to go look for him, and when he had left, Suzanne sank wearily into a pew. Reverend Tom looked at her and shook his head. "If you just had a cold, shouldn't you be over the worst of it by now?"

Suzanne made an effort to control her somewhat labored breathing. "I'm fine," she insisted. "I'll be fine. It's just...lingering a bit." Reverend Tom pursed his lips, but they all allowed her to rest in silence until Douglas returned.

He shook his head. "I can't seem to find him."

"Oh, for...," Suzanne snapped, and then caught herself. After a moment, she took a deep breath, heaved herself to her feet, and looked at Douglas. "Would you be willing to assist me?" Together, they headed back up the aisle of the sanctuary, with Douglas calling to the kids to stop and gather round.

Looking troubled, Reverend Tom slipped out without a word.

Rather than have them start immediately on the carols, however, Douglas announced that they first needed to warm up their singing voices. He soon had them tramping around the sanctuary belting out some simple marching songs. The activity, the change of routine, and the novelty of singing loudly in the normally quiet precincts of the church sanctuary brought harmony in more ways than one. Anne watched in admiration at his ability to unite the tired, fraying group.

Just as they finished, Brad came hurrying back into the sanctuary. "I'm so sorry," he called out. "I didn't realize we were going to work on the music." He cast a nervous glance at Suzanne, who was again seated in one of the front pews, and then hurried toward his guitar case to get out his instrument.

As he was about to lift the strap over his head, however, he looked at Suzanne again, and paused. "Mrs. Brady?" he asked uncertainly. He immediately set the guitar back down and hurried over to her. He was joined by Douglas and by Reverend Tom, who had just reentered the sanctuary, and a moment later by Anne, Wendy, and Helen.

Suzanne's breathing had become much more labored. "I'm sorry," she wheezed. "I think...I think I am feeling a little unwell after all. I just need a moment."

"Suzanne, I'm going to drive you home," said Reverend Tom decisively. He turned to Brad and Douglas. "Will you two finish running rehearsal, please?" They hesitated and then both nodded.

"Should we...?" Helen asked tentatively.

"No, we'll be fine. I'll get her home and her husband can put her to bed." He turned to Brad again. "If I need a ride later, I'll call you. Otherwise I think the best thing you can do is all go on with the rehearsal. Your time's almost up, anyway." He looked up at the children, who were all standing a little distance away, watching. "Don't worry," he said, "she's going to be fine. She just has this flu that's going around.

"Mr. Trowbridge and Mr. Pauthen are going to finish the rehearsal."

Brad and Douglas stepped forward to engage the attention of the children again while the pastor helped Suzanne get to her feet and don her coat. "I'm really going to be fine," Anne heard her say.

"Of course, you are," Reverend Tom said, "but you're going to have to spend some time in bed first." And he led her out of the building.

CHAPTER SIXTEEN

As soon as Anne arrived at the church the next afternoon, she realized that she would not find Reverend Tom there. When she and Helen had visited two weeks ago to test the key they had found, Sophie had told them that the pastor visited parishioners on Mondays. But still, presumably she'd find Sophie herself on duty. She had little doubt that Reverend Tom would allow her to go through the records of old church bulletins, but she wasn't sure if Sophie would do so, at least not without the pastor's permission. Sophie struck Anne as, well, a little insecure.

Still, she was there, so she might as well try.

"Hello, Sophie," she said, smiling broadly as she entered.

As before, Sophie seemed flustered and looked up at Anne like a scared rabbit, though she seemed to relax a bit when she recognized her visitor. "Anne!" she cried but said nothing more.

For a moment, Anne was at a loss for how to continue and found herself falling back on one of the clichés of the season. "So, ready for the holidays?" Unfortunately, this provoked a five-minute discussion on Sophie's gift-giving obligations, her choices for each person, and the circumstances involved in the purchase of each item. Anne smiled and nodded throughout, finally removing her coat and hat.

"Well, I must say, you're further along than I am," she said, realizing with a slight jolt how true this was. But she quickly regained her focus. "Say, Sophie," she adopted a conspiratorial tone, "do you remember that ring that we found?"

"Sure I do," Sophie replied eagerly. "Have you been able to figure out why Edie hid it there?"

"No-o," Anne said, "I'm still working on that. In fact, that's why I came by this afternoon. Helen Smith reminded me that the board members are responsible for finding people to stock the cabinet for the Advent season and that those people are thanked each week in the bulletin."

Sophie nodded uncertainly.

"I thought that if I could have a look at the bulletins from last year, I could get a sense of who was, you know, going into the cabinet. Just in case it might provide any insights. Do you think that would be possible?"

"I don't see why not," Sophie replied without hesitation. "The files of old bulletins are right back here," and she turned to a row of filing cabinets along the wall behind her reception desk. "What are you looking for? Last December?" She pulled open a drawer, plucked out a folder, and handed it to Anne. "We can look through it right over here," and she gestured toward a worktable off to one side.

But as she flipped through the bulletins from the previous December, Anne quickly realized a problem. "The donors are thanked," she observed, "but it doesn't say which day they were responsible for." Sophie gave her a questioning look. "I wanted to see if anyone was assigned specifically to the seventh. Nobody seems to know when the key was discovered missing. So somebody may have been assigned that date. That person might even be the one who left the ring and took the key. But these acknowledgements in the bulletin don't say which person is responsible for which date."

Sophie took the bulletin that Anne was examining. "Well, but it must have been Edie," she said. "Look, here's her name listed right here."

"But we don't know for sure," Anne insisted.

"Well, there's another file that relates specifically to the Advent cabinet." She looked innocently at Anne. "That has the schedule in it."

Anne looked at her incredulously but then regained her composure sufficiently to smile and ask, "Well, do you think we could see that one?"

Sophie nodded and returned to the bank of filing cabinets. It took her a bit more rummaging this time, but she soon straightened up with a thin file folder in her hand. She handed it to Anne, who opened it where she stood. Anne's eyebrows rose in surprise.

"Well," demanded Sophie. "Was it Edie?"

"You're right that Edie was down for that week, but it wasn't for the seventh." Anne looked up slowly. "The seventh was you, Sophie."

* * *

Sophie shifted uncomfortably on her feet. "Me?" she asked, glancing to one side.

"Yes, see here's the schedule right here." Anne thrust the open file folder toward her excitedly. "Your name's down for the seventh." Sophie glanced down at it but quickly looked away again. She made no effort to take the folder in her hands. Anne made an effort to control her excitement and think through the situation logically. "Okay, so you said you'd never seen the ring before the other day...," she began.

"I hadn't," Sophie snapped, suddenly defensive. "It's not that I just *said* I hadn't. I hadn't!"

Anne jerked her head up in astonishment at Sophie's sudden vehemence. "No!" Anne exclaimed, "Yes! I mean, I didn't—"

"Just what are you accusing me of, anyway?" continued Sophie, oblivious of Anne's surprise and dismay. "So what if my name's on the schedule?" she demanded.

"Sophie—" Anne stammered, "I didn't—I think you've got the wrong—"

"You think I stole that ring, don't you?" Sophie continued, her voice rising nearly to a scream. "You think I stole it and hid it in the Advent cabinet as a safe place. Well, I didn't!"

"Sophie, I never..." Flabbergasted, Anne struggled to make sense of the other woman's reaction. What had she said to set this off? What should she do to calm the increasingly distraught woman? And all the while, a line from Shakespeare's *Hamlet* pushed its way to the forefront of her mind: "*The lady doth protest too much, methinks.*"

Then to Anne's complete bewilderment and dismay, Sophie burst into tears.

And at that moment, the door opened and Reverend Tom stood silhouetted by the light from outside. Closing the door quickly, he said, "What's going on here?" It was the sternest tone that Anne had ever heard him use. Mortified, she stood rooted to the spot, unable to respond.

But Sophie immediately wailed, "She thinks I stole that ring!"

This was so wildly inaccurate that it broke Anne's paralysis. She opened her mouth and drew in a breath to respond, but Reverend Tom was already striding around the desk to the work area, and he held up his hand to Anne with a small shake of his head. "Anne," he said firmly, "could you wait in my office, please? I'll come and talk with you in a moment."

For a moment longer, Anne held herself poised to speak, but then she nodded and walked through the door into the pastor's office. She was already beginning to feel the reaction to the stress come on her, and her knees suddenly felt weak. She quickly made her way to one of the guest chairs and sat down. Her breath was coming in quick, shallow gasps, and she focused on making it deeper and more even.

Too late, she realized that she hadn't shut the door when she came in and she could now hear everything being said out in the reception area. She thought about standing up to close the door, but her legs still felt unsteady. Besides, she worried that the action would draw too much attention. The moment of opportunity had passed.

Hands clasped in her lap, she sat and listened to Reverend Tom calming the distraught receptionist. Feeling the need to take action of her own, she tried to form a prayer for strength, but at first she found it very hard to focus and her attention kept drifting to the conversation in the other room.

She heard the receptionist again claim that Anne had accused her of stealing the ring and hiding it in the Advent cabinet, and she tearfully insisted to Reverend Tom that she had not. The pastor said he knew perfectly well that she had not and that he would not allow Anne or anyone else to make such an unfounded accusation against her.

During this, Anne was continuing to try to pray in an effort to relieve her distressed state. She realized in her distraction that she was praying for strength and wisdom for herself. And she recognized that this was a mistake. She realized that the person in need of prayer here was not Anne herself, but Sophie. With that insight, the knot of tension within her loosened a degree, and she tried to put the thought into practice.

Gradually, almost as if in response, Sophie calmed down and their talk became softer and less distracting. As Anne prayed for Sophie, she could feel the beginnings of a greater clarity within her, though her emotions still threatened to overwhelm her with shame and anger.

After some time, Reverend Tom stepped into the office and closed the door behind him. Anne said a quick "amen" under her breath. By now, she understood that there was something more going on here than a simple misunderstanding, and yet she couldn't help defending herself as soon as he shut the door. "I didn't accuse her—" she hissed, but Reverend Tom waved away her words with a weary nod.

"I know," he said, "I'm sure you didn't." He removed his coat and hung it on a hook on the back of the door and then moved behind his desk and dropped into the chair with a weary sigh. "I'm sure you didn't," he said again, though it was more muttered to himself than directed at her.

After a moment, Anne said simply, "I'm sorry."

Again he shook his head. "She can be like that," he said in a low voice. "A little...volatile. Prone to taking things wrong in a rather extreme way. It cost her a job a couple of months ago. In fact, it's cost her several jobs. But when she's unemployed, when she has no structure or purpose, it just makes her worse." He glanced up at the closed door. "Her sister in California begged me to find some employment for her, so here she is. Not the ideal temperament for dealing with the public, I know, but in many ways, she's very efficient and able. And it's not like it's a frequent occurrence. I just...try to keep an eye out for situations that might set her off."

Anne wasn't sure how to respond. Finally, she asked, "Will she be okay?"

"Oh yes," Reverend Tom assured her. "She recovers pretty swiftly. Though she will continue to be very sensitive about that topic." He stressed the *will*.

"Should I apologize to her?"

He made little circles on his desk with his fingertip while he considered this. "I wouldn't make a big deal of doing so. It could set her off again. And whatever you do, don't mention the ring, either."

"Reverend Tom..." Anne struggled to voice her thoughts. "Maybe she really did?" Reverend Tom cocked his head and gave her a piercing look. "I mean, she got *so* upset. And I truly didn't accuse her of anything. But what if she really did have something to do with putting the ring in the cabinet?"

"'The wicked flee when no man pursueth,' you mean?" he said, quoting Proverbs 28:1. "No, I can tell you with absolute confidence that Sophie had nothing to do with the ring or putting it in the Advent cabinet."

"But she showed me the schedule of people responsible for providing things for the cabinet. Her name was down for that date." And in the back of her mind, she heard an echo of Sophie saying *"Perhaps we'll find some sort of treasure in there"* when they'd gone to try the key that Anne had found.

Tom sighed. "That was my doing. When we brought the cabinet out of storage last year, I noticed right away there was a key missing, but I didn't call attention to it because I wanted to talk... Well, I mean I hoped it would... turn up. But eventually it became clear that it would *not* turn up, so I added Sophie's name to the list for that date. I did it so that she would have the opportunity to be included in the process, and publicly acknowledged in the bulletin, but could plausibly be excused from actually providing something. After all, number seven couldn't be opened, right?" He shrugged. "It was a well-intentioned but poorly thought-out effort to give her a little boost, make her feel included." The pastor held Anne's gaze. "Besides, think about it, Anne. If Sophie had been the one to put the ring in the cabinet, it still doesn't explain how it ended up with Edie, does it?"

Anne sat back in her chair, deflated. "No," she said. "That's the question that seems to scuttle most of my theories. Why Edie?" Her eyes lost their focus as her mind returned to what had become well-worn grooves of thought. Absently, Anne continued, "Sophie seems to take it as a matter of faith that Edie put the ring in the cabinet, since the key was found among her things."

Reverend Tom studied her for a moment and then shrugged. "That would be the most straightforward explanation."

CHAPTER SEVENTEEN

The family Christmas tree was finally up, adorned with a mix of familiar ornaments from their Brooklyn apartment, plus Aunt Edie's beautiful, handblown glass orbs, and of course the wonderfully childlike ornaments Ben and Liddie had made in school.

Still, the worry over other tasks undone pulsed away at the back of Anne's mind, becoming ever more insistent until, by Tuesday, she was nearing panic. Christmas was now just one week away! She'd spent so much time and energy decorating the library that she had not yet bought a single present. The floor space around the glittering and beautiful tree was looking sadly empty, and she noticed that Ben and Liddie were starting to cast anxious glances that way.

She picked up the phone and called the one person who could help her out of this mess.

* * *

"Right," said Wendy, bustling up to the Gibsons' living area a short while later, "what's your plan so far?" Anne looked up and felt that her diminutive friend loomed over her, all energy, focus, and determination.

"Plan?" asked Anne.

Wendy brushed aside the humor. "I mean, where do you want to go? What stores do you want to hit? In what order? What's on your list?"

"That's the problem," said Anne. "I don't really know where to go. I was hoping you might have suggestions?" When Wendy didn't respond immediately, Anne continued, "I mean, I guess I've been to most of the big stores around here by now, but Christmas shopping is kind of its own beast. And I figure you must have lots of experience with it."

"You got that right," said the mother of seven. "And I say that the way to tackle it is through organization. And perhaps technology. Should we be shopping online?"

Anne frowned. "Do you think things would be delivered in time?"

"Well, perhaps not, unless you pay for expedited shipping, which gets expensive fast." Anne could almost see her friend striking that option off her mental list. "Okay, then it's shopping the old-fashioned way. Where's your list?"

"Uh...," Anne began.

"Nothing?" Wendy eyed her friend incredulously. "Not a single gift or store that you've thought about?"

"Well, some, but whatever we do, don't let me forget to pick up some gifts for Remi and Bella. And I think I'll get something for Sherri and the other volunteers as well."

Wendy nodded. "Okay, so a bookstore then?"

Anne gave her a reproachful look. "That goes without saying!"

"Anything else?"

"Oh, a fabric store," Anne said, remembering suddenly. In response to Wendy's quizzical look, she continued, "Liddie has specifically asked Santa for a new dress for her Cleopatra doll—though a dress won't cover all *that* doll's problems. But I'll have to find a doll-dress pattern, and..." She trailed off, since Wendy's jaw had dropped in a universal gesture of incredulity.

"I see." Wendy narrowed her eyes. "Well, desperate times, desperate measures. Get your coat." She checked her watch, and her face assumed a determined expression. "We'll get all your shopping done before school gets out. Grab the doll. Our first stop will be Minnie's. And then"—she turned and started out the door—"we're going to Deshler."

* * *

"Never?" demanded Wendy. "You grew up in Blue Hill and you never went to Minnie's Doll Hospital? It's an institution."

"What can I say?" Anne replied. "I had one doll, and I hardly ever played with it. I preferred books."

"I thought our mothers were the last generation to have just one doll," Wendy muttered. "Though it's true that kids nowadays seem to get new dolls on a whim. But you've heard of it, right? I mean, it was here long before Chad and I came to Blue Hill."

Anne, who only vaguely recalled the name, kept silent. Sometimes she felt like Wendy knew her hometown better than she did, even though the Pyles had moved to town only seven years ago.

"Well, it's run now by a couple named Zelinksi, Harriet and James. Harriet is the granddaughter of the original Minnie.

They're both antique doll collectors and dealers and restorers. And come the holidays, they have all sorts of clothes, which they make themselves, for all the major brands, plus dollhouses and doll furniture. It's wonderful Anne, and for me a real pocketbook saver."

Anne looked down at Liddie's Cleopatra doll, which she cradled in her arms just like an infant. Sadly, the doll was looking down on her luck at the moment. Her prim 1920s suffragette costume was torn at the waist, her hair was tangled, and she had lost her youthful glow. She'd gotten that way because Liddie took her almost everywhere. Anne admitted to herself she was proud of Liddie for keeping her so long, though.

Just as Wendy had promised, Minnie's was almost a museum itself with its stock of rare Kewpie and china dolls, some of which, Anne noted, bore astronomical price tags. Harriet wasn't wearing a nurse's uniform, although there was a picture of her grandparents standing in front of the store dressed as a doctor and nurse. But when Harriet saw Anne looking a little bewildered and holding Liddie's doll, she rushed over and took the doll in her arms and treated her as a caring nurse would treat a sick patient.

"Oh, what a lovely doll!" she exclaimed, and Anne couldn't help but beam. "Needs a bit of a bath, I see." Harriet ran her finger over the torn sleeve. "I can fix this too, if you like."

Anne was speechless but managed an enthusiastic nod just as Wendy came up with a gingham sundress, a woolen pleated skirt and knitted sweater, and a felted winter coat.

"Something for all seasons!" Wendy exclaimed.

Harriet gave them a receipt for the doll and promised she would have her ready by lunch.

* * *

Deshler was larger than Blue Hill and boasted the region's best and biggest shopping mall, which drew customers from a wide area. Wendy and Anne arrived to find cars bumper to bumper almost a mile from the entrance, with police officers on duty to direct the heavy volume of traffic in and out of the parking lots. Though it was not snowing, the sky was overcast and the air moist, and the officers were well bundled against the chill.

Anne suddenly felt weighed down by the traffic, the weather, the obligations. She sank back into her seat, feeling energy drain from her body. Exhaustion was setting in before they'd even set foot in the mall. She wanted to suggest to Wendy that they turn around and go home, that they flee, but she realized this wasn't, *couldn't be* an option. She felt trapped.

Once in the lot, they joined the steady, snaking stream of cars that circled endlessly looking for an open spot. After living in New York, Anne was certainly accustomed to crowds, but those were crowds of pedestrians, which she found much more manageable. A wall-to-wall throng of shoppers walking around seeing the famed Christmas store windows and the brightly lit ice-skating rinks in city parks was a vibrant thing, something one belonged to, while this throng of automobiles was anonymous and alienating. It was also more frustrating. In a pedestrian crowd, there was opportunity to step around or between others and move at your own pace. Trapped in cars, drivers were locked in procession as they crept around the lot.

For a moment Anne missed New York with a pang such as she had seldom experienced since returning to Blue Hill.

Fortunately for Anne, Wendy was an experienced navigator of the shopping mall sea, and she soon spotted a shopper about to make her departure. Wendy staked her claim by pulling up and turning on her turn signal, and she deftly scooted into the vacated spot as soon as the previous occupant's bumper had cleared the edge. The unflappable Wendy Pyle was undismayed by the traffic and crowds. She flashed a bright smile and said, "Let's go."

Anne had a sense that Wendy was now infected with the spirit of the hunt. Anne just hoped it would rub off on her.

As they crossed a vast stretch of parking lot from the car to the entrance, an eager Wendy in the lead, Anne tried to form a prayer for stamina to get her through the shopping and through the season. *For the sake of her children*, she thought, and the idea buoyed her. Whatever her own merits, or lack thereof, God would help her in her own determination to be a good mother to Ben and Liddie. They were what mattered. And hadn't He *already* sent help in the form of the irrepressible Wendy? She smiled and whispered "amen" as she stepped across the threshold and into the mall.

Once they were inside, Anne began to relax a bit. The carols playing on the PA system were not as blaring as they might have been, the fluorescent light not as glaring, and the crowd around her not as ill-humored. She unzipped her coat and allowed herself to be entranced by the colored holiday lights that had been hung throughout the mall. She had to admit it was festive. She looked at Wendy expectantly.

"You really have no idea what you're looking for?" Wendy demanded. "Haven't the kids asked for anything else?"

"They have, yes," Anne admitted. "Liddie asked for a scooter—you know, one of those that you kick along on. That sounds like a good idea. I thought about getting Ben a remote-control car or some accessories for his train. But he's asked for an iPad, and I don't think he's ready for that just yet."

Wendy snorted. "It's nice to have dreams. Well, I always build my list on the foundation of the Big Three: clothes, books, and games. So let's start there." She steered Anne deeper into the mall while she expounded on her theory of Christmas shopping. "Clothes can be handed down as they're outgrown. Books can be passed around from one to the next. And games are something that everyone can enjoy together. See?"

"I always feel a little bad giving the kids clothes as Christmas presents," Anne said wistfully. "They seem so...prosaic."

"Honey, you are going to be doing nothing but buying them clothes for the next ten years, so you might as well get credit for Christmas presents out of a few of them."

"All right," Anne sighed.

"And besides, they needn't be entirely dull." Suddenly, she stopped short and leaned in close. "And I'll tell you another secret."

Anne cocked an expectant eyebrow.

Lowering her voice still further, Wendy said, "Clothes come from Santa. Books and games," she waggled a thumb toward her own chest, "come from Mom."

* * *

Later they sat in one of the mall restaurants, enjoying lunch. "She'll love the dress," Wendy was assuring Anne about one of the presents she had bought for Liddie. "Just don't, you know, let her wear it outside to play."

A brief vision of the new dress reduced to rags flashed through Anne's mind. She shook her head. "It's a wonder kids' clothes survive at all."

"Well they don't, really," Wendy replied thoughtfully. "In my house they just seem to kind of vaporize after a while. I'm sure there must be some law of physics being broken, but I've never been able to determine which." She had been dragging a french fry through a puddle of ketchup on her plate, and she now popped it in her mouth with a grin. "And speaking of science," she continued after a moment, "I think Ben is going to love that telescope."

"I hope so," Anne said, "he's been going through the astronomy books at the library lately. But for all I know, he may be onto something else before Christmas even gets here."

"You've got to encourage them where they are," Wendy declared. "When they're young, you want them to develop as many interests as possible. Who knows how those will come back later in life. He may drop astronomy now only to pick it up again when he retires."

"Retires," Anne repeated. "Boy there's an idea to get your head around. Can you imagine the day when your kids retire?"

Wendy laughed. "We've got some time yet."

Anne's mind was filled with a brief vision of Ben as an adult, perhaps a graduate student, using the telescope she had bought today to gaze at the stars and planets. She hoped he liked it and perhaps would even be inspired by it.

For Liddie, she'd found an enchanting kaleidoscope filled with sea glass and colorful metallic flecks. She also had a jigsaw puzzle—which came in a big box and once wrapped would look impressive under the tree—and a set of paper dolls of a young woman horse trainer.

Wendy picked up the paper doll set and cocked an eyebrow at Anne. "Did somebody ask for a pony?" she asked.

"She always asks for a pony. And now that we have more of a yard, she thinks of it more frequently."

"*Hmm,*" Wendy said thoughtfully. "My kids have been going through a rabbit phase. They keep popping the question at me like I'm gonna forget one day and just say, 'Yes, we can have a rabbit.' Or rabbits, as the kids would like." She shook her head. "And we were so much more sensible, I suppose."

After a thoughtful pause, Anne gave her friend a fond look and said, "Wendy, thank you so much. I can't tell you how relieved I am to have this done."

Wendy responded with a pleased smile, but she merely replied, "You just needed a little push to get started. And I should be thanking you." She laughed. "It's always fun to shop when you're not spending your own money! I got all the pleasure and none of the responsibility." She turned her attention back to Anne's bags and picked up one of the gifts that Anne had purchased for her staff, canisters of fine green and black tea.

"Those are for the twins," Anne explained. "I bought a special book for all of the volunteers. I got a book about New York for Sherri."

Wendy gave her a quizzical look. "You know, you've got a whole building full of books that she can read for free. I know she reads a lot, but I don't think she's made her way through all of them yet."

Anne assumed a mock lecturing tone, raising a finger for each point. "Number one: Books are always good gifts, no matter how many you already have or have access to. That's just axiomatic." Wendy rolled her eyes at Anne's two-dollar word choice, so Anne amended, "Self-evident. Number two: There's a big difference between borrowing a book and actually owning it. As a librarian, of course, I'm in favor of both. And number three" — her tone became warmer and more knowing — "I think this book in particular is one she'll want to keep."

"Well," said Wendy with a laugh, "any argument that comes in threes is clearly unanswerable. Especially when it involves you and books."

Anne sat back in the booth and gazed around at the whimsy of the mall restaurant with a sudden and powerful sense of contentment. Spending time with her friend, or with her kids as she had on Saturday, selecting gifts for people she loved, and even trying to assist a stranger by restoring a lost ring — she was beginning to feel more in tune with the spirit of the holiday.

She recalled her frustration and pessimism earlier when they'd been in the car, and she smiled, feeling a rush of gratitude and affection for her friend. "Of course it is," she replied. Then, toasting Wendy with the plastic tumbler that held her soda, she said again, "Thank you."

* * *

Back at home, Anne placed the now beautiful and new-looking Cleopatra doll on Liddie's bed where she'd found her this morning. She wondered how long it would take Liddie to notice the washed and combed hair, the cleaned skin, or the patched shoulder. But in a way it didn't matter—she knew that Liddie always delighted in finding her doll just where she left her last.

Anne had a quiet hour to herself until the kids came home from school. She turned on the radio to the classical music station and retired to the easy chair, where Hershey happily curled up at her feet. She drifted into a light sleep with images of jewelry and dolls and Christmas lights and glittery bows and cards swirling through her head, until she heard the heavy clomping of an approaching pony. And then she realized that Ben and Liddie had arrived and were running up the stairs.

Chapter Eighteen

The next day, Anne sat at the circulation desk, wrapping gifts for Ben and Liddie. When she and Wendy had returned home from the mall the day before, they found that large boxes had arrived from both Anne's parents and her in-laws, Byron and Marlene Gibson, each filled with gifts for the kids. Sherri had again been on duty as a volunteer and she had spirited these away to the storage closet, but since neither set of grandparents had wrapped their gifts for shipping, Anne now had those to wrap as well as the ones she'd bought herself the day before.

She felt guilty doing this during work hours, but it was so much easier to get it done while the kids were in school. Though she tried to whisk away the evidence of her preoccupation whenever a patron approached the circulation desk, in fact most of them seemed delighted to have "caught her in the act" of her holiday preparations. She learned quite a bit about what was under the tree for a fair number of her library regulars, and had to explain her thinking for almost every gift that she herself had selected. As a result, it appeared that at least one other Blue Hill boy would be getting a telescope that Christmas.

Anne was very happy to have both the wrapping and the conversations to occupy her, because in another part of her mind, she was trying very hard not to think about the ring. She was even being slightly dishonest with herself about the reason. She'd been telling herself that worry about the ring, and the time she'd been spending on it, had been a contributing factor to her stress and unhappiness the day before.

But as she folded wrapping paper and tied up ribbons, she admitted to herself that she was also gun-shy following the incident with Sophie. She was genuinely curious about how Aunt Edie had been involved in the story of the ring—how *had* she come to have the key in her possession? But the extremity of Sophie's response to Anne's queries had shaken Anne profoundly, and she had been second-guessing her own behavior ever since.

In the end, however, she determined that she felt a responsibility to her great-aunt Edie to find the owner of the ring. She realized that she had developed an idea that the ring represented some sort of unfinished business on her great-aunt's part. She was convinced that Edie had intended to do something with or about the key and the ring, and that for whatever reason, she had not done before her death.

Anne sighed. A good deed for a stranger was one thing. An obligation to her great-aunt was another, and not so easily abandoned. She needed to keep trying.

Once she had finished her wrapping, she waited for a quiet moment and then ran quickly up to their living area and brought the ring down to the circulation desk. She opened the lid of the box and placed it squarely on the desktop before her.

What did she know for sure? She pulled a pad of paper from a drawer and jotted down some notes in an effort to organize her thinking. As she catalogued all the things she had learned about the ring, a nagging feeling struck her. There was something she was missing, some crucial bit of information she needed to gather that would make everything else fall into place.

She closed the ring box and flipped it over to stare at the logo on the bottom. Suddenly she recalled why she'd gone to the Diamond District in the first place: to ask about the engraving on the inside of the ring. But though Brockhurst had examined the ring quite closely, she'd forgotten to ask, and he never said a word about the engraving.

Anne opened the box again and withdrew the ring. She fished around in the drawer of the circulation desk for a magnifying glass and set about examining the engraving.

"You look very Holmesian," said a voice, and Anne looked up to find Douglas Pauthen smiling at her. "Marian would approve."

"Approve of what, dear?" said Marian, approaching the desk.

"I was just saying that Anne looks like she is hot on the trail of some clue in a mystery," her husband replied, "wielding her magnifying glass like a pro."

"That's just in books, dear," said his wife, setting three mystery novels on the desk. "I'm sure Anne has plenty to do in real life as a librarian. Is this the most recent Jan Karon book?"

Anne glanced at the title and nodded. She hesitated a moment and then asked, "How are the costumes coming along?"

This elicited a warm smile from Marian. "Wonderfully, Anne. I'm very pleased with how they're coming out."

Anne assumed this must be true, but she had a hard time reconciling the statement with the beat-up fabrics she'd seen.

"They're almost done, of course. After all, the performance is only five days away, and we have a rehearsal this afternoon. I hope to start getting them fitted then."

"I'll look forward to seeing them."

"So what are you examining so intently?" Douglas asked when Anne had finished checking out their books.

"There's an engraving on the inside of this ring," Anne said, "and I'm trying to figure out what it means."

"Ah, is this the famous ring that we've heard about?" asked Douglas. "The one that was found in the Advent cabinet?"

Anne nodded. "I've been trying to find out who it belonged to. I thought if I could figure out the significance of this engraving it might help me do so." She picked up the ring. "It appears to be some letters and a date. Possibly initials."

"May I?" asked Marian, taking the ring.

"A date suggests an occasion," observed Douglas, "and there are a number of occasions on which one might give someone a ring."

Anne nodded. "Yes, I've always kind of assumed that this was an engagement ring."

"But there are other occasions," said Marian, turning the ring about. "A birthday. Graduation. Even Christmas."

"Is that a hint, my dear?" Douglas asked, but his wife ignored him, so Anne continued.

"That's true, but without more information, I don't see how I can determine what it was."

"Well," said Marian, "if it *was* meant as an engagement ring and you have a date that goes with it, perhaps you could find an announcement in the paper."

* * *

"Anne, did you go to see the window displays every year?" asked Sherri. She had arrived a little early for her volunteer shift, and as she often did when things were quiet, she was quizzing Anne about life in New York City.

"Yes, every year," said Anne smiling.

"And the tree in Rockefeller Center? And the skating rink?"

"The tree is always gorgeous. And it's fun to watch the skaters, but you wouldn't actually want to skate there."

"But I love to skate!"

"That's not the point. The rink is tiny and crowded, and it costs an arm and a leg. You're better off going up to Central Park, or maybe Bryant Park."

"Well, I'd do it once anyway," said Sherri, "just to say I had." Sherri had never visited New York and was eager to do so. She thought she might even want to move there one day, and when she'd learned that Anne had lived there, she was in awe. Anne, who had loved New York, was happy to reminisce when Sherri asked her to. "Christmas in New York must be amazing," she said dreamily.

"You know, it truly is," Anne said with a smile. "I mean it's more crowded than ever, but there's a certain lightheartedness, a certain camaraderie at Christmas. People will always say that there's something in the air at Christmas, and it really does feel that way."

"What else did you do?" Sherri asked eagerly.

"Okay, here's something: People will tell you that it's just for tourists and not to bother, but I say, go to Radio City Music Hall to see the Rockettes. They know how to put on a Christmas show." Anne thought for a moment. "I could go on and on."

Sherri grinned. "I'd love to go to New York and do all those things."

Anne, who had gotten a little wrapped up in her memories, brought herself back to the moment and smiled. "I know you would," she said, "and for that reason, I got you this." She drew out a small package and handed it to Sherri. "Merry Christmas, and thank you."

Sherri's eyes lit up as she took the package. "May I?"

"Of course."

She ripped off the wrapping to find a small gift edition of E. B. White's *Here is New York*. "Of course, it's not exactly a current guide book," said Anne, "but you can get travel information these days on the Internet. And for many people" — she tapped the book's cover — "this is still remarkably true to what New York *feels* like."

"It must be so much more exciting than Christmas in Blue Hill," Sherri said wistfully.

"Oh, there's a lot to enjoy in New York," Anne told her, thinking about the ring and the key and their mysterious connection to Aunt Edie, "but I'm learning that Blue Hill has its own kind of excitement."

CHAPTER NINETEEN

When Anne arrived with the kids for the afternoon's Nativity play rehearsal, they found a subdued and thoughtful group. She urged Ben and Liddie forward and turned to talk with Wendy, who said in a low voice, "Suzanne is bedridden."

"Will she be okay?" Anne asked with concern.

"Oh yes," Wendy assured her, "but she won't be leading any more rehearsals. And we've lost some more cast members to the flu as well."

Up front, Reverend Tom was quietly consulting with Brad and Douglas, while the children all stood or sat silently looking on. Marian was fussing with some garment bags off to one side.

"Christmas Eve is less than a week away," Anne said as Helen joined them. "Will they go ahead with the play? Or will they cancel?"

"I imagine they'll forge ahead," Helen said, "if I know Reverend Tom."

Watching them confer, Anne noticed that Brad's expression was grim and Douglas's impassive, but Reverend Tom's was clearly upbeat, if serious. He was doing most of the talking, while the other two men nodded occasionally and, it seemed to Anne, reluctantly. She watched as Reverend Tom reached out with both hands and touched the other two lightly on the forearm. Then all three bowed their heads and closed their eyes, and Anne assumed that Reverend Tom was saying a brief prayer.

When they raised their heads again, Reverend Tom smiled warmly at Brad and then led Douglas to one of the front pews, where they sat. Brad took a deep breath and stepped toward the silent and expectant children.

"As you can see," he began, once he had their attention, "our production is facing a bit of a challenge thanks to this year's flu outbreak. So before we go any further, is there anyone here who feels that they're coming down with it?" He looked around at the group, but nobody spoke or raised a hand.

Anne noticed Reverend Tom giving a pleased nod where he sat.

"If you do feel sick," Brad continued, "please go home." There was some nervous laughter at this, but Brad continued earnestly, "I'm serious. This is not worth risking your health or anyone else's health. This play is a celebration, not an obligation. If you're not well, you owe it to yourself, and to everyone around you, to take care of yourself first. The rest of us will manage somehow. I want you to keep this in mind as we go forward. If you're sick," he repeated, "go home."

Nobody left, and they all attempted to look as healthy as possible. "Okay, then," Brad smiled warmly as he continued. "As I said, we'll get through this somehow. The first step is to determine which parts need filling and which we can do without. I'm afraid that some of the reassignments that Mrs. Brady made at the last rehearsal are going to have to be reassigned yet again. As you can see," he gestured at the group, "we've lost a few more people."

Brad had been clutching Suzanne's official clipboard, and he now raised it and started to look through some of the papers there. After a moment, he raised his head again and looked speculatively at the kids. "So, do you remember how Mrs. Brady told you it was important to familiarize yourself with the whole play? And not just focus on your own part? Well, now's the time when we learn just why that's important. Not only are some of you going to have to switch to new parts, as we discussed last time, but some of you with smaller parts are going to need to double up. What do you think? Can you handle that?"

There were tentative murmurings of agreement from the kids.

Brad broke out into a wide smile. Nodding, he said, "I think you can. So, let's see where we are."

As much as possible, Brad tried to avoid reassigning actors who had already been switched to new parts at the previous rehearsal. "I know those of you who switched last time," he explained, "have been cramming ever since to learn your new part. I really don't want to put you through that again."

The relief on a few faces was evident.

Though he wrestled with the same sort of domino effect that had challenged Suzanne at the previous rehearsal, Brad finally reached a point where most of the roles had been covered. The most significant unfilled parts were one angel, the camel, the innkeeper's wife, and, most troublingly, the narrator.

"The innkeeper's wife only has two lines," said Brad, now feverishly flipping through the sheets on the clipboard, "and we can give those to the innkeeper." He made some notes and then looked up. "And for the camel, we'll just use the cardboard cutout that you've used in previous years when there were fewer people available.

"As for the angels…" They had cast three angels, but only one was an older girl and she was to have led the singing. She was the one now sick. "Liddie and Becky will do a wonderful job as our two angels," Brad said, smiling at the two younger girls, "and I'll lead the singing myself." The smile faded from his face, however, as he continued, "But as for the narrator…."

The narrator was a new role that had been added to explain some of the historical background that Brad had wanted to add, and also to read the Bible verses necessary as transitions from one scene to the next. In previous years, Suzanne had read the verses, but Brad had expanded the role to make use of Carrie McAllister, one of the older teens who had more experience than the other kids in the production.

Carrie had seemed perfectly healthy at the last rehearsal but she was now ill.

Brad looked at the other teens in the cast. "Didn't any of you even look at the narrator's lines?" he implored, but they all hung their heads and shuffled their feet.

Then, from off to one side, Ben said, "I did" in a hesitant voice.

Brad looked at him skeptically. "The narrator's lines?"

Ben shrugged and then began to recite the narrator's lines from the beginning. As he went on, Brad's face slowly lit up, and after a while, he nodded and, "Okay, that's good." All the other members of the cast were looking at Ben with amazement, and Anne could feel herself practically glowing with pride.

"Ben," said Brad, "I think I'm going to switch your role. Will you be okay not playing a sheep?"

"*Baaaah*," said Ben.

* * *

"Before we get going," called out Marian Pauthen, "all these changes in the cast mean that I'm going to have to make further alterations in the costumes." She turned to Brad. "But I can start getting some of them fitted now, so as you can spare people, please send them one at a time over to me." He nodded his agreement and, checking his clipboard, told the first child to go get fitted.

For the next two hours, Brad and Douglas worked with the kids to get the production into shape. In order to keep up energy and interest, they alternated between working on the lines and stage business and rehearsing the singing. Brad was consistently upbeat and encouraging, though he reminded them that they had little time to prepare before the performance on Christmas Eve. Consistently, he expressed his confidence in their ability to be ready in time.

During the rehearsal, the kids were sent off, one by one, to a corner to consult with Marian about their costumes, and many came back wearing them. They had mostly been pinned up temporarily so that the kids could get a feel for what it was like to move around in them, and many indeed moved awkwardly or hesitantly. At first, Anne didn't really register the costumes, and more and more were added so gradually that she paid little attention, until suddenly she realized that a good number of the actors were now in costume.

And they were magnificent.

She could sense Wendy sit up and take notice at the same time. What had been ratty velvet drapes, old sheets, and stained tablecloths had been transformed into gossamer angel gowns, rich cloaks for the wise men, simple tunics for shepherds, and plain but dignified clothing for the holy couple. Marian had also fashioned amazing and delicate wings for the angels, as well as halos, and beards out of wool and denim for all the male parts.

Anne could see a change in the children too. She strongly suspected that, up close, the clothes didn't maintain quite the same illusion that they did when seen from the audience. But nevertheless, the children wearing their costumes seemed to inhabit their parts with more assurance and pleasure. They began to make the subtle transition from saying their lines to acting, and they knew they were doing so and enjoyed it.

The play was to close with a tableau with all of the actors on stage, and when they reached that point in their run-through, most of the actors were fully or partially costumed, and they struck and held their poses for the tableau with confidence. The ladies in the pews burst out in spontaneous applause, and the actors broke character, laughing in delight.

Though the costumes had transformed the actors, the play still faced challenges. There were still lines to be memorized, movements to be practiced, and tunes to be mastered. Indeed, the cast was not yet able to make it all the way through the play without a variety of mistakes, mishaps, and breakdowns.

But when Brad finally called a halt, there was a definite sense that things were coming together, even if it was clear that a great deal of work remained to be done.

"Don't forget, everyone," he said as they gathered up coats and hats, "our next and final rehearsal is Friday. Not Sunday. Dress rehearsal this Friday afternoon, and then the performance is Monday night. It'll be our last chance to get everything perfect." He glanced around the room, making eye contact with everyone present before adding, "And thank you, everyone, for today. Good work!"

"Why Friday?" Anne asked Helen as she waited for Liddie and Ben.

Helen shook her head. "Experience has shown us that trying to schedule a rehearsal on the day before Christmas Eve just doesn't work. People are too busy, and we end up with half the cast skipping the dress rehearsal."

"I'm afraid I won't be here," Anne said, "though I promise Ben and Liddie will. I just haven't been able to get coverage for the library for that afternoon. Alex is going to bring the kids. There's some chance I may make it for the very end, but I can't promise."

"That's fine," Helen said reassuringly. "The way things are going, I think the children will be far too busy with rehearsal to require much adult supervision."

CHAPTER TWENTY

The next day, Anne was ready to pursue Marian's suggestion. Once Remi and Bella were settled, and presented with their Christmas gifts, Anne headed down to the offices of the *Blue Hill Gazette*. She hadn't bothered to call first, and she arrived to find that her friend Grace was out, but Anne by now was a familiar face in the newspaper's offices, and the young receptionist was happy to let Anne go through the archives of old papers.

Since the issues Anne wanted were only eighteen months old, she found them piled in stacks on the shelves of the glorified closet that served as the morgue. Anne loved an archive of any kind, even one with dim light, narrow aisles, and tall shelves stacked with mounds of old newspapers. There was but a tiny table to one side for workspace, and naturally it was as far from the light as possible. The air was dusty and all sound was muffled by the piles and piles of paper. Anne was in heaven.

She decided to start with a two-month period, one month on either side of the date that was engraved in the ring. Since that date was in the spring, it had been a busy time for engagement and wedding announcements, and Anne pored through them all carefully, looking for names that corresponded with the two sets of initials she had. She found several cases where one half of a couple had the right initials, or where the couple's first or last names yielded matches, but she found no case where all four initials corresponded.

Slowly, she worked out further and further in both directions from the date she had until she had checked the papers for the entire first half of the previous year, but she found nothing. She leaned against the tiny table with a sigh, folding her arms and feeling discouraged. There were any number of possible explanations, she knew—the date might not represent an engagement, or the engagement might not have happened in the Blue Hill area, or the parties involved might not have chosen to announce their engagement in the paper. Still, having just recommitted to this search for the ring's owner the day before, she was frustrated to have come to yet another dead end so quickly.

She frowned at the shelves in front of her.

"Why so glum?" asked a voice, and Anne looked up to see the always radiant Grace Hawkins standing in the door of the tiny room. "I heard you were back here," she continued, "though it looks like you're not finding what you were looking for."

"I'm afraid not," Anne replied as she began to tidy up the newspapers she had disarranged. "And I don't think I'm going to, either."

"May I ask what 'it' is?"

Anne laughed. "An engagement announcement."

Grace's eyebrows shot up, and she craned her neck to see the dates on the issues that Anne had been examining. "From last year. Anyone I know?"

"Unfortunately, nobody *I* know—or should I say, I don't know whose." She twisted her mouth in a that's-not-right-either gesture. "I mean, that's what I'm trying to find out."

Grace laughed. "I think," she said, "that we need to get some lunch, so that I can try to make heads or tails of what you're saying."

* * *

Coffee Joe's shop, a few doors away, was offering a special mocha peppermint coffee in honor of the season, and soon Grace was sipping one and Anne was savoring her black coffee as she perused the lunch menu. After they'd ordered, Anne recounted the entire tale of the Christmas key and the ring it uncovered, right down to her fruitless attempt that day to put names to the initials.

Telling the story aloud to a fresh listener helped Anne organize her own thoughts but also just helped calm her down. As she spoke, she felt more relaxed and became aware of the pleasant warmth of the restaurant, the rich aromas, and the happy chatter of the other patrons around them. When she came to the upsetting episode with Sophie, Grace was sympathetic and indignant on her friend's behalf.

When Anne had finished, Grace sat for a while in silence while Anne ate her lunch and continued to absorb the soothing ambiance of the establishment. When she finally spoke, Grace harkened back to an earlier episode in the story. "So Henderson Brockhurst first claimed that it was the ring that had been stolen from him, but then later changed his story when he was questioned by the police?"

Anne was a little surprised that Grace had chosen to focus on this particular development, but she said, "Well, I don't think *questioned* is the word, if you mean it in the sense of interrogated. The alleged crime was one that he had reported, after all. One where he was the victim. It's not like he was a suspect."

"Except possibly suspected of making a false insurance claim on his stolen ring."

"Well, yes, but he now says this isn't the ring, and I don't see how the police could prove otherwise."

Grace didn't respond to that point but sat for a while longer in thoughtful silence. "The thing is," she said at last, "I remember that incident."

Anne was a little surprised at this. In the absence of an arrest and trial, she wouldn't have thought that the case would have made it to the attention of the newspaper editor, especially since it appeared that the police investigation never got very far.

"Oh yes," Grace said, responding to Anne's skeptical expression. "I remember because Brockhurst himself made such a fuss about it. Normally I get my criminal news from the police, but Brockhurst, as soon as he'd filed his report, made a point of bringing a copy of it down to the paper. He went so far as to accuse an employee of his, a David Something-or-other, of having taken the ring. Apparently, this guy had up and left town.

"Well, I tried to confirm the story with the police, but they would 'not comment on an active investigation.' So I ran a little story about the mysterious disappearance of the ring, but I didn't mention his accusation of the ex-employee because I had no independent corroboration of the charge. I figured Brockhurst was turning lemons into lemonade by trying to get some publicity for his store out of the misfortune of losing the ring. It seemed to me the ring might just as easily have been shoplifted."

She took a rapturous sip from her peppermint mocha, then continued. "But no, after the story ran, Brockhurst actually called up and complained because I didn't include the angle about his ex-employee. I would have thought he'd be embarrassed if anything. After all, he hired the guy in the first place. But he sounded like he was much more interested in smearing this guy than in retrieving his stolen property. It made me wonder about his motivation.

"Now I don't know. If he felt sure that this guy had done it, maybe he'd want to get back at him by blackening his name in public. But, on the other hand, I'd think a more satisfying revenge would be to make sure the police could catch him."

Grace looked off into space for a bit, and Anne could tell that her friend had bounced back and forth between these two arguments quite a bit at the time. She was apparently revisiting all the possibilities one more time, but after a moment, she shook her head and continued. "Anyway, there was just something about his behavior in all this that seemed off. You know what I mean?"

Anne, who'd had the same feeling about Brockhurst herself, nodded.

"So I told him that unless the police confirmed that this David fella was a suspect, I wasn't going to run that part of the story. And then he starts in with all these other accusations against the guy—there was 'the chance,' he said, that this guy had stolen other jewelry or had even embezzled from him."

Grace shook her head incredulously at the memory. "This was sounding ever stranger. I asked him if he had reported these other crimes to the police, and he said no. He said he was still 'gathering evidence.' Well naturally, if I wasn't going to run the other accusation without police verification, I sure wasn't going to run any of this stuff until there was an actual police investigation.

"Finally, I asked him outright, I said, 'It sounds like you don't like this guy.' And he got very huffy at that and made some noises about wanting to see justice done. I told him that's what the police are for, and he finally hung up. But it was very strange."

Once again, Anne was reminded of her own encounter with Brockhurst, his initial bluster, and how quickly he caved when his bluff was called. They sipped their coffee for a bit until Anne finally asked, "So what did you do?"

Grace gave a rueful snort. "Well, that's the thing, isn't it? I wasn't about to let Henderson Brockhurst tell me what to print in my paper. But on the other hand, there was clearly something going on here, and I wanted to know if there was a story in it. So, I asked around a little about this employee David."

Anne cocked her eyebrow, but Grace merely shrugged. "Apparently he was a nice guy. Anyone who recalled meeting him seemed to like him, but not that many people knew him. He wasn't from around here, didn't have family here. He'd moved here about a year and a half or two years before and had apparently worked for Brockhurst since arriving in the area. It's true that he seemed to leave town rather abruptly, but not so much as to be suspicious. At least his landlady didn't think so. And what's more, as far as I could tell, it seemed that he left town sometime before Brockhurst reported his ring stolen. But I had trouble nailing down actual dates, so it's hard to be sure."

Fascinated, Anne asked, "Where did he go?"

Grace gave a perplexed sigh. "That part is a little odd in that I couldn't seem to find anyone who knew. Or at least who would tell me. His fiancée didn't pretend not to know, at least—that would have been ludicrous—but she flat-out refused to tell me, the one time I managed to talk to her directly." She gave Anne an accusatory glance. "I think your aunt was running interference for her."

"My aunt?" Anne exclaimed with a mixture of confusion and anticipatory thrill.

"Yes, she was staying with Edie. Julie... but I can't recall her last name. I'm not sure that I ever knew it... Coincidentally, she never seemed to be there when I called."

Anne was dumbfounded at the reappearance of the mysterious lodger, Julie. And Julie's fiancé was this jeweler who had been accused of stealing the ring? Suddenly, Anne didn't like the sound of where this was headed. What if David had stolen the ring and passed it to his fiancée, who had then hidden it in the Advent cabinet at church and left the key among Aunt Edie's things? Anne felt slightly dizzy for a few moments.

"Anne?" Grace gave her a concerned look before continuing. "Yeah. She stayed with your aunt Edie for, I don't know, a few months I guess. I thought you'd have known all about it."

"I only recently learned about it," Anne said.

"She had some connection to the university, didn't she?" Grace continued after a moment.

"Yes, she had a postdoctoral fellowship, teaching, I assume. For two years. And apparently, she spent the last few months of it living with Aunt Edie."

Grace nodded. "That makes sense. As I say, I only managed to talk with her the one time. Then within a few months she was gone herself, and I had no way to follow up on the story any more. So I dropped it. The news waits for no woman, you know. I had other stories to pursue."

Anne suddenly remembered the engraved letters. "Grace, the initials in the ring are *JH* and *DC*. That could be Julie and David. What were their last names?"

Grace blinked slowly and then shook her head, frowning. "I'm sorry, Anne, like I said earlier, I don't remember at this point. I'm not sure I even knew Julie's last name, and though I'm pretty sure I had David's at one point, I never met him or talked with him. I just don't remember it now." She paused and thought some more. "But I guess the matching first initials would be a pretty big coincidence?"

"Yes," said Anne, "since there's also the apparent connections with Aunt Edie and with the Diamond District. But it's not proof. It's just not enough. And it doesn't explain enough." Grace gave her a questioning look, and Anne continued, "For instance, if we think this was their engagement ring, well, why would she leave it behind when she moved away? Why isn't she wearing it right now? Why would David steal an engagement ring from his employer? If that's what he did. You don't steal something that your fiancée is then going to wear for everyone to see. It makes no sense." She shook her head. "The initials in the ring certainly suggest a connection to Julie and David, but it's still not clear what the connection is or what it means. And we have a clear connection to Edie."

"So ask them," suggested Grace.

"You said yourself, nobody seems to know where they've gone. And without last names, how am I going to trace them? A jeweler named David? An academic named Julie? And that's assuming they haven't changed their names or professions."

"Why would they do that?" asked Grace in surprise.

"If they left Blue Hill because they had something to hide, they might. Neither you nor I trust Henderson Brockhurst, but that doesn't mean that he's not telling the truth. The fact is, we just don't know."

"Well," said Grace with a wry smile, "but you make another good point there as well. We may not trust Brockhurst, but we know for sure that he knows some things that we do not. The last name of his ex-employee, David, for starters."

CHAPTER TWENTY-ONE

Grace insisted on going with Anne to visit the Diamond District. "After all," she'd said, "it's an unfinished story for me. And besides, he may not be eager to see you again, but he should want to talk with me. He certainly did last year."

The air had turned sharply colder and the wind, while not strong, was persistent in snaking through coats and scarves. Both women had clutched their wraps and ducked their heads when they'd exited the cheerful warmth of the coffee shop.

By the time they pulled into the parking lot of the shopping center, it felt like the car had barely had time to warm up.

As they stepped from Anne's Impala, the wind rattled the naked trees under a leaden sky. Even the interior of the Diamond District, with its dim light, felt chilly. At first, Anne assumed that the store was empty as it had been on her first visit, but as her eyes adjusted to the gloom, she was surprised to hear a low murmur of conversation from the back of the store. As she and Grace moved toward the back, they saw two figures standing behind one of the far counters.

Anne recognized one of these as the stooped figure of Henderson Brockhurst. The other was a stranger, a smaller, younger man with a moustache that didn't suit his ferret-like face. The two men looked toward them, and Brockhurst appeared to give a little start. He touched the other man on the arm and spoke into his ear, whereupon the stranger slipped through a door in the back wall and disappeared.

Brockhurst eyed them as they approached and finally, in his bland tone, said, "Good afternoon. How can I help you?"

"Mr. Brockhurst," Anne said, "I don't know if you remember me. I was here a couple of weeks ago to ask about a ring that I'd...well, to ask about a ring." She paused for a moment, but he said nothing, so she continued. "You said that it was a ring that had been stolen from you. Do you remember?"

"I remember," he said simply.

Anne had forgotten how disconcerting his unresponsiveness could be. She wished that she had prepared herself better mentally. Perhaps she shouldn't have just rushed right down. But she also began to be curious just how unresponsive he could be. She drew a breath and tried, "We left it that I was going to take that ring to the police. I wanted to let you know that I did so."

"I'm glad to hear it."

Anne and Grace exchanged a glance. Grace, who, after all, got information out of people for a living, seemed amused. She stepped in to ask, "Is that the same stolen ring that you contacted me about last year, Mr. Brockhurst? You remember that we spoke? I'm Grace Hawkins of the *Blue Hill Gazette*."

Brockhurst hesitated a moment and gave a half bow. When he finally spoke, he said carefully, "I thought it was the same ring."

"But you subsequently told the police that you were mistaken, yes? That the ring Anne brought you was not the stolen ring?"

"That's right."

Grace's use of her name made Anne wonder whether Brockhurst knew who she was. She didn't think she had given her name when she came here before, and she didn't know if the police would have mentioned it. On the other hand, in a small town, it was always better to assume that people knew who you were. She realized that she had left anonymity behind when she came back to Blue Hill from New York.

"It seems an odd mistake to make," pursued Grace.

Brockhurst shrugged. "They look very similar."

"So I guess the police never found the ring or caught the thief?"

"No."

"And do you still think it was your former employee David?"

Another hesitation, and then a shrug. "I don't know who it was."

"Because last year you seemed pretty convinced it was him."

"I have my suspicions."

Grace glanced back at Anne, who resumed her own questions. "Mr. Brockhurst, because of the question whether it was your stolen ring, we didn't get a chance to talk about it beyond that." More stolid silence. "I'm still trying to trace information about the previous owner. Since you know now that it is *not* the ring that was stolen from you, is there anything that you could tell me about it?"

"I—I would have to see it again."

But Anne had not been so foolish. "I'm sorry, I don't happen to have it with me. But I remember you examined it quite closely. Is there nothing you can recall? It was in one of your boxes."

He merely shrugged at this.

"It also had some engraving on the inside. Perhaps you remember that? Do you offer engraving?"

Since there was a sign on the counter that said, *Ask us about engraving*, Brockhurst could hardly say anything other than, "Yes."

"But I'm afraid," he continued in a somewhat stronger tone, "that I cannot tell you anything more about the ring. I simply do not recall it well enough. And as you know, at the time, I thought that it was a different ring."

"Funny that you should have mistaken it for your stolen ring even with the engraving," Grace mused. "It seems like that would have been fairly distinctive." He made no response to this, so they thanked him for his time and turned as if preparing to leave. Just as they had reached the door, Grace suddenly turned back. "Oh, Mr. Brockhurst, what was the last name of that ex-employee again? The one you suspected? I know you told me last year, but I've forgotten. David . . . ?"

Brockhurst was silent for a long, long moment, and then finally said, "Courtney."

* * *

With a first name, a last name, and a profession, not to mention a connection to someone named Julie, Anne had hopes that she now possessed enough search terms to track down the elusive couple, at least, if all those terms were still valid. It still wouldn't be easy, however. After all, jewelry stores had no particular need to list their employees on their Web sites, and the names she had to work with were not especially distinctive. It would take quite a bit of searching and checking yet, but Anne was starting to feel more optimistic about getting some results.

She explained all this to Grace as they drove back toward the center of town, unable to contain the excitement bubbling up in her voice.

"Well, I'm glad to hear you say that," Grace said, "because I came out of there feeling like we hadn't gotten much information at all. But if you feel like you can trace these folks now, well, I'll be interested to hear what you find."

When they had parked back at the library, Grace asked, "May I see this famous ring?"

"Of course," said Anne, and she led the way into the library. At the circulation desk, she dispatched Sherri to do some shelving. Then she pulled open the drawer and took out the ring.

"You keep it here?" Grace asked.

"Well, I had it upstairs, but I brought it down yesterday to look at it further, and I haven't taken it back up yet."

Grace gave her a skeptical look.

"What? It's perfectly safe."

But Grace had already opened the box. "Oh my," she said softly. "Well, it really is a gorgeous ring, isn't it? Are you sure you just don't want to claim that it was Edie's and keep it?" She pulled it out of the box to get a better look, then she gave Anne a sly smile. "Have you tried it on?"

Anne leaned forward and, in conspiratorial undertones, admitted, "Too small."

Grace slipped it onto her own slim finger, which it fit perfectly. They both gazed at it. "You see," Anne said finally, "you could pull off a ring like that. It looks like it belongs on you."

Grace admired it for a few seconds longer and then tugged it off with a laugh. "Nah," she said, "I'm afraid I'd lose something this nice in a heartbeat. Down the garbage disposal, or something like that."

* * *

Later in the afternoon, Anne got a call from Wendy, who announced that she was picking up Ben and Liddie from school and that they would be with her for a while. She didn't want Anne to worry. She then rang off with a quick "gotta go," leaving Anne a little puzzled, but since she was busy with patrons she didn't worry too much about it.

It was almost dinnertime when Wendy came through the front door alone, calling a cheery greeting. Though her friend seemed unperturbed, Anne felt a quick stab of anxiety. "Where are the kids?" she said quickly.

Wendy smiled broadly. "It's okay," she said, "they went up the other stairs."

Relieved, Anne was still puzzled that they'd not come in with Wendy, and she gave her a questioning look. "You should plan to stay down here for a while," Wendy said with a broad wink. "They have some things to do up there." Seeing Anne's suspicious glance toward the stairs, she added, "I tell you what. I'll go on up in a minute myself and see how they're getting on."

When Anne continued to stare at her blankly, Wendy started to get impatient. "Anne, think what time of year it is." And finally, she resorted to, "What did I help *you* do the other day?"

Anne, finally catching on, gave an embarrassed smile, but then another thought occurred to her. "Wendy," she said in a brook-no-nonsense tone, "how much do I owe you?"

Chapter Twenty-Two

Anne had been relying heavily on her library volunteers during the busy holiday season, and she was feeling guilty about it. As a result, she had released them all and was alone in the library on Friday morning, the last weekday before Christmas Eve and Christmas Day the following week. As it happened, the schools had declared this the first day of the holiday vacation and the library was swarming with excited kids who were just days away from opening their presents.

It annoyed Anne when parents treated the library as a babysitting service, dropping off their children and not staying to supervise them. But she knew it was a problem faced by libraries all over the country, and she found it difficult to blame the children for the actions of their parents. And today she was in too good a mood to let it get her down.

Despite the lack of assistance, Anne was in her element, answering questions, making suggestions, and darting her patented "librarian glare" at any little miscreant who threatened to get too far out of hand. Unfortunately, her lack of help would continue all day since her troops had their own holiday chores to attend to. This meant that she would miss the dress rehearsal for the Nativity play that afternoon.

She was nurturing hopes of getting the library closed and scooting down for the end of the rehearsal, but if she couldn't manage that, both Alex and Wendy had volunteered to transport Ben and Liddie home afterward.

So for the time being, she sat at the circulation desk and smiled serenely at the chaos around her. She too was feeling the excitement of the approaching holiday. She made a halfhearted effort to begin her Internet search for David Courtney and the enigmatic Julie, but she was interrupted so frequently that she made little progress. She tried to keep a page of search results open in her Web browser, but even then she had to keep opening new tabs and windows to respond to the questions that came her way. Finally, she decided to put it off until a time when she could focus.

Once again, Anne thought back to the stress she'd been feeling at the beginning of the week. Thanks to her friends Wendy, Grace, and Alex, and thanks especially to her children, she'd been reminded that Christmas was about family and faith, about community and relationships, and she saw plenty of that in the enthusiastic children dashing around the library.

Reverend Tom walked through the door and stopped short, watching and listening to the pandemonium with an arched eyebrow. Finally, he walked over to the circulation desk with a broad smile on his face. "You are the calm center of the storm, I see," he said as he approached. "An island of tranquility in a" — he gestured at the room — "troubled sea. And on your own today with no assistance?" he asked, looking about. "Ben and Liddie upstairs?"

"They're in the Children's Room. All my usual workers are busy with their own holiday preparations. I'm afraid I'll miss the rehearsal this afternoon, or at least all but the very end. I've already mentioned it to Helen."

Tom nodded. "Then you should have some surprises to look forward to with the actual performance."

"I think I know how the story turns out," she replied, laughing.

"Yes, but you know," Reverend Tom said, suddenly serious, "that's really the value of the Christmas story, isn't it? Not novelty, but consistency and reliability. Every year in our performances, He is born afresh in our hearts."

Tom gazed off into the distance for a moment, and Anne wondered if this might be the seed of a future sermon, but she was distracted by a young girl asking the way to the restroom. When Anne turned back, Reverend Tom was smiling benevolently once again. "That girl," said Anne, nodding after her, "first came in a week ago to deliver her letter to Santa. Except for school, she'd never been to a library, and now she's been back twice. And it's the same story with some of these others. Now that the ice is broken, a bunch of them have been coming back on a regular basis. I'm so pleased at how that's worked out."

"They just had to see what was available here," said Reverend Tom. "And speaking of available...Douglas Pauthen has highly recommended that Johnson biography, so I came by to see if you have it or if it's checked out again."

Anne's face fell. "Oh, I'm sorry. Not only is it checked out, but there's a waiting list. Douglas was the first on the list."

"Not to worry," Reverend Tom reassured her, "that's just as well for me anyway. But if you could add my name to the list, I'd appreciate it." Looking down, he noticed a boy waiting for Anne's attention so he stepped to one side to give him access.

"Mrs. Gibson," said the boy, "do you have some colored markers I could borrow?"

"You know, I believe I do. The question is, where to find them? Hold on a sec." She pulled open the drawer and rummaged inside. "Well," she said after a few moments, "they're in here somewhere." She reached farther to the back of the drawer until she pulled the drawer's contents out altogether, piling them on the desk as she continued to search.

Finally, she pulled out a plastic case with six or eight markers in it. "Success at last!" she cried. "That, my friend," she said to the boy as she handed him the markers, "is a lesson in the value of persistence." He looked at her a little uncertainly. "Go!" she said, making a shooing gesture. "Draw pictures. Make art. Just be sure you return those," she called after him.

She smiled ruefully at Reverend Tom as she returned items to the drawer. "Naturally, those markers were the very last thing in there," she said.

But Reverend Tom's attention had been caught by something she had pulled from the drawer. "Is that the famous ring?" he asked, gesturing toward the box on the table.

"You know," said Anne, "that's almost exactly what Grace Hawkins said yesterday, 'the famous ring'." She glanced up at him. "Have you not seen it yet either? I've talked about it so much, but have I ever shown it to you?"

"I…don't think you have shown it to me, no."

Anne held up the ring box. "I'm sorry. And here I've bent your ear about it so often. You must have wondered what it looked like." She handed the box up to him, and he opened it. "Grace put it on her finger yesterday, and it looked just gorgeous."

"*Mm-hmm*," Reverend Tom said, gazing politely at the ring. After he'd looked for a few moments, he handed it back to her without even removing it from the box.

"Men," said Anne, and Reverend Tom took on an innocent expression.

"I assume you've been too busy to continue your inquiries?" he said.

"Sadly, despite all of my other obligations, I can't seem to let it go that easily."

Having asked in a jesting tone, Reverend Tom seemed somewhat taken aback by the response. "But surely you've explored every possible avenue."

"Well, that's what I thought too. But now I've got one new piece of information from Henderson Brockhurst that may break the—"

"Brockhurst!" the pastor exclaimed sharply. "You haven't been back to see him again, have you?"

"Why, yes, I have. Just yesterday. And he—"

"Anne, do you really think that's wise?" Reverend Tom's tone was agitated, and his face showed an expression of concern.

Anne was somewhat nonplussed. "Well, he wasn't much help, granted. But he—"

"But, Anne," Reverend Tom interrupted again. "What if he becomes desperate?"

"Desperate? Brockhurst? About what? He's told the police that the ring isn't his after all, that is, it's not the one that had been stolen from him. I don't think he would try to claim it at this point. And besides, we didn't take it with us."

Tom hesitated. "We?" he finally asked.

"Oh, Grace Hawkins went with me. She thinks there may be a story somewhere in all this. Or at least in the story of his stolen ring. Or something." Impatiently, she gave up trying to clarify that point and exclaimed, "But that's not the big news."

"Oh?" said Reverend Tom weakly.

"No, the one new piece of information we got from Brockhurst was…wait for it…the name of his former employee, David Courtney. Brockhurst thinks that Courtney was the person who stole his ring, though the police don't seem to agree, or at least they wouldn't say that to Grace.

"But, guess who David Courtney also is." She waited, but Reverend Tom said nothing. "He was the fiancé of the mysterious Julie, the lodger who stayed here with Aunt Edie!" It was impossible to hide the triumph in her voice. "Isn't that amazing? I'm sure this must be more than coincidence. And now with this much information, I should finally be able to track them down!"

Just at that moment, there was a loud crash from the second floor followed a few moments later by the sound of crying. "Uh-oh," Anne said jumping up. She rushed from behind the desk and ran up the stairs.

On the second floor, she found two chairs knocked over and a couple of older boys looking sheepish and trying to comfort a crying younger boy.

"It was an accident, Mrs. Gibson," said one of the older boys looking up. "Honest!"

Ben and Liddie were also there, looking discomfited, but they confirmed that it had been an accident.

It turned out that there had been a little playful roughhousing among the older boys, which had resulted in the overturned chairs and an overturned boy. But he proved more surprised and dismayed than hurt, so Anne told him he could come down and sit with her at the circulation desk. She told the older boys to take their rough play outside. Though she fretted about singling them out, she also sent Ben and Liddie upstairs to the residence.

As she came down the stairs, coaxing the boy along, she called out ahead, "It's okay, Reverend. Just a little tumble, and all's well now. Right, Jeffrey?" But when she looked up, she was surprised to find that Reverend Tom had vanished. Frowning, she glanced around but had to return her attention to Jeffrey.

She pulled over a chair for him and got him set up with some crayons and paper, and only then did she look down.

The ring box was missing from the desktop where she had left it.

* * *

Anyone could have taken it. At least, that's what Anne kept telling herself. She'd been gone for several minutes, the library was full of people, and she had foolishly left the ring out on the desktop. She'd had a vague notion that Reverend Tom would be able to keep an eye on it for her, but clearly he'd been called away. By some emergency or something. And so the ring had just been left lying there and someone had seized the opportunity and grabbed it.

It could have been anybody.

Except, in her heart, Anne knew that it was not anybody. Yes, the library was busy but it was mostly full of kids, and youngish kids at that. And they were mostly upstairs, especially following the commotion that had drawn Anne herself. The first floor had been much quieter, especially the area around the circulation desk. Nobody had been anywhere near the desk when she came back down. And if Reverend Tom had received a call about an emergency, he would have come up and told her before he left or shouted up the stairs or something. That's just the way he was.

But Reverend Tom had disappeared without a word.

And the ring had disappeared too.

And the only explanation that made sense was that these two facts were connected.

Reverend Tom stole the ring.

It was quite some time before Anne could even articulate this thought to herself, even though she had intuitively known it to be true from the moment that she noticed that the ring was missing.

First, she had continued to fuss over Jeffrey for a while, as a way to postpone thinking about the matter. Recovered from his upset, the boy soon grew annoyed at the attention and returned to the second floor. Then Anne had simply sat and stared at the desktop for a while, as if the ring box might rematerialize. And then she'd gone carefully through the drawer, though she was certain that she had not stopped to put the ring away before she rushed upstairs. After all, Reverend Tom had been right there. And then she'd gone through the other drawers in the desk, even though the ring had never been in any of them.

She stopped herself before she went to look for the ring upstairs.

And then she slowly and reluctantly worked her way through the logic that led to the inevitable conclusion: Her pastor had stolen the ring.

At last, resistance and disbelief gave way to indignation. Reverend Tom had stolen the ring! Why would he do such a thing?

Look at the position that he had put her in. What was she supposed to do now? Call the police? On Reverend Tom? Well, clearly she just wasn't going to be able to do that. Then what? Confront him? *"Reverend, why did you steal my ring?"* She could no more imagine herself doing that than calling the police. But then, what *would* she say the next time she saw him? Just pretend that nothing had happened? She didn't think her own emotions would let her do that.

But if it were true, and she still struggled to accept the possibility, then why had Reverend Tom stolen the ring?

Well, and that was the point, wasn't it? Anne felt herself calming a little. Suppose Reverend Tom did take the ring. The thing was, she fully believed that there *was* a "why." He must have had a reason for doing what he did. She might not know the reason. It might be completely unfathomable to her. But she realized she had faith that such a reason existed. She trusted Reverend Tom, and whatever the motivation for his action, well, she was going to have to put her faith in that trust.

She took a deep breath, held it a moment, and let it go.

Yes, acknowledging her trust in Reverend Tom helped, it helped a lot, but it didn't solve everything. She was calmer but not fully at peace, and she probably wouldn't be, she realized, until she had an explanation for his behavior. Trust was one thing and understanding was another.

CHAPTER TWENTY-THREE

Over the course of the next few hours, Anne slowly regained greater control over her emotional response, but a part of her mind was continuously turning the question of *why*. Why had her pastor done it? Despite her decision to trust the man's integrity and motives, she could find no reasonable explanation.

At noon, Alex came by to pick up Ben and Liddie. Since there was no school, they were to have lunch with Ryan and spend the early afternoon with him until Alex took them all up to the rehearsal. Though he entered the library in a jovial mood, Alex seemed to sense that there was something troubling Anne. As soon as he'd dispatched Ryan to find Ben and Liddie upstairs, he stepped close to the circulation desk and asked, "What's wrong?"

Anne was sorely tempted to tell him what had happened. But if she were truly putting her faith in Reverend Tom, she decided, then it would be inappropriate to discuss the matter until she understood it better herself. Otherwise, she risked misrepresenting Reverend Tom and his actions. In addition, the idea of saying it out loud—"Reverend Tom stole the ring"—forced her to confront the fact that she had no real proof.

These things flashed through her mind almost as a single thought when Alex asked his question, and she barely hesitated before pasting on a smile and cheerfully responding, "Nothing.

Just a busy morning." She could tell from his expression that Alex didn't believe her, but she had at least succeeded in deflecting his question.

"Okay, then," Alex said doubtfully. "Well. We're, uh, we're having soup and grilled cheese for lunch. Do you have something?"

"Oh yes, I brought something down with me this morning," Anne said. "And Alex...thanks." She also meant, "Thanks for taking the kids," but also "Thanks for not asking more questions." Before Alex could respond, Ryan, Ben, and Liddie were back and clamoring to depart. Anne kissed her children and wished them luck with the rehearsal. "Or am I supposed to say 'break a leg'?"

"I think that's just for the performance, Mom," said Ben.

"We'll see you toward the end?" Alex asked as they prepared to head out.

"I'm not sure," Anne replied. "We'll see."

As the afternoon wore on, many of the children went home or went off to play elsewhere, so that the library gradually grew very quiet, and in the waning sunlight of the winter's day, Anne brooded over Reverend Tom's mysterious behavior. She hardly noticed the gradual exodus until finally she looked up and realized that she was practically alone in the library.

With most of her patrons gone, Anne was able to emerge from behind the circulation desk and start cleaning up the considerable mess that a large number of children can make in half a day. Lost in thought, she only partially registered the sound of the front door opening and closing. She had assumed it would be yet another child, so she was startled to look up and see a grown man shaking off a blue parka and looking about. He was no one she'd ever seen before: slight build, mustache, wire-rimmed glasses, and an unfashionably wide, sky-blue tie.

Since he was peering about with an air of purpose, Anne moved back to the circulation desk and said, "May I help you?"

He stepped forward briskly and asked, "Mrs. Gibson?"

Anne was surprised. "Yes," she said, and repeated, "May I help you?" because this man was apparently not in search of the librarian, but of her in particular. For no reason she could identify, she began to feel nervous.

"My name is Russell Haines," the man said. "I'm with Jewelers Mutual Insurance Company. I understand you've found a ring?"

After a long moment of flabbergasted silence, Anne stammered, "How did you know?"

"Your local police department was kind enough to inform us," Haines replied, taking another step forward and placing a briefcase on the counter. From his shirt pocket, he produced a business card that he handed to Anne. Then he snapped open the briefcase, pulled out some papers, and began to sift through them. "I understand that it may be a ring that was reported stolen from the Diamond District last year?"

"Well, no," Anne responded stammering again.

Haines gave her a sharp look. "No?"

"The man at the Diamond District, Henderson Brockhurst, said that it wasn't that ring. Or that is, he said at first that it was, but then he changed his mind and said that it wasn't." Haines nodded, but Anne couldn't tell from the gesture whether he meant to indicate that he'd already heard this, or just that he understood.

"So there's some question about the matter."

Anne hesitated. "I guess so."

"Which is why the company has asked me to come here. I'm hoping, Mrs. Gibson, that you will allow me to examine the ring myself. Would you be willing to do that?"

"Oh," said Anne weakly.

"I can perform an initial examination right here." He pulled a jeweler's loupe and a small lamp from his briefcase as he spoke. "You may observe the entire time. Possibly we would determine that we wish to examine it further in a lab. In which case, you would be given a receipt, of course," he looked into her eyes as if to reassure her on this point, "and we would guarantee that no harm would be done to the ring in the process. But I think it unlikely that we would need to do that." He gazed at her expectantly. "Would you be willing?"

"Well, uh—"

"Mrs. Gibson, my company settled a fairly large insurance claim on the report of this stolen ring. You can understand that, if there's a chance that the ring has now turned up, we'd want to ascertain whether this is the case. Can't you?" Haines was clearly trying to adopt a winning and confidential tone.

"Yes..."

But Anne was making no move, and Haines began to show signs of impatience. "Then what is your hesitation?" he asked. And trying again to sound more conciliatory, he added, "I'm sure we can allay any fears you may have."

Finally, Anne managed to stammer, "I — I don't have it."

Haines froze and his gaze turned icy. "I beg your pardon?"

"I mean, it's not here. Not right at the moment." But now that she had blurted out the words, Anne began to regain her confidence. "A friend is looking after it for me.

"The fact is, this isn't a convenient time," she continued more forcefully. "Yes, I'm willing to have you examine the ring but not right now." She brandished the card that he'd handed her. "I've got your contact information here. I'll be in touch about scheduling a time that's more suitable."

Haines continued to glare at her suspiciously. "I appreciate that, Mrs. Gibson. But what do you mean when you say that you 'don't have' the ring?"

"A friend is looking after it for me."

"Looking after it? Why? Have you given it to this person?"

"No," Anne said quickly, "it's not that. It's just as I say. A friend of mine has it at the moment. Temporarily." She endured his suspicious glare another moment before flaring up a bit herself. "Look, Mr. Haines, I'm sorry I can't accommodate you right now, but that's just the way it is. I'll be happy to allow your company to make its own examination of the ring," she glanced down at the card, "after I've checked you out a bit myself, but it's just not possible to do it right this minute." She gestured at the desk. "I have a library to run. As I say, I'll be happy to call you to schedule a time after... A time that will be more suitable."

Haines pursed his lips and began to return the equipment and sheaf of papers to his briefcase. "I see," he said, snapping it closed. "Well, I appreciate your... theoretical willingness to assist, Mrs. Gibson. As you might imagine, it is a question of some concern to my company." He recovered his blue parka and shrugged back into it.

"I'll look forward to your call to schedule an appointment." With that, he picked up his briefcase and left the library.

Anne drew a long, shuddering breath as she stared thoughtfully at the door he had closed behind him.

* * *

Anne now had three things to stew about as she sat out the afternoon shift. First, Reverend Tom's inexplicable behavior. Second, the insurance claims adjuster's sudden appearance on the scene. And third, the bad timing of the first two.

She was at least able to determine through a quick Internet search that not only was the company legitimate, but even that Russell Haines was indeed one of their adjusters, since the company listed its personnel on its Web site. They didn't provide pictures, but she'd had no real reason to doubt him anyway. She was just feeling the need to confirm whatever information she could.

She pondered everything that she had learned. The suspicion that Brockhurst had committed some sort of insurance fraud had always seemed like a real possibility, and apparently the insurance company itself now thought so as well. Presumably, Anne thought, this involved the reporting of the stolen ring as being more valuable than it actually was – a real sapphire rather than an imitation gem. And now, possibly, the ring in question had unexpectedly turned up.

She considered Brockhurst's behavior. First he had claimed that the ring was his stolen ring, and he'd tried to avoid returning it to her. If this were the ring and he'd falsely reported its value, his first panicked impulse might be to get the ring back in his possession in an attempt to control the situation.

But he had returned it eventually, even though she had declared she would take it to the police. Well, she hadn't left him much option there, had she? She'd threatened to call the police right then and there to the store. He might have made a calculation—if he let her take the ring there was at least a chance that she would not go to the police, whatever she might be saying, while if she called the police on the spot, their involvement was unavoidable.

Too bad for him that she was a woman of her word.

By the time Michael Banks went back to talk with him about the ring, they had learned the truth about its value. In fact, she recalled Michael saying that he had confronted Brockhurst with this information. In retrospect, she wondered if Michael had tipped his hand too soon. If he'd been more circumspect, he might have led the jeweler into some sort of incriminating statement. But since he had long ago filed a claim and received settlement on the basis of a high value for the ring, Brockhurst then had no choice but to say, "Sorry, this isn't the ring after all." It sure looked suspicious, but what could the police do in the absence of proof?

Tip off the insurance company, which as Haines himself had said, was highly motivated to conduct a more thorough investigation.

But how had this all come about in the first place? Had Brockhurst somehow arranged the theft of the ring so that he could file a false insurance claim? No, that didn't add up, Anne decided. To begin with, the man just didn't strike her as bright enough for the role of criminal mastermind.

But more importantly, it didn't square with his behavior at the time. If he had set out to commit fraud, would he have been so eager for publicity about the theft? Would he have called the newspaper to get them to run a story? Presumably the insurance company would require a police report but not a newspaper clipping, so why deliberately court the extra exposure?

And finally, if Brockhurst had arranged the theft, how did the ring end up in the Advent cabinet and the key in Edie's house?

No, it seemed much more likely that Brockhurst had found himself confronted with the theft of his ring and only then decided to make the most of the situation through a creative insurance claim.

Which still left the question: How did the ring and the key end up where they'd been found?

Anne looked at the clock and started in surprise. It was just about time to close the library, and she was now confronted with another decision. Should she try to make it to the end of the dress rehearsal? And if she did, what would she say to Reverend Tom when she saw him?

She was hesitating over this dilemma when the door opened and Officer Michael Banks walked in. "Michael!" she exclaimed, both relieved at the distraction and annoyed because it was closing time.

"Anne," he said, giving her a nod and then coming to a stop. He hesitated for such a long moment that she was about to ask him what was wrong, when he finally said, "Anne, there's a guy down at the station. He thinks you might be involved in stealing the ring and the filing of a false insurance claim based on it."

Chapter Twenty-Four

M e?" Anne said weakly. Without knowing quite how she'd gotten there, she found herself seated in the chair behind her desk.

Michael didn't bother repeating it but allowed Anne to absorb what he'd said while he took off his jacket. The look he gave her was sympathetic but serious.

After a moment, she took a long, shuddering breath. "That," she said, "would be Mr. Haines, I guess." Her police officer friend's silence confirmed her deduction. "Michael, you know that can't be true, right? After all, I wasn't even here when the ring was first reported stolen. That was last year. I was still in New York." He nodded but made no reply.

"And then, I'm the one who brought the ring to you. Once I'd found it. And I went with you when we went down to Hank's and he told us that it wasn't real." Though she knew the charge was groundless, just the awareness that she herself had been accused was making Anne increasingly fearful. And Michael was not providing the reassurance she was looking for.

Finally, in a mixture of fear and bravado, she demanded, "Are you here to arrest me?"

At that, Michael grimaced and shook his head. "No, of course not. But the thing is, Anne"—he looked at her with concern—"Haines says that you claim you don't have the ring anymore."

Anne dropped her head. "Oh."

"I have to ask you, Anne, is it true? Because, you remember that I asked you to keep me informed about the ring? I asked you not to do anything with it without checking first with the police."

"I remember," Anne said meekly.

"So, what about it? Haines said you claim that somebody else has the ring now. Is that true? And if so, will you tell me who has it?"

Now Anne was in a real dilemma. She certainly didn't want to tell the police, not even her friend Michael, that Reverend Tom had taken the ring without asking or saying anything to her. At least, she didn't want to say anything like that until she had a better understanding of what he was up to. Even if she herself trusted his motives, the police might not be able to see things in the same light.

Whatever the pastor's reasons, what he'd actually done might have to be counted as theft in the eyes of the law.

But at the same time, of course, she had her own responsibility both to the law and to her friend Michael Banks.

"Well?" asked Michael again.

"Michael, I don't...It's true that I don't have the ring right at the moment."

"So you gave it to someone? Where is it, then?"

"To tell you the absolute truth, I'm not one hundred percent sure." Anne suspected that this was about the worse thing she could have said. But it was the truth.

Michael's incredulous tone confirmed her suspicion. "You're not...Anne, what on earth has happened?"

Clearly there was no easy way out of this dilemma. Michael had a duty as a police officer to keep asking her until he knew the facts. Much as she was reluctant to do so, it looked like she was going to have to tell him about Reverend Tom.

She was about to open her mouth to do so when her phone rang. She almost jumped out of her seat in surprise.

She looked up at Michael and reached out toward the phone. He glowered, but he did not tell her to ignore it.

"Anne," said Alex's voice, "you're still there? Isn't the library closed by now? We'd hoped to see you down here for the end of the rehearsal."

"Alex," she said, a little light beginning to gleam at the end of the tunnel. "Alex, is Reverend Tom there with you? Could you put him on, please?"

Apparently something in her tone discouraged all questions. She could hear a muffled, "She wants to talk to you," in a puzzled voice, and then Reverend Tom's voice came on the line.

"Tom, the police are here," Anne said, looking directly into Michael's eyes.

"The police?" He sounded concerned but not alarmed.

She decided to take her chance. "They're asking about the ring," she said. "They want to know where it is."

There was the slightest of pauses, and Reverend Tom replied, "I see." There was no surprise in his voice. "Please tell them I'll be right there."

* * *

Anne still wouldn't give Michael an explanation, but she promised that Reverend Tom would do so when he arrived. "Do you know him?" she asked.

"Only by reputation," he said. While they waited, Anne finished closing up the library, but left the front door unlocked. When Reverend Tom arrived, he walked right in and Anne introduced the two men.

Tom pulled off his overcoat, reached into his pocket, and set the ring box down on the circulation desk. "Anne, I'm terribly sorry," he said in a matter-of-fact tone.

Michael looked first at the box, then at Reverend Tom. He turned to Anne. "Why didn't you just tell me that you'd given it to your minister?"

"Because she didn't give it to me," Reverend Tom said. "I took it without permission."

Michael gave him a startled look. "You stole it?"

Reverend Tom said, "Yes," but Anne spoke at the same time, saying, "No."

Both men looked at her. "Well, not really. I mean, I would have given it to him, if he'd asked." It occurred to her that Reverend Tom *had* asked, or at least hinted that she should do so. "That is, I want it understood that I don't object to what he did. I wouldn't want to press charges, for instance."

Michael gave her an exasperated look and then turned to Reverend Tom. "Meaning no disrespect to a man of the cloth and all, but would you care to explain yourself, sir? When did you take the ring? And why?"

Tom described how he had grabbed it off the desk that morning when Anne had been called away to a disturbance on the second floor. "It was a foolish thing to do," he said. "An impulse, acted on as a result of desperation."

"But why?" asked Anne, who had been wrestling with the question all day.

"Because I was worried for you," he said, turning to her. "You told me you'd been back to see that jeweler, that Brockhurst."

"You went to see Henderson Brockhurst again?" Michael cut in sharply.

"You didn't say I couldn't," Anne said.

Obviously fuming, Michael said, "No, but I would have thought you'd have the sense to mention it to me first." His eyes darted back and forth between them. "What happened?"

Anne recounted the conversation that she and Grace had had with the jeweler. "Okay," said Michael, turning to Reverend Tom. "So why did you find that so alarming?"

"In a way," Reverend Tom replied, "Brockhurst and his crimes are the reason why the ring was in the Advent cabinet in the first place."

Chapter Twenty-Five

"First of all, I want to apologize for not having shared any of this before," Reverend Tom said. His hint that he knew the history of the ring had set both Anne and Michael staring at him, so with a sigh, he had suggested that they all sit down, since it was a bit of a story.

"Everything I knew about it," he continued, "I was told in confidence, by your aunt Edie," he nodded at Anne, "and by the others involved. I've been struggling to find an appropriate path that would not involve breaking those confidences, but it's clear now that I'm not going to be able to do so.

"But ever since you found that ring, Anne, I've been concerned. And I have grown more and more concerned as time went on and as you continued your search for its owner. You may recall that on several occasions, I have tried to convince you to drop it, or at least put your efforts on hold."

Anne nodded.

"I was unsuccessful, of course. You are much too determined a woman to simply drop it. And I worried that if I pushed too hard without being able to provide a reason, it might only further pique your curiosity and cause you to redouble your efforts." He gave her a rueful smile.

"This morning," he continued, "when I realized how close you were to learning everything on your own, well, I panicked a bit. I needed to buy myself some time to think things through. So I grabbed the ring when you went upstairs. Of course, you would know it was I who took it, but I thought it would at least distract you while I considered what to do. I have thought and prayed today, and I had already determined that it was time to tell you everything.

"But in the meantime," Reverend Tom gestured to include Michael, "things had progressed without me."

"Perhaps more than you know," Michael said. "I've got an insurance adjuster now who thinks that Anne is part of a conspiracy to file a false claim on this ring."

"Oh dear," said Reverend Tom, frowning in concern. "Well, I'll be able to clear that all up for you, I trust."

"I'm sorry I didn't do a better job of picking up on your hints," Anne stammered. "I certainly didn't mean to put you in an awkward position."

"Of course you didn't," the pastor said with a smile. "The fault is entirely mine."

"So what about this ring, then?" Michael asked. "Is it the stolen ring or no?"

Despite the gravity of the situation, Reverend Tom gave him an impish smile. "Yes and no," he said. But before Michael could get irritated, he held up his hands as if to ask for patience. "This is the ring that was reported as stolen, but in fact, it never was stolen. This ring belongs legitimately to Julie Helzl."

"Julie...? Aunt Edie's lodger!"

"Yes, Anne. This is her engagement ring, given to her by her fiancé, David Courtney. David worked for Henderson Brockhurst, and as you may recall," he nodded at Michael, "David was the man that Brockhurst accused of stealing the ring. But in fact, David bought the ring legitimately, at cost, through Brockhurst's store. Brockhurst subsequently accused David of stealing it in an attempt, I believe, to besmirch David's reputation, to rob him of credibility. I assume that Brockhurst has adjusted his own records to conceal that fact the ring was legitimately purchased."

"But didn't David defend himself?" Anne asked.

Tom shook his head. "He'd already left town by then. Indeed, I think his departure is what precipitated Brockhurst's action in filing the police report. I think it was a preemptive measure."

"Preemptive?" Michael said. "Why, what did David know that scared Brockhurst so much?"

Tom smiled and nodded at this deduction. "David knew that the store was falsely selling imitation gems as real ones," he replied. "This had been going on for some time, and not just here. That store is part of a statewide chain, and the chain is owned by Brockhurst's family. Apparently they are all involved." He hesitated a moment. "What's the name of the store again?"

"The Diamond District," Anne supplied.

"Yes, that's right. Well, David, you see, had moved to this area from Philadelphia in order to be closer to Julie, who had a fellowship down at the university. He's an experienced jeweler and he found a job at the Diamond District, so he settled in

Blue Hill. But he'd been working there for, I don't know, six or eight months, when he began to suspect that something was amiss."

Tom spread his hands as if to suggest David's growing knowledge. "David says they hid it very well. It's his opinion that the chain probably has many employees who are completely unaware of the scheme. The family members control these particular transactions themselves. But since the Blue Hill store is smaller than most of their others, it was harder to keep David in the dark. Or perhaps Brockhurst is just not as bright as his relatives. A chain is only as strong as its weakest link.

"And then they made a big mistake." Anne saw Michael lean forward as Reverend Tom said this. "As an employee, David had arranged to buy an engagement ring at cost. But what he ended up getting was one of these rings where the stone was not real. David thinks there must have been some sort of communication breakdown between Brockhurst and the other members of his family who were responsible for making the switches."

Tom shrugged and continued. "As I say, he'd already had some suspicions, although they had been admittedly vague. But now, rather than confront the family about the ring he'd received, he started digging into their records more thoroughly. Well, they were clever, but they couldn't hide their tracks entirely from someone who was determined and had inside access. David learned that while some of this fraudulent activity went on here in Blue Hill, much more of it was happening in their stores in the Philadelphia area. He soon had a pretty good idea how it worked, but he didn't have any real proof, apart from his own ring."

"He still could have taken his suspicions to the police," said Michael.

Tom held up a finger. "I'll get to that. But in the meantime, you see, he and Julie had their own developments to deal with. They'd met back in Philadelphia when Julie was a graduate student in art history. And then she got the fellowship down at the university and eventually he followed her out here. For a while, they had hoped that Julie's fellowship would lead to a permanent teaching position, and they thought they might settle around here.

"Back in the early part of last year, however, it had become clear that Julie's job was not going to last beyond the initial two-year appointment. But God had indeed opened a window for her when He closed a door, because back in Philadelphia, the curator of a small museum had unexpectedly announced his retirement, and Anne's old graduate advisor had secured her an interview for the position. Well, they offered her the job, so she and David knew that once her fellowship was done, she would be moving back to Philly."

Reverend Tom paused and seemed to be making some calculations. "This must have been in March or early April of last year, and it was about the same time that David had become convinced that the Diamond District had been engaging in fraud.

"David didn't go to the local police," Reverend Tom gave Michael an apologetic shrug. "He seemed to think that the police would be more inclined to believe a local businessman than someone who had moved to town only a few months before."

Michael harrumphed but said nothing further.

"And besides," Reverend Tom continued, "David has a cousin that he is quite close to who is on the force in Philadelphia, so he took the story to him. Since it now looked like David would be moving back to Philadelphia anyway, they decided that he would do so right away, and he would try to assist the police there in building a case against the Diamond District chain. And so he moved away again."

"But how did you become involved in all this?" Anne asked.

"Ah, well, Julie had come to our church once or twice, you see. She'd been trying out different churches in the area, I think partially with an eye to where she might eventually have her wedding. Anyway, I had met her that way, and then one Sunday, she was telling me that she had to find a new place to live because the family she'd been renting from suddenly needed the room back. She only had a few months left on her fellowship, and she was having trouble finding someone who would agree to anything less than a year's lease. So I introduced her to Edie."

"But Aunt Edie didn't take in lodgers," Anne exclaimed.

"No," Reverend Tom agreed, "but she would talk about it from time to time." He smiled. "In fact, she said that you were always pushing her to do so. She thought highly of your opinion."

Anne blushed.

"I thought this might be an opportunity for her to give it a try," Reverend Tom continued, "knowing that this particular lodger would be gone in a few months. Though I think, in the end, she agreed to it more out of a desire to help Julie than to have a tenant. The two of them got along like a house afire, and yet even still, once Julie left, Edie told me that she'd never do it again." He smiled at some memory of that conversation.

"But they hit it off, you say?" Anne asked.

"Oh yes, so much so that in pretty short order, Julie had confided to Edie everything about her fiancé and the dark doings at the Diamond District. And she was upset about the publicity concerning the 'stolen ring'."

"After David left town, Brockhurst must have gotten suspicious that something went wrong about that ring," Anne said, the pieces beginning to fall together. "So he reported it as stolen. Like you say, it was a preemptive move. He couldn't know what, if anything, David had said to the police, so he tried to destroy any credibility that David might have." Reverend Tom nodded.

"And that's why he was so eager to have it written up in the newspaper too," Anne continued. "It was all part of his smear campaign. And that's why he was upset that Grace didn't run his accusation of David."

"But even though Grace was perceptive enough not to run it," Reverend Tom said, "the rumor still got around town. I think most people who knew anything about the incident were under the impression that David had done it."

"And I suppose Brockhurst had to file an insurance claim as well, if he hoped to pull off his ruse," Anne added, "The police might have noticed if he didn't. Though I suppose greed could have played a part there too. After all, he had to claim the higher value for the ring."

Reverend Tom nodded again. "That was how we reasoned as well." Anne cocked an inquiring eyebrow at "we," so Reverend Tom continued. "When Brockhurst started making noise about the allegedly stolen ring, Julie got very upset. After all, she had the ring in her possession. Well, she confided in Edie, and then they came to see me. And I agreed to help hide the ring."

He looked at Michael, who had been following the conversation intently. "I want to stress that I saw nothing wrong with this course of action. I absolutely believed that Julie and David were the legitimate owners of the ring, that it was not, in fact, stolen property. And I was also aware from Julie that David had been in touch with and was even working with the police in Philadelphia. So the authorities had been informed. At the same time, I didn't believe Julie to be in any danger on account of the ring. If the police learned she had it, well, she had a perfectly legitimate explanation to give them. I tried to reassure her about that. Unfortunately, she was extremely upset about the matter. Moreover, she was afraid that Brockhurst might learn that she had it, even though David had never told his former employer who his fiancé was."

Tom's face was thoughtful as he recalled his conversation with the young woman. "But Julie was frantic," he continued.

"The ring had to be kept safe because it was still their one solid piece of evidence. But she was too frightened to keep it near her."

"So you hid it in the Advent cabinet," said Anne, "and gave the key to Aunt Edie, so that it was locked up but they could still get at it any time they wanted."

Reverend Tom continued. "It seemed like a good idea. We have a filing cabinet that locks, but I didn't want to give them a key to that. The Advent cabinet is practically nothing *but* keys and locks."

"And then what?" Anne asked.

"Julie moved back to Philadelphia over the summer and left the ring behind. Edie tried to convince her to take it then, but she insisted she felt much safer leaving it where it was. I confess that I thought at the time that Edie might have tried harder to convince her, but it was too late to say so." He gave Anne a sheepish look, as if apologizing for even suggesting some criticism of Edie.

"Julie called Edie once or twice," continued Reverend Tom, looking at Michael. "She told her that the Philly police department was still pursuing their investigation with David's help. But in the meantime, she and David were planning their wedding and were very busy with that. She promised to get in touch when they were ready to reclaim the ring.

"When the Christmas season started to approach, Edie and I talked it over a little, but nobody seemed too surprised that one of those numerous keys should go missing. So we just announced that number seven was the cubby without a key and worked around it. We assumed that Julie and David would come back for the ring sometime before the next Christmas, that is, this Christmas, and then the missing key could be 'found' again."

Tom's face clouded a bit with old sorrow. "And then Edie passed away this year. And I didn't know how to contact Julie or David, nor did I know exactly what Edie had done with the key. So I decided I would just wait until I heard from them. There would be time enough at that point to come to you and start a search for the missing key. But in the meantime, you found it yourself."

Chapter Twenty-Six

E vents the next day moved quickly. In the afternoon, Anne was bringing Wendy up to date on the story of the ring, when she was surprised to receive a call from Michael Banks, asking if it would be convenient for her to come down to the police station for a few minutes. He didn't give details except to say that she might be able to help him with the case.

Wendy immediately shooed Anne out the door. Wendy herself was expected at home, but she told Anne she would await a full report.

When Anne arrived at the station, Michael greeted her and led her to the back of the building and into a room that looked like a large storage closet. But set into the wall was a window that looked into the next room, and through it, she could see six men all standing with their backs against the far wall. They were all shuffling their feet and looking about nervously, and a uniformed officer seemed to be watching over them.

The glorified closet in which she stood was dim, but the room beyond was brightly lit.

"It's one-way glass, as you've probably guessed," Michael said. "Have a look and tell me if you recognize any of those men."

Surprised and a little perplexed, Anne stepped up to peer through the glass. But she frowned as she did so, wondering just who it was she was supposed to be looking for. Brockhurst? Surely the police didn't need her to identify him. For a wild moment she thought of Russell Haines, but of course there was no reason for him to be in a line-up.

Michael rapped on the glass and the officer in the other room apparently spoke to the men. They all stopped fidgeting and held up small placards with numbers on them.

"Do you recognize any of them?" Michael asked again.

"No, I...Wait!" Anne gave a small gasp as a ferret-like face clicked in her memory. "Yes. Yes, I do."

"Which man, and where do you know him from?" Michael asked calmly.

"The second from the end. Number five, I mean. He was at the Diamond District the other day when Grace Hawkins and I went in to talk to Brockhurst."

"And you're sure about that?"

Anne nodded emphatically. "Oh yes. I mean, I don't know who he is or anything, but he was there when we arrived. And he slipped out, to the back of the store." She turned to Michael. "Who is he?"

He gave a slight smile. "I tell you what," he said, "if it would be convenient for me to come by this evening, I'll give you an unofficial update." He paused and added, "Perhaps you could arrange to have Reverend Tom there too."

* * *

"The first thing I did this morning," said Michael that evening, as he sat with a cup of tea cooling in front of him, "was call a buddy of mine on the Philly PD."

When dinner was over, Anne had packed the kids off to their rooms and awaited the arrival of Michael and Reverend Tom. When they were settled, Michael explained that, given their involvement in events up to the point, he was willing to bring them up to date, but that they had to treat the information as confidential. Both Anne and Reverend Tom had readily agreed, of course.

Now Michael continued, "He was able to connect me with someone working on the Diamond District business." He looked at Reverend Tom. "Even though you haven't heard from David or Julie for a while, it turns out that the investigation has been moving forward all this time. In fact, they've been making pretty good progress. They had one suspect they were all set to arrest when he disappeared from Philadelphia."

After a pause, Reverend Tom asked, "Was he the mastermind of the operation?"

Michael shook his head. "No, he was a junior member of the family, a cousin. More junior even than our Henderson Brockhurst. But he was stupid enough to slip up and give us something we could charge him with. And the police in Philly thought that he was weak enough that, with a little pressure, he could be persuaded to give evidence against the entire operation.

"The thing is, his own family doesn't think much better of young William than the Philly cops do, and they apparently figured out that the guy had made himself vulnerable, so they somehow spirited him away. And Philly PD has been trying to track him."

He gave them a satisfied smile. "They e-mailed a picture to me."

Suddenly, Anne said, "Was that the man today?"

Michael nodded and explained to Reverend Tom about the lineup. "After the things you told us yesterday, Reverend, my plan had been to go have another talk with Henderson Brockhurst. It was just fortuitous that I decided to check with Philly first. Mostly because I was in early on a Saturday and Brockhurst wasn't going to be open yet. But I knew that my buddy in Philly would be around, and it happened that I was able to connect with the other guys there right away.

"So imagine my surprise, when I get down to the Diamond District and there's Philly's fugitive suspect, big as life. That was more luck, because the two of them weren't paying attention, and I walked right in before they knew I was there. If they had been on their toes, he might well have slipped out before I spotted him."

Michael gave another little smile. "Actual foot chases aren't as exciting as what you see on television. The guy tried to run out the back but he didn't even make it as far as the rear exit before I had him. Now that we've got him, he's trying to blow a lot of smoke and confuse the issue. One of the things that he claimed was that he just arrived in Blue Hill this morning. And that's when I remembered you saying, Anne, that you'd found someone with Brockhurst when you went in the other day. So I thought I'd just have you come down and see if this is the same guy. Every lie that we can catch him in just gives us more leverage to make him talk."

"I couldn't imagine why you wanted me to come down," Anne interjected.

"Every little bit helps," Michael said. "And in the meantime, one of my colleagues from Philadelphia was already on the way. Once he got here, the two of us were able to break this guy completely. He's given up the whole scheme."

"So what becomes of Henderson Brockhurst?" Reverend Tom asked.

Michael hesitated and smiled. "I can't share all the details of an ongoing investigation just yet."

Anne cast him a shrewd glance. "He's got somebody watching Brockhurst right now," she concluded, "to make sure he doesn't run. He's probably just waiting on an arrest warrant."

Michael's grin broadened and he tried to hide it by sipping his tea.

"But won't Brockhurst have warned the rest of his family?" Anne asked. "I mean, if cousin Billy's been picked up. They can't know for sure what he's said, but it can't be good." Michael continued to maintain his silence and sip his tea. "The Philadelphia police must be watching the rest of them," Anne decided. "Probably while they wait for their own warrants." Though Michael still didn't respond, Anne was confident she had guessed correctly.

"Well, that's wonderful," Reverend Tom said. "I'm so happy to hear that it all seems to be working out." He cast his own sly glance at Michael. "It was very kind of you to come by to tell us all this."

Michael acknowledged the implication with a laugh. "Well, yes, you're right. I didn't come by solely just to bring you up to date." He pulled a folded piece of paper from his pocket and set it on the coffee table before him. "You may not have heard from David and Julie, but the Philly PD has been in touch with them regularly. My colleague brought their contact information out with him.

"If you're still interested in returning that ring," he added with a wink.

* * *

On the last Sunday before Christmas, all the "treasures" from the Advent cabinet were on display on a special table in the fellowship hall. One of the church's board members had found the time to do a brief write-up on what each of the items symbolized. The mix of odd items included toys, shells, a photocopied poem, and an old yellowed piece of sheet music. Much of the fun of the Advent cabinet had been the revealing of the treasures in the cubbies and the ways in which they were associated with Christmas. This day there had been a hand-knit dish rag, an unshelled walnut, a short pair of chop sticks, a packet of flower seeds, a domino piece, a votive candle, and — quite ironic to Anne — a ring.

This ring was just a child's toy. It was made of pink plastic and had a gaudy blue stone in the center. Still, Anne looked around nervously to see who might have put the ring in and what sort of message that person was trying to send. She wondered if it might have been Sophie, trying to make some strange accusatory gesture. Reverend Tom had told her that Sophie was planning to move to California to be with her sister. Could this be some sort of parting shot? When she cast a quick glance in her direction, however, Sophie's face was blank as usual.

Of everything that had happened in her search for the ring's owner, the incident with Sophie was the one thing Anne felt worst about. It was a lesson to be careful of unintended consequences, no matter how good one's intentions are. She smiled to herself: She had managed to come up with her own little lesson for that particular Advent treasure.

Reverend Tom betrayed no special reaction to the ring, but he chose the packet of seeds to focus on, with a short message about hope and new life. Afterward, when most of the parishioners had left and only Anne and Helen were still drying dishes, he commented on the ring.

"I happen to know that Evie Bronski put the toy ring in. It's a bit of a coincidence, actually. She initially stuck it in there because her three-year-old had picked it up from someplace and Evie was afraid she was going to put it in her mouth and swallow it. You see? She put it in the cabinet to hide it. Then later when she told me about it, she decided to leave it in there as a treasure. I think she intended it as a bit of a compliment to you."

CHAPTER TWENTY-SEVEN

O n Monday, Christmas Eve Day, Anne was very glad that she had long before decided to close the library for the holiday. It turned out she had quite a bit to do that morning to get ready for the guests who were driving out from Philadelphia: David Courtney and Julie Helzl.

Between the imminent arrival of Christmas, the Nativity play scheduled for that evening, and now the arrival of unexpected guests, Ben and Liddie were practically bouncing off the walls with excitement. Since the library was locked up, she sent them down there to play, but they were too keyed up to stay in one place and were soon back in the kitchen, clamoring for attention. Even Hershey, picking up on the kids' excitement, was bounding around underfoot.

Finally, Anne set them to rehearsing for the performance, with Ben practicing his lines and Liddie "helping." The focus at least calmed Ben a little bit.

One of the disadvantages of living in an apartment in Brooklyn had always been that there was no place to send the kids when they were keyed up. She might banish them from the kitchen while she tried to prepare a Christmas dinner, say, but they really couldn't go very far. She'd thought that one of the advantages of living in her aunt's rambling Victorian would at least be the opportunity to send the kids to the other end of the house, so that they were still safe inside but out of her hair. But her children insisted on staying only one or two rooms removed from her, as if they were still in their Park Slope apartment.

She heard a muffled crash from the living room. "What's going on out there?" she called, a warning edge to her voice.

"Nothing," came back the chorused reply. She cocked an ear for more sounds. No further crashes, no crying—apparently nobody was hurt. She decided she'd let them work it out.

She smiled, suddenly glad to have them close by after all.

Soon Reverend Tom arrived, and he graciously amused the kids in the living room while Anne finished up the last of the preparations.

Even though it was only lunch, she spread out one of Edie's holiday tablecloths and set out plates and glasses. As she worked, she reflected on the ring and how it had consumed her attention over the course of the season. *Why?* She wondered. Yes, she was curious and tenacious by nature, and yes, she had sensed from the start that the ring wasn't just misplaced but was lost to its owner. Yes, she had wondered what Edie's involvement was in the story. And, yes, finding the owners and reuniting Julie and David with the ring was rewarding. But somehow that didn't satisfy her.

She stepped back to appreciate the table she had just set. Something was not right about that either. She tapped her finger against her lips as she made a mental list of everything she needed to set out on the table. "Oh," she blurted, when she thought of it. "The centerpiece." A simple arrangement of garland ends, baby's breath flowers, and pinecones finished the setting.

David and Julie arrived on time and rang at the family's entrance to the house. Reverend Tom went down to greet them, since he already knew them and Anne was still putting the finishing touches on the things in the kitchen.

Reverend Tom brought them up the back stairs and made introductions. Julie was just as she had been described: Tall and willowy, her blonde hair was pulled back in a loose ponytail and her expression reflected the seriousness of a scholar. Then she smiled and presented Anne with a simple bouquet of flowers, and her face was full of warmth and kindness. David stepped forward, shook her hand with both of his, and then, noticing Ben and Liddie standing shyly behind Reverend Tom, he leaned over and shook their hands effusively as well.

"I hear you two are going to be stars tonight!" David said. He had brown hair that just brushed the tops of his ears, and eyes that crinkled when he smiled. The kids responded immediately to his outgoing nature and stepped forward to tell him more about the play.

As Reverend Tom took charge of the coats and the kids chatted with David, Julie said solemnly to Anne, "I'm so sorry to hear about Edie. She was a wonderful woman and very kind to me. And I'm sorry to think how out of touch I've been that I've only learned of her death in the past few days." Anne noticed that there was a wedding band on the woman's finger, and Julie saw her observe it. "Yes," she said, "it's true that we've had some things to distract us in the meantime. But I still feel bad."

"I think it's perfectly understandable," Anne said, "and I'm sure Aunt Edie would think so too. Congratulations to both of you!" David and Julie both beamed.

"I suppose that, without further ado," Anne continued, "I should go ahead and return this to you." She picked up the ring box from the table and handed it to Julie.

Julie opened the box slowly and stared for some time at the ring. Her eyes held a hint of tears when she finally said, "It's even more beautiful than I remembered."

"Yes, well," said David, "it's taken us on quite a little journey too."

Julie withdrew the ring, put it on, and held out her hand to admire it. When she looked up again, the tears were falling down her face. "Thank you," she said quietly to Anne. "You don't know what this means. A *completion*, I guess, is the word I'm looking for. It's just a symbol, but now I feel that David and I can move on from that terrible business."

As she spoke, David was nodding his head vigorously. It suddenly struck Anne that Julie was speaking what David would have said. They seemed to be so in concert with one another. Anne saw that they were not only in love but were best friends as well. Just as she and Eric had been.

Anne felt herself starting to tear up, so she said quickly, "Wouldn't you like to see how the house has changed?" and she gave them a thorough tour, going somewhat more into the details of the renovation than was strictly necessary. Though she knew that Julie had briefly been her aunt's lodger, she was still caught by surprise occasionally when a comment from Julie revealed her former intimate familiarity with the house. She remarked on some changes that Anne herself had long since ceased to think about, so accustomed had she become to the modifications that had turned the home into a library.

But through Julie's eyes, she once again caught startling glimpses of her great-aunt Edie's home beneath all the changes. And she was reminded afresh just how thoroughly that home had been transformed for the sake of its new role in the community.

They returned to the large open living area on the second floor to have their meal, and Anne began to feel that sense of disorientation diminish. As lunch progressed, she, Julie, and Reverend Tom exchanged many stories and anecdotes about Edie and about Blue Hill. Hearing Julie talk about her beloved great-aunt reminded Anne once again what a strong, but understated, force for good Aunt Edie had been.

Over the course of the meal, David questioned Ben and Liddie about their roles in the production. David mentioned that he had once played the shepherd in a Nativity production when he was small.

"I spent the next month telling everyone that I wanted to grow up to be an actual shepherd," he recalled with amusement. "They had a hard time convincing me that there wasn't really much call for shepherds any longer."

After the meal, Julie and David stayed to help Anne clear the table, while Reverend Tom made his excuses and dashed off to church. Although Anne had invited the young couple to attend the Blue Hill Community Church's Nativity play, she hadn't expected them to stay for it, so she was surprised when she overheard David assure Ben and Liddie that he would be there and would be sitting as close to the front as he could.

They left to get a little more shopping done while they still had time, but they assured Anne that if they got to the church first, they would save her a seat.

* * *

At last it was time to head down to the church for the evening performance of the Nativity play. Anne bundled up the costumes for Ben and Liddie, double-checking to make sure she had all the accessories. As the narrator, Ben didn't need much beyond a jacket and his clip-on tie, but Liddie still had a costume to worry about. "Okay, here are the angel wings," Anne said, looking about, "but halo...halo?

"Liddie, have you been playing with your halo?" Anne asked sharply, but Liddie just looked at her blankly. "Well, it's not here."

"I'll look in the library," Ben cried and jogged off, as Anne shouted after him, futilely, not to run in the house.

"Liddie, you look again in your bedroom, and I'll look in the living room." But a thorough search didn't turn up the halo. As the time was nearing for them to be at the church, Anne's mind raced to think of an alternative. She thought perhaps she could crinkle up some aluminum foil, and even congratulated herself that this was a brilliant idea as she dashed for the box still on the kitchen counter, when Hershey, who'd been napping in a corner of the kitchen, gave a grunting sigh and rolled over, revealing Liddie's halo, rumpled but intact.

* * *

Even though the performers were required to arrive early, they found the parking lot already filling rapidly when they pulled in and took a spot in the last row. Ben and Liddie jumped out and went racing off to the church offices, which were serving as the production's greenroom. Anne followed with Liddie's costume, forgotten in the excitement.

Walking in, she was surprised by the level of activity. It appeared that quite a few parents had come backstage to give their children a pre-performance pep talk. More than a few of the kids seemed to be suffering from jitters, and the nervous excitement in the room was palpable and cheerful.

Having delivered the angel costume to Marian, who was overseeing the dressing of all the actors, Anne turned to leave. She was suddenly surprised to find Suzanne amidst the bustle, albeit looking somewhat lost. "Should you be out of bed?" Anne asked.

Anne received a doleful look in response. "Probably not," Suzanne said, "but I've never missed a performance yet."

Privately, Anne hoped Suzanne's presence would not cause a problem. After the way Brad had stepped in to lead the production in her absence, Suzanne's return could prove to be a distraction. She looked about for Brad and spotted him conferring with Alex. She briefly wondered at Alex's presence there but turned back to Suzanne with a sudden decision. "Well, it may be that you've never missed a performance," she said, "but from the looks of you, this may be one that you should enjoy from the comfort of the audience."

Suzanne looked around sadly. "I think you may be right. I may have pushed myself too much." She began to walk out with Anne. "Every year I've done this, the pageant always seems to be on the verge of falling apart at the last minute, then somehow it all comes together."

"I'm sure that will be the case this year as well," Anne assured her and led her out toward the sanctuary.

Anne spotted Wendy and Chad Pyle sitting near the back. Every one of their seven children was involved in some aspect of the evening's production, and Anne suspected the outing served as a sort of date night for her friend and her husband—a rare occasion when their children weren't clamoring for their attention. Wendy waved at Anne with a happy smile.

Mildred Farley sat near the middle of the church with a woman Anne didn't recognize. Perhaps a family member in town for the holiday. Mildred was turned out elegantly, as usual, in a blue pantsuit and her gray hair falling in soft curls around her face. She gave Anne a warm smile and mouthed "Merry Christmas!"

Sherri Devereaux caught Anne's attention eagerly from the other side of the aisle and waved her over. Her eyes shone with excitement as she leaned forward to talk with Anne and gestured to the man and woman sitting next to her. "My parents told me we're all going to New York in the spring!" she said. The young woman did a little happy dance right in the pew where she sat. "I can't wait!"

Anne smiled. "How exciting for you. I'll try to put a list together of places you should see on your trip."

Anne turned her attentions up the aisle. True to their promise, David and Julie were seated near the front, waving eagerly for Anne and Suzanne to join them. Just as she was about to sit down, however, a truly devastating thought occurred to Anne.

"I forgot my camera!" she cried, loud enough for the people in the pews nearby to turn and look sympathetically. Anne pawed frantically through her pocketbook in the forlorn hope that it had somehow snuck in by itself, berating herself silently the whole time. She did find her phone and decided it would have to do, though she knew from experience that the quality of the video it produced was very poor. What should she tell her parents?

Just then she felt a nudge in her side. It was Julie, drawing Anne's attention to David, who said in a stage whisper, "I've got you covered," as he held up a digital camera.

* * *

The sanctuary was decorated throughout with candles, boughs of evergreens, and holly. As the lights dimmed a little over the pews, a solemn hush came over the crowd. The pianist played a meditative piece by Brahms, which was the perfect background for quiet reflection.

Then Reverend Tom stepped forward and welcomed the audience to Blue Hill Community Church, and he said a brief prayer before stepping aside for Brad's introduction of the play.

When Brad stepped to the podium and looked over the packed sanctuary, it was clear that he was a little nervous, but Anne noticed that he did something she'd seen Douglas do many times. He squared his shoulders and pulled himself up as if a string were lifting him from the crown of his head, and he slowly inhaled. Anne wondered if the ex-military man had been giving Brad some tips on public speaking.

When he began to introduce the play and to explain the novelty this year of having more speaking parts, she saw almost a new person. Brad was confident, less pedantic, and more at ease with himself. He spoke to the audience in an intimate yet commanding way. It was amazing how he'd grown over the course of the season from a kid who seemed to have bitten off more than he could chew to a young man who had risen to the challenge.

Next up to the podium came her son, Ben, the narrator of the pageant. His voice quivered just for a moment as he launched into his recitation, but he soldiered on and he too began to relax into his role of providing background into the world that Joseph and Mary lived in.

As he spoke, the two young angels, Liddie and Becky, stepped forward. Off to one side, Brad led them in singing "O Come, O Come Emmanuel." Their clear, thin voices were supported but not overwhelmed by Brad's tenor, and after the first verse, they were gradually joined by the other members of the production. At the third verse, the angels raised their hands for the audience to join in.

Following the hymn, most of the performers cleared the stage area, and the story of Joseph and Mary unfolded. As the innkeeper cast the travelers away with comic gusto, fans quietly set up in the back added a bit of chill to the air so that the audience got a sense of the winter night that the couple faced. The young cast gathered again and sang "Silent Night" a cappella, then parted to reveal a hay-filled manger, an inviting respite for the exhausted couple.

As the entire congregation sang "Away in a Manger," though, the lights flickered out. For a moment, the audience faltered in its singing, but the kids and Brad continued at extra volume, as if nothing had happened, so Anne, like everyone else, hoped it was a minor glitch and kept going also.

Then came the sound of a small thud overhead. Everyone looked up to see a weblike structure descend over the stage and slowly start to glow. A large white star crafted from webbing and small white Christmas tree lights majestically unfolded over the manger. The audience was entranced. Anne cast a sideways look at Brad, who was glowing, but she also noticed Alex standing beside him with a satisfied grin on his face. So that is what he'd been up to all this time!

The three wise men Gaspar, Melchior, and Balthazar, presented their gifts, resplendent in the colorful velvet robes Marian had sewn from curtains, and they sang "We Three Kings."

As the cast assembled for its closing tableau, the entire congregation joined in "Joy to the World," and a brilliant light beamed out from Alex's complex star to illuminate the infant in the cradle, a dramatic and inspiring climax to the seasonal tale of hope and joy.

After the performers had taken their bows, Reverend Tom stepped up to wish everyone a Merry Christmas, and the pianist played "Joy to the World" again, as everyone seemed to stand up and start talking at once. Chaos had once again—joyfully—descended on Blue Hill Community Church.

Next to Anne, Suzanne was weeping and thumping her hand over her heart. "I've never seen anything so beautiful in my life," she said, then sneezed. David held up his camera to show Anne that he'd gotten lots of pictures. "Wonderful production!" he exclaimed.

Anne shouldered her way through the crowd to collect Ben and Liddie and congratulate them on their wonderful performances, and to commend Brad for his deep and moving production of the Nativity play. Suddenly a word, one Julie had used earlier in the day flashed into her thoughts.

"Completion!" she whispered aloud, though no one heard her.

Her life had been turned upside down in recent years, but in Blue Hill she had found a home for her family, a calling in the community, and the awareness that, whatever the route she had taken, she had come full circle to where she needed to be.

About the Authors

Emily Thomas is the pen name for a team of writers who have come together to create the series Secrets of the Blue Hill Library. *The Christmas Key* was written by the wife-and-husband team of Jolyn and William Sharp.

Jolyn is a magazine editor; her husband, William, is a fund-raiser for a university. After a number of years in New York City, they now live in New Hampshire with a bossy cat and a cowed dog. Jolyn enjoys knitting, weaving, and gardening, and William leads book discussions at their local library. They read more detective novels than is good for them.

A Conversation with the Authors

Q. How did you get started as a writing team?

A. Since we've been married we've always shared our writing with one another, but we started working as a team when we wrote a few of the books in Guideposts' Tales from Grace Chapel Inn series.

Q. What are the challenges and rewards of collaborating with not only other authors on a series but with a spouse? How does it compare to writing a stand-alone novel?

A. Despite the image we generally have of the lonely writer toiling away in a garret, collaborative writing is not really that unusual. Think of the teams that write films and television series, the latter also featuring continuing characters and settings, despite the multiple authors. The success of series with multiple authors depends upon good editors who ensure the tone and continuity of the series.

We find, working with one another, that our imaginations really blossom when we start hashing out a story or plot together. We have to know when to compromise, but sometimes our compromises lead to more interesting ideas.

Q. *Describe your writing process.*

A. We talk constantly about where the book is going and what the next scene should be. Generally, one of us will start working on a chapter, then the other will tidy up that piece and expand it. In *The Christmas Key*, Jolyn wrote the subplots separately, then William wove them into the main body of the novel.

Q. *When you are not writing, what are your favorite activities?*

A. Jolyn loves to knit and weave. William is an avid reader and now is totally addicted to audio books. Both enjoy crossword puzzles, word games, and (weather permitting) kayaking and hiking.

Q. *What advice would you give an aspiring novelist?*

A. Read. Read everything, especially contemporary fiction, and the sort of books that you want to write. Also read your own work out loud to hear what is good and what is infelicitous, what races and what drags.

Q. *Which character in Secrets of the Blue Hill Library are you most like? Why?*

A. We're very much involved with our local library, so it's interesting to compare our real-life library to the fictional one in the Blue Hill series. We share Anne's enthusiasm for reading and for sharing her passion with others. Mildred is someone we see as having the life skills to pick up and run with any situation. In *The Christmas Key*, when Anne is fretting about so much to do for the Dickens of a Christmas event, Mildred steps right up and handles the refreshments for her. We'd like to have a little more Mildred in us.

Q. *Which scene in this story was your favorite to write? Which was the most challenging for you?*

A. We had a lot of fun with the whole Dickens of a Christmas arc, and the final scene where Santa visits the library. The most challenging was writing about Brad because we wanted to show him — and the congregation — growing and blossoming as the Nativity came together, fell apart, and came together again.

Q. *Anne Gibson likes to drink her coffee without cream or sugar. What are your coffee-shop favorites?*

A. We both drink our coffee with cream (no sugar), but we disagree on strong versus mild coffee.

Q. *What are your favorite Christmas books?*

A. William: If any writer can be said to own Christmas, it is Charles Dickens.

Jolyn: *The Polar Express.* I didn't discover it until I was an adult. But I like how vividly realized it is.

RECIPES FROM THE LIBRARY GUILD

Mildred's Ginger Cookies

2 tablespoons candied lemon
    or orange rind (optional)

⅞ cup sugar

¾ cup butter, softened

1 large egg

¼ cup molasses

2 cups flour

1 teaspoon ginger

1 teaspoon cinnamon

⅛ teaspoon freshly ground
    pepper

½ teaspoon salt

2 teaspoons baking soda

Preheat oven to 350 degrees.

    If using candied lemon or orange rind: mince the candied rind and combine with one-eighth cup of sugar. Set aside. Cream together the butter and remaining sugar, add the egg and molasses, and mix well. Sift together the dry ingredients and combine with the butter mixture.

    Roll the dough into balls, about the size of a large marble, then roll in the sugar mix. Place on ungreased cookie sheet about two inches apart (they will flatten out as they bake). Bake for twelve to fourteen minutes. Sprinkle a little sugar on the tops of the cookies when they first come out of the oven, then cool them on racks.

FROM THE GUIDEPOSTS ARCHIVES

The following story by Dina Donohue originally appeared in the December 1966 issue of Guideposts *magazine.*

For years now, whenever Christmas pageants are talked about in a certain little town in the Midwest, someone is sure to mention the name of Wallace Purling. Wally's performance in one annual production of the Nativity play has slipped into the realm of legend. But the old-timers who were in the audience that night never tire of recalling exactly what happened.

Wally was nine that year and in the second grade, though he should have been in the fourth. Most people in town knew that he had difficulty keeping up. He was big and awkward, slow in movement and mind. Still, Wally was well liked by the other children in his class, all of whom were smaller than he, though the boys had trouble hiding their irritation when Wally would ask to play ball with them or any game, for that matter, in which winning was important.

They'd find a way to keep him out, but Wally would hang around anyway—not sulking, just hoping. He was a helpful boy, always willing and smiling, and the protector, paradoxically, of the underdog. If the older boys chased the younger ones away, it would be Wally who'd say, "Can't they stay? They're no bother."

Wally fancied the idea of being a shepherd in the Christmas pageant, but the play's director, Miss Lumbard, assigned him a more important role. After all, she reasoned, the innkeeper did not have too many lines, and Wally's size would make his refusal of lodging to Joseph more forceful.

And so it happened that the usual large, partisan audience gathered for the town's yearly extravaganza of crooks and crèches, of beards, crowns, halos and a whole stageful of squeaky voices. No one on stage or off was more caught up in the magic of the night than Wallace Purling. They said later that he stood in the wings and watched the performance with such fascination that Miss Lumbard had to make sure he didn't wander onstage before his cue.

Then the time came when Joseph appeared, slowly, tenderly guiding Mary to the door of the inn. Joseph knocked hard on the wooden door set into the painted backdrop. Wally the innkeeper was there, waiting.

"What do you want?" Wally said, swinging the door open with a brusque gesture.

"We seek lodging."

"Seek it elsewhere." Wally spoke vigorously. "The inn is filled."

"Sir, we have asked everywhere in vain. We have traveled far and are very weary."

"There is no room in this inn for you." Wally looked properly stern.

"Please, good innkeeper, this is my wife, Mary. She is heavy with child and needs a place to rest. Surely you must have some small corner for her. She is so tired."

Now, for the first time, the innkeeper relaxed his stiff stance and looked down at Mary. With that, there was a long pause, long enough to make the audience a bit tense with embarrassment.

"No! Begone!" the prompter whispered.

"No!" Wally repeated automatically. "Begone!"

Joseph sadly placed his arm around Mary and Mary laid her head upon her husband's shoulder and the two of them started to move away. The innkeeper did not return inside his inn, however. Wally stood there in the doorway, watching the forlorn couple. His mouth was open, his brow creased with concern, his eyes filling unmistakably with tears.

And suddenly this Christmas pageant became different from all others.

"Don't go, Joseph," Wally called out. "Bring Mary back." And Wallace Purling's face grew into a bright smile. "You can have my room."

Some people in town thought that the pageant had been ruined. Yet there were others — many, many others — who considered it the most Christmas of all Christmas pageants they had ever seen.

Read on for a sneak peek of another exciting book
in *Secrets of the Blue Hill Library*!

Off the Shelf

The three- and four-year-olds squirmed, trying to see the
pictures in the book as Anne Gibson read. They pushed to
their knees, leaning forward, restless.

"Oh, the places you'll go," Anne read on. Her voice filled with
wonder as a dozen pairs of little eyes grew round. This was what
she loved most about being a librarian, seeing the anticipation that
each new story brought to young readers and knowing the
limitlessness of where those stories could take them.

She glanced toward the window in the Children's Room of the
Blue Hill Library. A dreary Monday. Rain drizzled down the wavy
pane. It was chilly for April. She tugged her sweater tighter against
her shoulders and turned the page.

A row of mothers sat in the back of the room listening in.
Bobby Phillips scooted closer. He was practically in Anne's
lap. Anne motioned with a finger for him to move back and he
obeyed.

She read on, imbuing her voice with wonder. The heavy
footfall of men's dress shoes on hardwood came down the hall of
the old Victorian house that now served as the library for the small
town of Blue Hill in rural Pennsylvania. Mayor Bultman squeezed

into the room. He was a shorter man, 5'4", stout. He had eyes that sparkled and a nice, albeit crooked, smile.

Though his wife volunteered often at the library, Mayor Bultman rarely made an appearance. Anne wondered what brought him in. Today was twice in three days. That was a new record. She kept reading, though she could hear the rumble of his deep voice as he talked to the mothers throughout the rest of the story. The kids' squirming intensified. Heads turned back, curious to hear what the man was saying. Anne glanced up, scolding him with a finger to her lips. The man's face turned red, but he nodded quickly and stopped his conversation.

Finally, when the story was complete and the children dispersed to pick out books to take home, Anne stood and moved toward the adults, including Mayor Bultman. He held out a hand to Anne. "I didn't mean to distract them like that. I forgot how short the attention span of youngsters can be." He said "youngsters" as if it were a foreign word he was testing out for the first time.

"They were pretty antsy before you came," Anne admitted, shaking hands with him. His hand was cold. "I'm sorry but you missed Betty," Anne added. "She left for her hair appointment about fifteen minutes ago."

The mayor shook his head. "I'm here to see you, actually."

"Oh?" Anne raised an eyebrow.

"Yes, ma'am." He glanced around the room.

"Are you looking for something to read? I just got a few political biographies in that you might like—"

"Oh no, no," he interrupted. "I'm far too busy for reading. I wanted to talk to you about the new tax levy that's coming up for a vote with the town council in a couple of weeks. You know" — he paused to run a hand across the back of his neck — "the library could really benefit from such a tax. There'd be money for new library programs, maybe some of those Internet things people are always talking about..."

Anne smiled. She knew exactly the types of things he meant — she'd been dreaming of expanding their services for a while now as she recalled the plethora of options the public library she'd worked for in New York City had offered, a virtual treasure trove of information. Things like online access to paid informational databases, more staff so they could have more open hours, books in new technologies, tutors for after-school homework help and language learning... And there were never enough computers.

She liked to think that someone could come to the public library and get a college education for free just by checking out books, requesting interlibrary loan titles that weren't on hand locally, and researching information available online. That was the power of the library — the freedom it gave to any person regardless of status or income. That was, if those resources were available. As it was here in Blue Hill, Anne couldn't even afford to pay most of her regular helpers at the library. Which meant the work fell mainly to her — with two young children who could be difficult at times. Most of her helpers were volunteers, even Wendy Pyle, though she helped at the library as often as any part-time employee. And Anne's salary was paid for by the grant her great-aunt Edie had created when she'd left Anne the house with the stipulation that the town of Blue Hill use it as its library. The town council had signed a fifty-year, dollar-a-year lease, granting the town of Blue Hill use of the first floor and a good portion of the second for the purpose of a library, but the maintenance and operation still required a sizeable amount of funding.

"So this levy is just for the library?"

The mayor shook his head. "Oh no, indeed. We have plans to build a community center as well." He told her about the multimillion dollar complex that would house an Olympic-sized swimming pool, an indoor ice skating rink, racquetball courts, a gym and workout room with weights, as well as a meeting room for various activities. "This kind of center could put Blue Hill on the map, give folks in surrounding towns a reason to come here." His face glowed with excitement.

"Wow. That sounds great," Anne said, truly impressed by the proposal. "But what exactly do you need from me?"

He ran a hand down the lapel of his dark suit and shifted his stance as a four-year-old boy darted between them, a stack of books in his small arms. His mother followed right behind him, offering Anne a look of apology.

The mayor cleared his throat. "I need help getting the word out. Letting people know how this could benefit us...them."

"So, maybe you could hold an informational meeting here at the library?" Anne offered. "To let people know what the levy is all about?"

Bob nodded. "Exactly! And some radio spots, flyers around town..." Several businesses had community bulletin boards in their entryways for just such announcements. "I'd want to do that meeting soon since the vote is coming up."

He pulled out a pocket calendar and a stubby pencil. "Would next Monday work?"

Anne tried to recall if she had any conflicts in her schedule, or if the library's Reference Room, where they would hold the meeting, was already booked. "I can't think of anything. But that's awfully soon—it'll be hard to get the word out in such a short time." She hadn't even said yes and already she was running into obstacles.

"Well, we don't have to decide that now." He waved a hand.

Anne studied him for a moment before the man pressed on. "I've got some *Vote Yes* signs for people to post in their yards as well. I was hoping you or maybe some of your volunteers here at the library could go door-to-door... With the election coming up I don't want people to think I'm just out campaigning. This is bigger than me and whether I get reelected. It's about helping the people of Blue Hill. With someone like you out stumping for it, the levy is bound to get support. The mayor can only do so much. It takes the support of upstanding citizens like yourself to make this kind of thing happen."

Anne was flattered that the mayor thought she might have any kind of influence in the small town, especially having just moved back after being away so many years. But, though she didn't let her face show it, she groaned inwardly at the suggestion. She hated the time such a commitment would take away from her family. Time was a precious commodity for a widow with two children of her own. She already put in almost fifty hours a week at the library. Yet she could see the mayor's point. And the library could definitely use the added funds, if only to pay for more part-time help so she could reduce her hours.

"Is there a lot of opposition to the levy?" Anne asked.

The mayor's face puckered and he pulled out a cloth handkerchief to blow his nose before answering. "Well...," he hedged. "Yes, actually. There are always those who'd rather not pay taxes at all. I don't know how they think libraries and the like are funded, but... that Jim Tousley —" He spit the insurance agent's name out as if it were a curse. The mayor had always appeared on the ballet unopposed, until now. This year the unassuming Jim Tousley was giving Mayor Bultman a run for his money, running against him in the upcoming election. Jim came in often to the library, looking for a good novel or nonfiction book to read.

"He's out there poisoning the water." The mayor scowled. "I don't know what he's trying to prove. I'm doing a good job here in Blue Hill." He looked straight at Anne. "Aren't I?"

"I'm sure it's nothing personal," Anne said.

The man took a breath and that crooked smile returned. "So...?" he pushed after a moment's wait.

"Aunt Edie always told me to sleep on things before giving an answer. Can I think about it? Get back to you tomorrow?"

"Fair enough." The mayor nodded, turning to leave the room as Marianne Cummings, his own personal assistant came in. A petite brunette, she looked younger than her thirty-some years.

She seemed surprised to see him. "Oh, Mr. Mayor!" she said.

"I thought you were at the office."

Her face turned red. "I was, and then I realized I promised Todd that I'd pick up a few books for him before he got home from school." The young woman was a widow who was often found in the library getting books for herself and her children.

"Well…" He was about to go on, but Wendy Pyle came bustling in.

The forty-two-year-old mother of seven had more energy than almost anyone else Anne knew. She volunteered at the library several times a week and kept up with her children's many and varied activities, from soccer to Girl Scouts to basketball.

"Anne, have you seen any of these books?" She handed Anne a list of children's titles. "I have looked high and low for them." Her gaze turned to the mayor as Anne scanned the list. "Hello, Mayor," she greeted with a nod.

The list named four titles, all children's classics: *Goodnight Moon* by Margaret Wise Brown; *Curious George* by H. A. Rey; *Alexander and the Terrible, Horrible, No Good, Very Bad Day* by Judith Viorst and Ray Cruz; and *Harold and the Purple Crayon* by Crockett Johnson.

"You know," Anne said, an image from only two days prior flashing through her memory, "I saw these titles on the table in here Saturday right before the Easter egg hunt." She pointed to the short table in the bright, colorful Children's Room where several kids were devouring picture books at the moment, whispering to each other and giggling about the silly drawings. The previous Saturday the library had hosted its first annual Easter egg hunt outdoors, on the expansive lawn that surrounded the large Victorian. A crowd had shown up for the event, making it a huge success.

"I know!" Wendy said, nodding her head. "That's what's bugging me—I saw them too, but now I can't find them anywhere."

"Did someone check them out?"

The mayor, who had been ready to leave only a moment before, now watched Anne and Wendy with mouth slightly agape. Marianne too seemed almost stunned.

Wendy shook her head. "I looked. They haven't been checked out in a few weeks, and they're all listed as returned and on the shelves."

"What are you suggesting?" the mayor piped in, his body stiffening, his brow furrowing. "That someone stole them?"

"Well, if they were stolen, we'll need to replace them—those four are classics," Wendy said. "And *Curious George* was a signed original."

That piece of news surprised even Anne.

"Why would you have such a valuable title on your shelves to be checked out by anyone?" the mayor asked, his gaze turning to Anne.

"I had no idea it was a signed original," Anne admitted, a bit puzzled by the news. If she'd known it was so valuable, she would have at least put it in the historical display at the front of the library and looked into its worth.

Wendy waved a hand. "Don't go blaming Anne," she said to Mayor Bultman. "I donated it when the library first opened. We have so many books lying around our house…Truth is my mother—she was an artist, liked to dabble in painting—met H. A. Rey years ago and had it signed. Mother had hundreds of signed books. It was kind of her thing, to go to book signings, meet authors. Some titles were so obscure, but she'd drive down to Philly whenever she heard of a signing. Maybe that's why I love reading so much." She shrugged. "It didn't seem like a big deal to me, to give it to the library. I have several signed H. A. Rey books at home."

"And now it's been stolen," the mayor repeated.

Anne lifted a calming hand. "The titles were probably just put in the wrong spot on the shelves. It happens all the time. Someone comes in, thinks about checking a title out, then puts it back in the wrong place."

The mayor leaned close, as if he were telling a secret, and said in a low voice, "You really don't want the people of Blue Hill to hear that their precious books are going missing. If they think you aren't responsible with their resources, our levy is dead in the water, Anne. You understand what I'm saying, don't you?" His glance flicked to his assistant. The woman was motionless, eyes round, watching them.

"Well…" Anne opened her mouth to speak, but no words came out.

"I'm telling you." The man took a deep breath. "I'm serious. If you let word get out that your inventory is disappearing, residents will think that their money will be wasted. Trust me. Just keep quiet about this."

"I'm sure this isn't a *theft*," Anne said again, raising an eyebrow at Wendy over the man's shoulder. "There's nothing to worry about."

Finally he gave a nod and said to his assistant, "Marianne, we need to head back."

"I'll be along in just a few minutes," she said. "After I find Todd's books." Then she turned to search the shelves.

He said his farewells, then disappeared down the hall once again toward the entrance. Anne could hear his dress shoes tapping on the hardwood floors. She turned back to Wendy. "Is he always so high-strung?"

"Like a violin," Wendy said with a chuckle. "I better go tell Mrs. Thompson she'll have to come back later for those books."

Anne nodded. "I'll keep looking."

Once the crowd thinned down to its usual Monday ebb, Anne and Wendy went back through the shelves. Children often shoved books in the wrong spot. No doubt that was the reason the titles were missing. But after a full search of the shelves they didn't find even a single one of the four books.

"Maybe they got put in another room," Wendy suggested. So they moved into the other rooms, looking, scanning, but nothing. Anne even went upstairs to check Liddie's room. Her five-year-old daughter loved to read almost as much as Anne did, and Anne wouldn't put it past her to take her favorites up to her room for bedtime enjoyment. After all, living on the third floor, above the library, gave the sense that this was all their home and the books downstairs merely an extension of that. Anne tried to iterate the distinction, but she wasn't always sure Liddie comprehended.

Hershey, their chocolate Labrador retriever, stared at her with curiosity, his head tilted as Anne bent to look under the bed, in the closet, behind the dresser and bookshelves.

Finding nothing upstairs, Anne returned to the checkout station and popped open the computer screen, typing in the first title, *Curious George* by H. A. Rey. There had been eight checkouts in the past five months. But each time they were recorded as returned. Perhaps the last person who checked out the book didn't actually return it, even though the record said they had. She knew it wasn't likely but it was worth checking.

She hated to think there might be more books missing than the four they'd discovered. The niggling thought grew — but there was simply no way to know if other books were gone too. If only she hadn't seen those very titles on the table in the Children's Room on Saturday — there had to be something to that.

She picked up the phone and called the last name on the list — Beth Wilson. The young mother of five picked up on the fourth ring.

"Hello, Beth," Anne said. "This is Anne Gibson from the Blue Hill Library." Anne could hear the sounds of children shouting in the background.

"Oh, sure," Beth said. "What can I do for you? Do I have overdue books again? Reggie, stop it!" she shouted at one of her kids.

Anne pulled the phone away from her ear for a moment to keep the shrill sound from piercing her eardrum.

"Sorry," Beth returned. "That boy is such a stinker today! He's actually climbing the curtains. Reggie!"

Anne smiled. Even in her short time in Blue Hill, she knew the four-year-old was all bullfrogs and mischief.

"I'm trying to track down some books," Anne began. "You checked out *Curious George* about a month ago. I have it listed as returned, but I thought I'd see…"

"Oh, I returned that," Beth said. "I specifically remember asking Reggie if reading it changed his mind about getting into mischief. He looked at me like I'd grown a third eye."

Anne chuckled. "Okay." She thanked her and hung up the phone. Next, she called the last person to check out *Goodnight Moon*. Amy Richter also claimed to have returned the book. It was the same with the patrons who had checked out the other two titles.

"Well, I'm stumped," Wendy said with a sigh, coming back to the checkout desk and taking the chair alongside Anne after she'd hung up the phone from her final call. Wendy leaned in with her arms on the desk and rubbed her chin with one hand. "I've looked over every shelf in the place. It's as if the books just vanished."

"I hate to think that."

A library was built on a foundation of trust—items borrowed would be returned. But only with the proper recording of who took what. Otherwise it was a free-for-all with no sense of order or accountability. For its patrons to break that trust destroys the whole system. "People in Blue Hill don't steal."

Wendy raised an eyebrow. "They don't? Where've you been living, in a fairytale?" She chuckled.

"You're very funny." Anne couldn't help but smile at her friend's jibe. "I just don't want to assume the worst." She shook her head.

Just then Mildred Farley came in the front door. The older woman looked sharp in an aqua-blue pantsuit with a white blouse. Matching aqua earrings dangled from her ears. She lifted her eyes to Anne and Wendy in greeting. Mildred had been Anne's great-aunt Edie's oldest and dearest friend, and Anne could see why. She had a deeply caring way about her, a wisdom that exuded from her core. She'd extended that wisdom and grace to Anne since her return as well, treating Anne like family, welcoming not only her but her children. Anne gave her a wave.

"There are some pretty complex security systems out there," Anne went on to Wendy. "I've been in libraries where every book has a security tag—if someone attempts to walk out the door without checking out a book, an alarm goes off." She shook her head. "It costs a fortune though. There's no way Blue Hill can afford something like that, even if the levy does go through. Besides, who wants to spend money on something like that when there are other resources the citizens of Blue Hill need far more?"

"What are we talking about?" Mildred asked as she slid library books into the book drop at the checkout desk.

"Some books are missing," Wendy supplied.

"Oh?" She turned a concerned gaze to Anne.

She hated to admit it, but the mayor's advice to keep the problem a secret echoed in Mildred's worried glance. Anne shook it off.

"I'm sure there's a good explanation," Anne said.

"But you look troubled."

"Oh, it's just one of those things," Anne said. "You know, you can't find something and it bugs you till you do."

"Don't I know it." Mildred gave her a knowing smile. "That malady gets more and more common at my age."

"The books will show up." Wendy patted Anne's hand.

Anne was beginning to wonder about that. She glanced around the old Victorian mansion. Hardwood floors creaked. Rain patted at the wavy windowpanes behind lace curtains made by Aunt Edie. A couple of patrons lingered in the Nonfiction Room, heads tilted as they gazed at titles on the shelves.

There was more at stake here than just a few missing children's books. To Anne this place represented a life of trust, honesty. This place was her heritage. For books to go missing... Her thoughts drifted to Aunt Edie, the woman who had made possible her return to this small town by leaving her, and Blue Hill, this house. That woman had had such spunk, such tenacity, championing causes for those who couldn't defend themselves. Standing for justice.

"What do you think Aunt Edie would do in a situation like this?" Anne turned to Mildred.

Mildred gave a soft chuckle and placed a hand on her hip. "She would've done exactly what you're going to do — get to the bottom of it!"